The Time Traveller's Nephew

The Displacers Series

Book 1

Simon Brading

First published 2015

This edition published 2025

Copyright © Simon Brading 2015

The right of Simon Brading to be identified as the author of this work has been asserted by him in accordance with the Copyright, Designs and Patents Act 1988.

This is a work of fiction. Names, characters, businesses, places, events and incidents are either the products of the author's imagination or used in a fictitious manner. Any resemblance to actual persons, living or dead, or actual events is purely coincidental.

All rights reserved. No part of this publication may be reproduced, distributed, or transmitted in any form or by any means, including photocopying, recording, or other electronic or mechanical methods, without the prior written permission of the publisher, except in the case of brief quotations embodied in critical reviews and certain other non-commercial uses permitted by copyright law.

Cover design by Andrėja Dikšaitytė

www.forgottenscriptorium.com

ISBN: 978-1-917470-50-6

For my grandfather, who was supportive of me no matter how many times I changed my idea of what I was going to do with my life.

CHAPTER 1
THE WATCHER

Italy, 9th August 1173

'The big day is finally here, Your Excellency,' the priest in black robes said with a smile as he placed the cardinal's cloak around his shoulders and brushed off a few pieces of lint that were so small as to be almost imaginary. 'And it seems that the heavens are smiling on your great work.'

'Indeed, Father! It is most auspicious.'

The old cardinal beamed as he peered short-sightedly at his indistinct reflection in the large mirror in the sacristy of the cathedral. It had been raining solidly for almost two weeks and, as the appointed day had approached, he had begun to despair, thinking that he would have to shout into a gale with water streaming down his face as he blessed the undertaking. However, the weather had finally broken during the night and the new day had dawned clear, bright and warm. He couldn't hope for a better sign of approval for his plans, and it was just as well, because more and more voices were rising up against his great endeavour from among the congregation, complaining that he was taking away from them the field where they grazed their sheep and played games and held fairs in the summer.

Satisfied with what he saw in the mirror, the cardinal turned to face the door.

'I am ready. History beckons.'

Watched by thousands of men, women and children from the city, the procession came out of the main entrance of the cathedral and moved slowly around the beautiful building to the far end, where the new bell tower would be situated. Wooden boards had been laid down on the mud for the cardinal so that he wouldn't be at all inconvenienced and his expensive and highly decorative robes wouldn't be spoiled and he was helped along them by the priest. Everyone else had to make do, though, and the otherwise beautiful hymn the choir was singing was marred every so often by discordant squeaks and squawks as one or other of them stumbled or slipped.

The builder in the embroidered brown apron signifying a master of his art turned from his contemplation of the large pit in which the foundations to the tower would be laid and came towards the group approaching from the cathedral. He went down on one knee and kissed the ring that the cardinal held out, then stood and gestured towards the hole.

'Your Excellency. As you commanded, we are ready to lay the first stone of the foundation, but I have concerns. The ground is soft. And not just because of the rain – we have not encountered the rock we expected and a bell tower of this design may become unstable. It would be best...'

'*May* become unstable?' The man in the black priest's robe standing behind the cardinal asked. '*May*?'

'Yes. *May*.' The master builder shrugged, brushing off the question without even glancing at the priest. 'It is not a certainty, Your Excellency, but in my experience it is likely. We should dig deeper and wider and bring in more stone to reinforce the foundations.'

'Then do that!' The cardinal ordered.

'Very well, Excellency.'

The master builder bowed his head and made to go back to his place with the workers, but was brought up short when the priest loudly cleared his throat.

The cardinal turned to him. 'You have something you wish to say, Father Marrone?'

'Yes, Excellency,' the man in black said, stepping closer to the cardinal and lowering his voice. 'I am concerned about the expense of this extra work. The donation only covers the existing plan.'

The cardinal waved away the priest's words. 'We can afford it. If need be I will pay from my own pocket.' He looked at the builder. 'You may begin.'

'Immediately, Your Excellency. It should only delay us a year or two at most to do the necessary studies and the extra work.'

The master builder smiled and bowed again, but there was a hiss as the priest sharply drew in air between his teeth and he sighed as he straightened back up.

'Yes, father?' the cardinal asked, irritation creeping into his voice. 'What is it now?'

'Well, Your Excellency,' the man said as humbly as he could, 'your appointment to Rome may come before these new preparations have been made...'

'And my successor would naturally take the credit for my contribution to the church,' the cardinal mused, finishing the thought. 'This is supposed to be *my* legacy...' He looked at the builder. 'Just how unstable will the tower be?'

The builder shrugged. 'Not very, Your Excellency. The tower will gradually subside, that much is certain, but it may take two or three hundred years for it to topple. Or it may never.'

The cardinal pondered the man's answer for a moment, then nodded. 'That is acceptable. We will trust that future generations will do what they need to do to keep it standing.' He dismissed the builder with a wave. 'We will proceed.'

'Yes, Your Excellency.'

The builder bowed once more. He wasn't happy, but who was he to argue with the cardinal or his adviser? He had informed them of his reservations and it was up to them whether they took his advice or not. They were the ones paying, after all.

He signalled the waiting men who took up the strain in the ropes, preparing to begin the task of lowering the huge ceremonial stone into place. Carved with the cardinal's name, it would forever form an important part of the foundations of a beautiful new bell tower for the cathedral of the nearby city of Pisa.

The priest in black watched, soaking up the sheer history of the moment, as the stone descended into the pit. However, when the stone touched the muddy bottom and the cardinal began the first of what he knew would be an extremely long and tedious series of prayers he folded his hands together and closed his eyes. He relaxed, reached out for home and...

...opened his eyes in his study back in Barcelona.

'Well? You had a successful Displacement, I presume? No need for medical attention this time, I trust?'

Andrew looked up at the bank of twelve monitors on the wall in front of him in three rows of four. Only one of them was on and displayed the face of James Hudson, observing via Skype from his home in London.

James was an older Displacer, an "Elder". At a certain age, people with their particular talent became too old for their bodies to withstand the extreme stress of time travel, so they lost the ability, going through what was known as the "Transition", and becoming Elders. James was the leader of the council of Elders and as such was Andrew's chief adviser in his role as head of the Displacers. He was in his nineties, thin, sparsely liver-spotted and mostly bald, but the light, the humour and the intelligence in his eyes was that of a much younger man and certainly not that of a man who had lived for several centuries.

Andrew nodded. 'I'm in one piece, thank you for your concern! And yes, disaster averted - the tourists will not be deprived of the opportunity to take a photograph holding up the leaning tower.'

James huffed with amusement. 'The Elders were more worried about Galileo not being able to carry out his experiments, but you're right, the loss to the tourists of the world would probably be far more devastating. I will make sure to adjust the files accordingly once you have submitted your report.'

Andrew grinned. 'I'll upload it to the servers this evening.'

'I look forward to reading it.' James smiled in return.

With the job of watching the Displacement and making sure that the Displacer returned safely completed, this was when whoever had been assigned to the task would normally sign off, but James hesitated.

'Something bothering you, James?' Andrew raised his eyebrow and played the innocent even though he knew exactly what else was on the man's mind. He wasn't going to make it easy for him, though, it was far too much fun to prod the normally reticent old gentleman into expressing his feelings.

The old man's eyes screwed up and his lips thinned. 'You know damn well what I want to know, Berry. Don't make me fly over there and beat you with my walking stick.'

Andrew chuckled and shook his head. 'Please don't do that! I can still feel the marks you left me with when I forgot to stock up on Glenfiddich. Twenty years ago.'

James grinned in satisfaction. 'Never forgot again, though, did you, boy?'

'No, sir!'

They shared a complicit grin, but quickly became serious as their sharp minds turned back to the problem at hand, one that was far more important than the mission that had just been successfully carried out - Sam Vives, James' grandson and Andrew's nephew.

'Sam is...' Andrew frowned as he thought back to the real reason why he was in Barcelona and not home in London at Displacer Headquarters. He shrugged. 'Sam is the same, actually - I'm still getting exactly the same feeling from him. It's strange and ambiguous, like he's one of us, but something else as well. I can't quite explain it.' He tugged at his hair in frustration. 'Gaah! I wish you could spare an Elder to come over and take a look at him; they'd be able to tell right away. No doubt about it.'

'I wish we could spare someone too, but you know how it is right now. You're just going to have to cope.' James grimaced and shook his head. 'I just don't get it; all the signs are there: he's introverted, quiet, studious, and you've seen the look he gets in his eyes when confronted with a problem. Those are all the things we usually see in a Displacer on the verge of getting their powers.'

'I know, but even so...'

James grunted and shifted around in his seat, momentarily making the face following software go a bit crazy. 'I don't like it; if he's one of us we need to know it so that we can train him before something potentially disastrous happens.'

'I know, and believe me, James, I'm doing the best I can.'

'I know you are, but the other Elders and I are worried just the same.'

Andrew grinned cheekily. 'When aren't you?'

'It's different this time, and you know it. There is a shadow looming over us that we can't explain and we can feel the time-line shifting. It's like a constant buzz in the back of our heads and it's making the lot of us grumpy.'

James saw that Andrew was going to make another smart comment and pointed his finger at the camera to forestall him.

'Yes, yes, I know, we're always grumpy. It goes with the age. And don't worry; *you'll* be an Elder soon enough, and I guarantee you'll be just as upset all the time as we are.'

Andrew laughed again, but didn't say anything more as the old man continued.

'You know that we need all the people we can get right now. We can't afford to lose anyone else. So if Sam is one of us we need to know it sooner rather than later and it is imperative that you get to him before something happens.'

'Don't worry, I'm sticking as close to him as I can. If I feel him Preparing I'll be on hand to stop him before he can Displace.'

'Thank you.' James nodded, truly grateful. 'Just look after my grandson, please, don't let anything bad happen to him. We've had enough...'

The old man stopped speaking suddenly as his eyes started to cloud up.

It was always a tragedy when a Displacer died in the past and it affected each of them deeply, but one of the members who had died most recently, Susan, Andrew's wife, had also been James' daughter. Her loss had been a heavy blow to the old man and one that he was only now starting to recover from.

Andrew suppressed his own welling emotions and forced himself to give the Elder a reassuring smile. 'Don't worry, James, nothing will go wrong. Sam will be fine.'

The old man nodded his thanks and disconnected.

Andrew sighed and relaxed back in his chair.

He stared at the screen that had held the face of his mentor and friend, and that now showed the two-hundred-year-old crest of the "Honourable Society of Displacers".

Unfortunately, James was right; recent losses and a distinct lack of new blood meant that they were thin on the ground. If the shadow James was talking about was an actual threat then they were going to be hard pressed to do anything about it; they were already falling behind as it was.

If Sam Vives was indeed a Displacer he was sorely needed.

However, despite his assurances to James, he really wasn't sure that he'd be able to fully protect his nephew.

CHAPTER 2
A RAINY DAY

It was a rainy May day in Barcelona when Sam Vives found out he was different.

Aside from being a bit short for his age there was nothing to distinguish Sam from any other boy of fifteen, nothing to set him apart from any of his classmates, and with his brown hair, brown eyes and sun-browned complexion, even he himself thought that he was truly unremarkable.

To all outward appearances then, Sam was just a normal boy; as normal as any teenage boy could be anyway. However, there was one thing that made Sam very special, but nobody knew it yet, not even Sam himself.

He had been born in Barcelona and lived there his whole life. His father was originally from a small village in Catalonia, but had lived and worked in the city for so many years that it was his home now. His mother was English - she'd come out to Barcelona for a job, met his father and then stayed.

Sam had a Spanish passport because of where he had been born, but he liked to think of himself as being at least a bit English. He recognised his mixed parentage as a distinct advantage - he wasn't "just" bilingual like most of the other students; he spoke English too, although not nearly as well as Spanish and Catalan. It also meant he had holidays with his British grandfather in London every year, which was always fun, especially when it snowed over Christmas.

Every day Sam would go to school and he would work very hard and play even harder. He would come home to do his homework and be with his family and then would go to sleep at night, content to be able to wake up the next morning and do everything all over again the next day. He thought that this was how things would always be and he would have been perfectly happy with this. If it wasn't for Rafa Sánchez.

Rafa Sánchez was the boy who had gone through puberty first in Sam's year at school, who had gotten bigger than everyone else, and had then let the rest of his classmates know it whenever he could.

He was a bully.

Rafa had many targets for his bullying, but Sam was by far his favourite. Sam had always been one of the smallest boys in his class, which made him easy pickings for Rafa and a piece of cake to stuff into a locker.

They had met several years before, on Sam's first day of school when they were seven years old. Sam had answered a question that Rafa hadn't been able to and had been awarded a gold star. This had been at a time when gold stars actually meant something and were hotly contested. Rafa had never forgiven him for that and, even now, eight years later, when the original reason for his dislike of Sam was long forgotten, he still took every opportunity he could to hurt Sam either physically or mentally. Sam tried to stay away from the bigger boy whenever he could, but it was almost impossible to avoid him completely. Not only was he in Sam's class, but they were usually in the same football game at break and he took every opportunity to trip or elbow Sam, whether he was on the same side or not. It was all part of the fun to him.

Unfortunately, they were also in the fencing team together.

Sam loved fencing, and had a real talent for it. At the moment it was his favourite sport, much more than football, which he didn't particularly like, but that all his friends were crazy about - half of them even wore "Barça" shirts to school.

The inventiveness of a bully is such that, even in an activity like fencing, where there are strict rules of conduct, they will always be able to find ways to circumvent them, violently if possible, especially if nobody was looking, and Sam was fairly sure that Rafa had joined the team just to find new ways to torment him.

This particular day Sam had been paired with Rafa for free fencing at the end of the session after the technical lessons, something he tried to avoid as much as possible. To make matters worse, they were using épées. That was bad because it was the biggest, heaviest type of sword and it already hurt when you got hit with it in the wrong place, even if it was used normally. In the hands of someone like Rafa it could do a lot of damage, especially because he never just used the minimum of force, but deliberately hit with all of his malice. It also meant that the whole body was a target and Rafa always made sure to aim for the most painful places.

He had known he was in trouble when the bully had flashed him that especially malicious grin of his, just before covering it with his mask; that look always meant that someone was going to be in pain soon, and there was only one possible target for Rafa on a fencing piste. It also didn't help that Rafa had his own mask and that he had painted the grill to look like a skull, a skull that was now grinning at Sam the same way that Rafa had.

Nervously, Sam saluted and pulled his own mask on. It was one of the school's old, battered ones. Unlike Rafa, whose parents were rich and spoiled him, giving him everything he asked for, Sam wasn't so vain as to want or need his own equipment when the school provided it.

They went into their "en garde" positions, sword extended in front of them, and their other hand behind their back.

The point of Sam's sword wavered slightly as his hand shook. Even though Sam usually won their matches he never looked forward to crossing swords with Rafa; he always got hurt in some way and his victory would be soured.

He took a deep breath and concentrated on trying to steady his hand, but it was too late, Rafa had seen and was chuckling evilly. 'What's the matter, Vives? You scared?'

Sam didn't answer; anything he said would just play into the bully's hands, so he just concentrated on the match.

The referee, one of the teachers in charge of the fencing club, called out for them to "fence".

The bully immediately went on the offensive. He ran forward and stabbed out repeatedly, trying to hit Sam as hard as he could. He had no finesse and little technique and instead just put all his strength behind each strike, jabbing indiscriminately at Sam's face and body. Despite his lack of skill he came closer and closer each time as Sam desperately tried to stay out of his reach, constantly moving backwards.

Sam was understandably scared, because a hit from any of the strikes would give him a huge bruise at the very least. However, he managed to push aside his fear enough to concentrate on the bout, after all it wasn't unexpected; this was Rafa's way of winning, his only way - the bully tried to intimidate his opponent in fights, giving up points sometimes, but always making sure to hurt the other boy as much as possible. In this way the other boy would become so scared that Rafa would be able to chase him around the piste at will and pick up an easy win. It worked just about every time, except with Sam, which only served to infuriate Rafa even more.

Sam was well-used to Rafa's bullying tactics and he retreated continuously using footwork that he had practised over and over for just this eventuality, barely staying just out of reach. He moved lightly on his feet, knowing that any misstep would cost him dearly, and waited, knowing that the right time would come.

He was almost at the end of the piste and in danger of going out of bounds when he finally saw his chance. Rafa overextended just a little bit too much in trying to reach him and with a quick flick of his wrist Sam got a neat touch on the inside of Rafa's sword hand before the big boy could react.

The buzzer went off and the box lit up. The referee halted them and announced that Sam had scored the point.

Rafa growled and pulled his mask up onto the top of his head and glared threateningly at Sam while he backed away to his starting position.

'Lucky point, Vives, bet you can't do it again.'

Sam grinned behind his mask and just walked calmly back to the line where he stood waiting for the referee to restart the match.

He did do it again, though. And again. And once more after that. All of the next three more points went to Sam in exactly the same way, as Rafa continued to charge ahead predictably and was easily countered by Sam each time. In short order Sam was winning four points to zero and needed just one more to win the short practice match by a whitewash. Rafa on the other hand was quickly becoming more and more frustrated, angry, and out of breath, he was stabbing at the floor beside the piste angrily between points, making the box buzz and light up repeatedly, as if unwilling to believe that his sword was working correctly.

Sam knew that this was when Rafa was at his most dangerous, but he was enjoying himself too much to care and besides, he wanted to get his own back, even if only in such a small manner, and he fully intended to teach Rafa a lesson the only way that he could - by beating him and showing him that he couldn't always have everything his own way.

They faced off again.

'Fence!'

Rafa knew no other way to fight so he charged straight ahead much faster than before, roaring in anger. His arm was pulled right back in order to stab Sam as hard as he could. It was a last ditch effort to intimidate Sam enough to score and start to take over the match.

Sam had anticipated this tactic, however; he'd seen Rafa use it before when things weren't going his way. He stepped calmly to one side just before the bully got to him and extended his arm almost casually, letting the big boy's own momentum do all the work.

Rafa had no time to stop and ran straight into the sword, bending it, compressing the tip, and giving Sam the point.

The buzzer went off and the box lit up.

'Halt!' called the referee.

Rafa ignored the order and stabbed out. He contacted with Sam's inside thigh as hard as he could, thankfully missing what had probably been his real target by inches.

Sam cried out in pain and fell backwards off the piste, his leg suddenly numb. He cursed himself; he should have known that Rafa was going to make sure to get at least some satisfaction out of the encounter, but he had let his guard down when he had gotten the point and consequently hadn't been ready to defend himself.

'I SAID HALT!' the referee cried out angrily.

Rafa slowly took off his mask and looked at the referee with a sheepish grin. He shrugged and looked apologetic as he replied, 'oh, I'm so sorry, I didn't hear you, sir.'

To Sam's eternal annoyance, for some reason all the adults in the school seemed to be blind to Rafa's bullying tactics. He suspected it was because the boy's father was a Member of Parliament as well as being rich. This teacher was no different and he nodded in acceptance of the weak apology before calling out the final score. 'Sam wins five points to zero.'

The man turned away to watch the other matches that were still going on and didn't see Rafa standing over Sam in a threatening manner, preventing him from getting up. 'Awww... Did the little baby get hurt? Are you going to cry, Vives?'

Sam looked up at Rafa and smiled, refusing to show the pain he was in. 'Not even close. You hit like my little sister.'

Rafa snarled and curled his hand into a fist in preparation to throw a punch, but he stopped and looked up when the fencing master called for the end of the practice session.

Suddenly there were too many people busying around and tidying up the equipment for him to be able to safely get away with whatever he had been about to do. Instead, he had to content himself with bending down to hiss a threat in Sam's ear. 'I've had enough of you, Vives. I'm going to get you, once and for all, if not here, then between classes or after school. Make sure you watch your back.'

Rafa turned away and stormed off, leaving Sam on the floor rubbing his leg, trying to get some life back into it.

Sam usually walked home from school on his own, but that day he had run into his mother and his seven-year-old sister Violeta outside the school and decided to accompany them.

His leg was hurting and he was limping slightly because of Rafa's unsportsmanlike attack, but he made sure not to let his mother know that there was anything wrong. He needn't have worried, though; his mother was far too busy taking care of Violeta and hurrying them along the road to notice the trouble he was having walking or the dark bruise on his leg.

Sam wasn't the kind of boy to run straight to a teacher or his parents when he got into difficulty with a fellow student. It wasn't as if there was anything wrong with that, but rather that he was too proud to do so, and he was certain that one day he'd be able to sort out his problems with Rafa on his own, although he didn't quite see how at that moment. He also didn't want to give his mother and father anything to worry about; he thought that they had enough trouble on their plates already with their jobs and bringing up his sister. Consequently, they had no idea that he was even being bullied.

There was only one person that Sam felt that he could really confide in and talk about these kind of things with and that was his Uncle Andrew; Sam knew that Andrew would keep his secrets and would just listen when all Sam wanted was talk and be there when he needed advice.

Andrew was English like Sam's mother and was a friend of hers and her father, James, Sam's grandfather. He wasn't actually related to them, but they called him "uncle" anyway because he was one of those people who had been around long enough to almost become part of the family.

Sam often went round to his uncle's flat when he wanted to get away from his family for a while. It was only a few streets away from his home and he had permission to drop by whenever he wanted. It was filled with knick-knacks of all different kinds from many different countries and Andrew himself had a treasure trove of interesting facts at hand to entertain a curious teenager. The best thing, though, was that Sam could ask his advice about anything and not have to worry about his mum or dad finding out and he frequently went round to see Andrew after school or over the weekend to talk to him about schoolwork or seek comfort whenever something happened with Rafa, which was far too often.

Andrew had been invited over for dinner that night and Sam was hoping that he'd get a chance to talk to him on his own for a while about his latest run-in with the bully and the threats that he had made. They were actually stopping by his flat on the way home from school; apparently Sam's mother had lent him her pressure cooker months ago and needed it back to cook the meal, but he knew that he wouldn't have a chance to say anything privately with his mother and sister there.

The door opened to reveal Andrew's grinning face and untidy mop of light brown hair. 'Afternoon, Margaret! I have the pressure cooker ready for you in the kitchen. I washed it, but it's probably dry by now. Do you want a cup of tea while you're here?'

'No, thank you, Andrew, I need to get the kids home and start on the food.'

'Right-oh!' He looked down at Sam and Violeta. 'Hi guys! How was school?'

Violeta looked up at him and smiled before sticking her fingers in her mouth and hiding behind Sam shyly.

Andrew laughed before turning to raise an eyebrow at Sam. 'How about you, Sam? Anything interesting happen? Got a girlfriend yet?'

'Of course not.' Sam forced a laugh, but he could feel his cheeks heating up in embarrassment. His lack of a girlfriend was too often a subject of debate in his family and to his chagrin his parents couldn't quite understand that he didn't like talking about that fact, or that he wasn't particularly bothered about have one; most of the girls in his year were rather self-centred and not particularly interesting. Besides, none of the girls, or boys for that matter, wanted anything to do with a boy who was constantly being beaten up and humiliated.

Sam's mother rolled her eyes. 'Sam, stay here and keep an eye on your sister while I go to get my cooker back, please.'

Grateful for the change in subject and chance to regain his composure Sam readily agreed. 'OK, mum.'

The adults disappeared towards the kitchen leaving the two children standing in the entranceway.

Sam looked around at the items Andrew had cluttering every surface. He picked up what looked like a Russian triptych from a nearby shelf. He marvelled at the intricate detail and ran his finger ever so gently over the gold leaf that formed the halos of the saints that were portrayed on it. Even though he didn't understand the motivations behind the creation of such an object he could still appreciate it as a work of art and it was indeed remarkable. He set it back down in its place, carefully placing it between what looked like a jade geisha and a vividly painted boomerang, then almost knocked it over again when he jumped at the loud metallic sound of things dropping to the floor behind him.

He turned and looked down to discover that Violeta had found what looked like coins in a little wooden box and had, none too delicately, tipped them out to play with.

He winced and sighed. 'Come on, Violeta... Those aren't toys...'

Sam knelt down next to her. He picked up the wooden box that his sister had discarded and started to put the dozens of flat metal disks back into it, but stopped and looked at them closer; instead of the modern coins he had expected, they were ancient ones. They were roughly made, most of them not quite round, and far heavier than their present-day counterparts. Some of them had languages and scripts on them that were vaguely familiar, like Greek or Chinese, but others only had symbols that he had never seen before, almost like meaningless squiggles, or pictures of animals. He was surprised at how new they all looked, as if they'd been minted only a few years ago and not dug up from the ground, the inscriptions on them fresh and the metal relatively untarnished.

He shrugged; they were probably cheap reproductions such as you could buy in the local museums.

He put the rest of the coins back in the box and was about to close it when he saw that Violeta still had one of the biggest coins, a gold one a good couple of inches across. She had it in her mouth and was smiling at him as she bit down on it.

Sam sighed. 'Violeta, don't do that, you'll hurt your teeth! Come on, give it to me, please.'

She shrugged and held the coin out. 'It tastes funny. Not like the ones on the Christmas tree.'

He took it and wiped the saliva off of it. It was actually really heavy. He was just about to put it in the box when he noticed that it had teeth marks in it.

'Oh, god...'

He looked closer at the coin, turning it over in his hands. Violeta's teeth had sunk quite deep into it, probably in an effort to get to the chocolate that usually came in gold coins of this size. The marks had obscured some of the writing but he could still make it out clearly enough - it was a Roman coin and had the name Julius Caesar on it.

He held it up to the light and stared at the face of the famous general and emperor in relief on it, it was so clear, so distinct, and just as detailed as any of the coins in his wallet.

For a while, he had been quite interested in Roman history. He had read some books about ancient Rome and particularly liked the *Cato* series by Simon Scarrow, he had also visited a lot of the Roman ruins in Barcelona and in nearby Tarragona. Now he felt like he had a piece of that history in his hands, even though he knew that the coin couldn't possibly be real.

He closed his eyes, feeling the heavy weight of the lump of gold and running his thumb over the face of the long dead ruler.

He thought back to the battles that he had read about and the fantasies he'd had of being a soldier in that all-conquering army.

He could almost hear the clash of swords against shields, smell the coppery tang of blood and feel the mud beneath his feet and the weight of the armour on his shoulders...

'Sammy, give it back! It's mine!'

Sam's eyes flew open and he blinked and looked around, as if seeing the entranceway for the first time.

Violeta was tugging on the coin in his hand, jerking his arm and she smiled when she saw him look at her. She stopped pulling at the coin and instead sat down with a soft thump, wrapping her arms around her legs and chuckling gently as she rocked back and forth, watching him.

He blinked at her, puzzled at her behaviour and was about to comment on it when he heard his mother and Andrew returning from the kitchen. He hurriedly put the coin in the box and placed it back on the shelf where it had come from.

He put his finger to his lips, telling Violeta not to say anything and put an innocent look on his face as the adults reappeared with the pressure cooker.

Sam's mother took one look at her daughter and rolled her eyes again. 'Oh, Violeta, don't sit on the floor, please, you'll make your dress dirty. Come on, get up, it's time to go home.'

Sam helped his sister to get to her feet then glanced back at the adults.

His mother was looking stressed; he knew that she had a lot to do with the dinner that night and didn't have time for his sister's playing around. He resolved to do as much as he could to help in the kitchen with the preparations to make things easier for her.

Andrew, on the other hand, had a funny expression on his face as he looked at Sam. 'Everything alright, Sam?'

'Uh, yeah…' Sam didn't think now was the right time to tell him about the new teeth marks in his gold coin, and he also didn't want to speak about Rafa and his bullying problems in front of his mother; that conversation could wait until the evening.

Andrew nodded slowly. 'OK, then… I guess I'll see you later tonight.'

'OK, bye!'

Sam smiled, then scurried after his mother as she whisked Violeta out the door.

Andrew frowned as he watched Sam leave. The feeling he got from the boy was just as confusing as always, but today it was stronger than ever, and for a moment, while he'd been in the kitchen with Margaret, he thought he'd felt something more…

He shook his head, if Sam had Displaced he would have said something, would have been far more in shock than he had been.

Probably.

Maybe.

He used the sound of the door closing to cover his swearing, then angrily stomped off down the hall to the kitchen to make himself a cup of tea.

He was completely out of his depth and he knew it; this kind of thing was usually handled by at least one Elder, if not a team of them. There was no way in hell he was going to be able to cope on his own.

Unfortunately he knew what he had to do, but doing the right thing in this case was going to bring him a whole heap of trouble from the council of Elders, not to mention a ton of grief from a certain person who hadn't exactly been happy when he'd been elected to lead the Society.

However, no matter how strict the rules were about talking to someone before it was absolutely confirmed that they were a Displacer, he was going to speak to Sam tonight and damn the consequences.

He needed to know what was going on with the boy and the risk of losing him was just too high to leave him in the dark about what he almost certainly was.

Sam walked behind his mother and Violeta as they made their way home from Andrew's flat. He was thinking about food, homework, his favourite TV programs and the day at school, anything to ignore the ache in his leg - a constant reminder of his bully problem.

There had actually been some interesting lessons today - he'd gotten to blow up some stuff in chemistry, which was always good fun, then history class had been about pirates and he'd learnt about Blackbeard and the golden age of piracy in the Caribbean. Best of all there had been no maths class because the teacher had been ill. Everybody always liked it when that happened and they never thought to ask how the teacher was.

They were only a few steps away from home when it started to rain.

His mother called out for him to hurry then ran ahead with Violeta, but Sam paused and turned his head up to catch the first drops. He quite liked the feeling of the cool water on such a hot and humid day and it was more than welcome after the unseasonal heat of the last few days.

The pleasant light rain didn't last for very long, though, as it quickly began pouring down in earnest. A light drizzle was one thing, but this was another matter entirely.

Sam dropped his head, tucking his chin to his chest, and was just about to run to catch up with his mother when he noticed that his white t-shirt was turning brown where the rain was soaking into it. For a second he thought it was just the dirty rain that fell in Barcelona sometimes when it hadn't done so for a while, but it was clearly more than that, and even stranger his bare arm seemed to be changing colour as well - in places it looked like it was covered with some kind of brown cloth.

He rubbed at his arm, trying to get rid of the marks, but only succeeded in spreading them even more and he noted with alarm that the rest of his clothes were changing colour as well, as they became wetter and wetter. It almost seemed like he was wearing two sets of clothes, one over the other, but the one on top was indistinct and hazy, like a mirage.

'Come on, hurry up, Sam, you're getting wet!'

Sam looked up to see his mother beckoning from the shelter of the street door of the block of flats where they lived. Violeta was peering around her skirts and laughing at the sight of her brother getting soaked, standing in the rain like a statue.

He shook his head and chuckled at his mother's insistence; it was far too late to say that he was "getting" wet; he was soaked through, all the way to his underwear. Hurrying wouldn't make much difference now.

There was a flash of light accompanied by a thunderclap almost directly afterwards and suddenly the rain was streaming down in sheets. Water ran down his face and he blinked, unable to see. He idly wondered if the pirates he had heard about in class ever had this kind of problem; after all, sailors were surrounded by water all the time and it wasn't as if they had swimming goggles in those days.

He lifted his hands and scrubbed at his eyes, trying to clear them, and as he did so a voice filled with fear and urgency rang out in his ear.

'What are your orders, Captain?'

Sam slowly took his hands away from his eyes and squinted in the sudden light.

Somehow he was standing in bright sunshine and it wasn't raining anymore.

He was also no longer wet.

All those things were strange in themselves, but none of them was the most obvious change in his circumstances. In fact, he didn't notice any of them at first, because what immediately caught and held his attention was the sight of the great wooden ship stretching away in front of him, rolling and pitching gently in an endless ocean.

CHAPTER 3
FIGHT OR FLIGHT

Sam was standing on a raised platform at the back of the ship next to a huge wheel and there was a crowd of raggedly-dressed and unshaven people looking up at him expectantly from the deck below.

'Captain! What are we going to do? The French are closing fast! Do we fight or flee?'

Completely mystified, Sam turned to the man who was talking to him, staggering slightly as the ship moved beneath his feet. Aside from the steersman at his post, he was the only other person on the quarterdeck with Sam. He was sun-browned, dressed in a white shirt and brown breeches, and had long curly hair as well as a short, well-kept, dark brown beard. There was a keen glint in his eyes that spoke of intelligence as well as a healthy dose of mischief.

He was exactly how Sam had imagined a pirate would look.

'F-f-fight?' Sam stumbled over the word, still not quite understanding what he was being asked or in fact much of what was going on at all.

Before he could elaborate on his question, though, the man spun around and shouted to the assembled crew.

'WE FIGHT! The crew of the Mermaid runs from no-one!' He thrust his right hand into the air and a mighty cheer rose from the men gathered below.

Even before they had quietened down again, the man started bellowing orders. 'Make ready the guns and let out the topsails, I want every stitch of canvas she can carry! Get to it, lads!'

With another cheer, the men ran off. Some went to start the loading process of the cannon that lined the main deck, while others began to swarm up the ropes on their way to the sails.

The pirate turned back to Sam and the eager grin on his face was instantly replaced by one of worry. 'Are you all right, Captain?'

'Wha... whe... Sorry, who are you?'

The man gave Sam a very puzzled look as he replied. 'It's me - Smithy, Mr Smith, your first mate... Are you sure you're all right, Captain? You're looking a bit seasick. And that's not like you, if you don't mind me saying.'

The man leaned in to peer at Sam with concern and Sam swayed back, not out of fear, but rather to get out of range of the man's bad breath.

He coughed. 'Huh? Oh, uh, yes, I'm fine, I think. It was probably something I ate. Thank you, er, Smithy.'

Sam smiled at his first mate and the man nodded, then turned away to see to the crew.

There was finally a chance for Sam to think and he tried desperately to work out how he could possibly have gotten onto a ship in the middle of the ocean, somehow becoming a pirate captain along the way.

He failed dismally; he could find no explanation for what he was doing here or why, beyond the very real possibility that he was either dreaming or hallucinating.

With no answers forthcoming he looked around. From his position on the quarterdeck at the stern of the ship he had a good view of everything and he drank it in, marvelling at the activity and the life around him. He wondered how his subconscious could possibly have created it all.

The Mermaid was a fairly large ship, certainly larger than most of the yachts that were moored in Barcelona.

The three masts towering overhead were covered with dirty looking canvas sails that had probably been white at one point, but which were now a dingy grey. They were full of wind, tugging the ship along strongly, making the masts and yards creak and the rigging sing with the pressure that was being exerted on them.

Near where Sam was standing by the wheel there was a short flight of stairs that led down to the main deck. Twenty or so crewmen had leapt up them while he'd been speaking with Smithy on their way to man the guns stationed around the quarterdeck and were even now busily loading them with shot and powder. The guns on the main deck, on the other hand, were almost loaded and a few of the crews were already standing back from them and waiting for further orders. Sam started to count how many cannons there were in total, but stopped when the number "twenty-eight" popped into his head - for some reason he just knew that was correct.

As the men completed their assigned tasks, the activity on the main deck began to slow and Sam turned his gaze upwards. He squinted to look up at where about a dozen men were unfurling the small sail at the very top of the main mast. Dozens more were hanging off of the ropes, or "ratlines" as they were called, up and down all three masts in order to be at hand if orders were given to change the sails.

The sun was blinding and he put his arm up to shield his eyes from the glare so that he could see the topmen better and this was when he noticed his clothing for the first time.

His t-shirt and jeans were gone and in their place were a rough brown cloth jacket with frayed gold lace down the sleeves and loose off-white cotton trousers. Reaching up he brought a black three pointed hat down from his head. It had a large red feather in it and he almost laughed at its strange flamboyance before grinning and putting it back on his head at a jaunty angle. Finally, when he looked down, he found that the heavy weight banging against his hip was a large curved sword - a cutlass. The blade was so long, and he was so short, that it was almost touching the wooden boards of the ship; however, its presence there was somehow familiar, and he found it strangely comforting as he rested his hand on the pommel.

Sam grinned; despite still not knowing how he had gotten there, he found that he was warming to his circumstances - he'd always enjoyed fancy dress, had even dressed up as a pirate a couple of times when he was younger, and the sword at his side was just the icing on the cake.

He turned to walk to the side of the ship and stumbled slightly as the ship pitched up and down. He winced as his bruised leg gave a twinge - evidently the injury had followed him into the dream, or whatever it was.

He leant against the rail next to one of the huge cannons, taking some of the weight off the leg, and looked down. Blue water was running past at what seemed like a very fast pace, foaming as it passed, and creating a white wake that stretched out behind the ship as far as the eye could see. It was all very beautiful and peaceful, even with Sam menacing presence of the gun next to him.

When he looked up at the horizon a whitish object caught his eye. There were no clouds in the sky to speak of, so the only thing that it could be was another ship, coming right towards them. Only the sails were visible above the horizon as an off-white smudge, which meant it was a long way off yet, but it was heeled over at a fairly steep angle, meaning that it was going as fast as it could and bearing down on them. It wouldn't be too long before it was in firing range.

'It's the Medusa, a French frigate of forty guns. We're out-gunned and it'll be a tough fight, but nothing you haven't brought us through before, Captain!'

Smithy was back at his side and Sam glanced around to see who he was talking to before realising that it was he himself that had just been called "Captain".

He smiled. Like most other boys and girls of his age, Sam had spent a lot of time daydreaming, especially in his more boring classes, but his dreams were never normally this real, this vivid or this detailed. It was promising to be a very good dream, though, with a sword by his side and a sea battle in the making.

Sam shook his head and chuckled to himself. 'This has to be a dream, it can't be real.'

Mrs. Martínez from next door was always watering the plants on her balcony and soaking the people walking in the street underneath; one of them had probably gotten overfilled in the rain and had broken its support and fallen on his head.

'Captain! You're not dreaming, you're wide awake, but the French will see us sleeping with the fishes if you don't do something soon. I know you're not feeling very well, but we need you!'

The urgency of Smithy's words shook Sam out of his thoughts and he turned to look at the man standing at the rail beside him as he considered the situation. A further glance around the ship showed that everyone was now silently watching him - the entire crew and officers, all tough-looking men, were waiting for him, a fifteen year old boy, to tell them how they were going to face the enemy.

However, it wasn't all those faces turned to him in expectation that struck Sam as being strange about his circumstances, rather it was how much he was able to think and reason. Usually when he was dreaming he had no power over anything; most of the time it was more like he was watching a movie than actually living the events, but this time it seemed he was firmly in control of the direction that the dream could go in. Unfortunately for him, that meant he still retained enough awareness to know there was no way he was capable of leading the ship into a fight. He didn't know the first thing about seamanship and it would be a complete and utter disaster, probably make him look quite foolish and would undoubtedly make him too embarrassed to have any fun.

He sighed and was about to tell Smithy that it would be for the best if he captained the ship against the enemy frigate, but didn't when he realised that, somehow, it wasn't true. Impossibly, there were all sorts of plans and tactics floating around in his mind about how to fight the coming battle, along with an extensive knowledge of nautical terms and the best way to handle the ship that he found himself in command of.

Yes, he'd read a few books about sailing because his English grandfather had been in the navy in the Second World War, and the *Hornblower* series of books that the old gentleman had introduced him to were his favourites, so he fancied he knew a little bit about how battles at sea worked. However, that didn't even come close to explaining the expertise he suddenly seemed to have, and he didn't think that watching *Pirates of the Caribbean* about a dozen times with his sister had contributed much either; drinking rum and walking funny weren't going to help him here.

Sam chuckled at the memory of the week, not long ago, that he and Violeta had spent saying "Arrr!" instead of "yes" after seeing the latest film, until their mother screamed at them to stop. Even though it was just a dream, this promised to be fun, and he would have loved to share it with his sister; she had loved playing at being a pirate. He would just have to have as much fun as he could and make do with telling her all about it when he woke up.

He leaned on the rail again and peered out at the enemy ship that was drawing ever closer. He could see some of its hull now as a brown mark under the white of the sails as it came up over the horizon.

'They seem very eager to come to us, don't they, Mr Smith?'

'Aye, Captain.'

A plan formed in his mind, almost by itself, and he smiled; her captain's impatience would be her undoing. 'They most likely expect us to be intimidated enough to give up and strike our colours in the face of their superior firepower, but we'll show them that being bigger and stronger doesn't mean everything and that we refuse to be bullied by the likes of them. We'll hold our course and wait for them, then give them our broadside when they get close enough. Have the men aim for their sails and masts please, Mr Smith - we may have fewer guns than they do, but that doesn't mean it won't hurt if we can hit them right where it hurts.'

'Aye aye, Captain!' Smithy grinned, obviously delighted with the plan, but the smile was quickly replaced with a fierce scowl. 'We'll teach them that they can't burn us out of our homes then continue to persecute us at sea! It's their damn fault we're here and it's time we got our own back!'

Smithy hurried off, leaving Sam on his own by the rail.

With his first mate taking care of his orders he found himself at a loss for what to do until the enemy were in range. He wondered if he should walk about the ship, encouraging to the crew before the battle, or maybe climb up one of the masts to get a better view, but as he turned around looking for inspiration something caught his eye and he knew exactly what he wanted to do.

Sam walked to the nearest gun. It was very similar to the ones that he had seen on the HMS Victory in Portsmouth one time on holiday and he supposed that most cannons looked more or less the same, just different sizes.

He nodded and smiled at the crew of the gun. 'If you don't mind, I'd like to have a go, please.'

The biggest man on the crew replied with a wide grin as he looked around at his companions. 'We don't mind one bit! Do we, mateys? Go right ahead, Cap'n, she's all yours.'

The rest of the gun crew also appeared very pleased to have him there and they smiled indulgently as Sam ran his hand over the cannon.

While some of the cannons that Sam had seen in museums had been ornate, this one was essentially a plain metal tube, undecorated and smooth. Like most nautical guns it was functional, made for use, and it looked like it had seen a fair amount of action, which wasn't to say that it hadn't been looked after, because it obviously had been, and the men's pride in it was obvious as they watched their captain inspect it.

He made a complete circuit of the huge cannon, running his finger around the inside of the wide barrel as he passed it, before going to the end and bending down to look along its length.

Sam still couldn't believe he was actually here and not dreaming. The feeling was even worse now because, from this perspective, peering down the barrel of the big gun at the approaching enemy ship, it looked very much like he was in a first-person shooter or something.

The French ship was coming nearer all the time and he could feel the sailors around him starting to get a bit nervous, wondering when their captain was going to give the order to open fire.

However, Sam knew that the worst thing he could do was waste his first broadside by shooting it off before the enemy was even in range and was watching carefully, waiting for the right moment. He did a quick calculation, again inexplicably knowing what he was doing, and reckoned he still had a few minutes to wait.

He smiled at the men gathered around him.

'What's your name, sailor?' he asked the big man, the leader of the crew.

'Brown, sir. Bosun Brown.'

'I'm sorry to butt in like this, Mr Brown.'

'Think nothing of it, sir; nobody lays a gun like you do!'

There were nods of agreement and smiles from the rest of the men. They were a violent-looking lot, with multiple scars on every single one of them, but even so they all seemed genuinely happy to have him there and surprisingly friendly.

'Nonsense! Every man jack on this ship is capable of laying a gun just as well as I am, and very soon you'll all get a chance to show it.'

Sam made sure that he said this loud enough so that the surrounding gun crews could also hear and he smiled before he bent down again to look over the gun at the French frigate. If there was one thing that the *Hornblower* books had taught him it was that good morale was very important before a fight, and he could hear the nearby crews repeating his words to other crews throughout the ship, spreading the captain's words.

He straightened up, but was prevented from saying anything more by the distant report of two cannons; the French were firing their "bow chasers", the forward facing guns mounted on a ship's front to fire at the enemy while you were chasing them.

Sam smiled wryly, the French were obviously supremely confident of an easy victory and were charging straight into the teeth of his broadside - the overly direct tactics of a bully who was used to getting his own way. In fact they were remarkably similar to the tactics that Rafa used in his fencing matches; they were trying to intimidate them into giving up and they probably expected him to surrender after they had fired a few shots.

He kept watching and saw two large splashes off the port side of the Mermaid, about two hundred metres away, as the shots flew far wide and very short. They hadn't even come close to hitting them.

He tutted and shook his head, playing up for his crew. 'Far too soon! I think the French have shot to spare.' Sam looked back at the frigate, carefully gauging the distance again - the French had indeed shot too early, but were now creeping into range. He turned to the gun crew. 'What do you say, shall we give them some back?'

His men roared in reply, bloodthirsty and very keen to get into the fight.

Sam bent down to begin aiming the gun at the target. He took his time as he gave the crew instructions and they used big levers to move the gun around. He made a few final adjustments to his aim, letting the enemy get just a little bit further within range, and then stepped to one side of the gun. 'Everybody clear, please!' The bosun handed him a slow match and he held it to the touch hole, hearing the fizz as the priming powder ignited.

With a huge roar the gun shot backwards and an immense cloud of smoke burst out of the mouth along with the cannonball.

A big cheer came from all the men watching and as the smoke cleared around him Sam could see the top of one of the Frenchman's masts slowly starting to topple, taking with it some of the rigging. He blinked and stared, unable to believe the incredible luck of the shot.

'The Captain's shown us the way, lads, now give 'em everything we've got!'

Smithy's shout could barely be heard over the cheers, and with another yell of delight the men bent to their guns and fired. Whether they had been encouraged by Sam's words and example or not, the fact was that the shots had been so well aimed that a good few of the cannonballs that flew over to the French ship had cracked a mast, parted a rope, or blown a hole clean through one of the sails, and the damage they had caused was considerable, even after just the one broadside.

While Sam had assessed the damage, the crew had reloaded and run out their cannon again. They were looking expectantly at him and he smiled, pleased that they had such confidence in him. He feigned reluctance, but smiled and shrugged. 'Very well, if you insist. I would love to have one more go, thank you!'

He bent, looking down the length of the gun again and gave directions to the crew. He waited for the ship to pitch to the exact right angle, then touched the match to the hole. Once more the cannon roared and raced backwards on its small wheels before being pulled to a halt by the ropes that were attached to it.

Another great cheer rang out and Sam saw that a shot had broken the Frenchman's main mast.

'That was us! That was us'n the Captain what did that!' Bosun Brown was boasting, crying out to the surrounding crews while he organised his men reloading.

The enemy ship was no longer heading towards them, but had been stopped and dragged around by the weight of the sails and masts that had fallen into the water. Not only were they dead in the water, but the debris was completely blocking their cannon and stopping them from firing back.

Sam shouted down to the main deck where Smithy was organising the rest of the gun crews. 'Well done, Mr Smith, well done indeed! Now cease fire, ship the guns and let's run down to them while they're still trying to clear away all that mess. We'll board and steal their ship from them while they've got other things on their minds!'

'Aye aye, Captain!' Smithy went about his work with a grin, shouting orders one after the other, bringing in the guns and changing the sails, and only a few seconds later the Mermaid heeled over sharply as they changed course towards the enemy frigate.

Sam handed the slow match back to Bosun Brown and smiled at the gun crew. 'Thank you, lads.'

They grinned back at him, touching their foreheads and nodding. As Sam walked away he heard them good-naturedly teasing the surrounding gun crews about their crew being the best and chosen specially by the captain.

He went to the rail and leaned on it. There was a moment of inactivity while they bore down on the enemy and he used it to reconsider his strange situation.

This dream, or whatever it was, had him puzzled, and there were a couple of things about it that struck him as especially strange. For a start he kept getting the impression that the men were talking to a point above his head; their eyes kept sliding slightly upwards as they spoke to him, as if they were addressing someone that was taller than him. Then there was his general sensation of being subtly different - he couldn't quite grasp it, but he felt as if he was older, more experienced somehow. Although, if that were true it would go some way to explaining why he was able to command respect from men who were more than double his age and quadruple his size.

However, while these things were peculiar, they weren't particularly worrying, so he filed his doubts away for later and turned his full attention back to the job at hand - he didn't want to miss a second of the fun, especially since the boarding action would give him a chance to test out his skill with a sword.

The crew were busy running around making preparations. Grappling hooks were brought up from below and Smithy directed the men to gather by the starboard side rail, ready to cross over to the French ship.

Sam stood next to the wheel and looked forward along the ship. It hadn't taken long to cover the distance to the French ship and they were now close enough that he could make out the men aboard her. They were running around, trying to free her of the wreckage that covered the decks in an attempt to get her under way again. They were so busy that they still hadn't noticed that the Mermaid was creeping up on them.

Sam ran down to the main deck to join his crew where they were silently waiting by the rail, gazing out towards the enemy with hungry eyes, every single one of them eager to go into hand to hand combat.

Despite the coming violence it was almost peaceful; there were no sounds of engines, just the rush of water past the hull, the flap of the sails overhead and the creaking of the ropes and wooden hull and masts. It was quiet moments like these that would usually be covered with rousing music in the movies, but Sam found that he had no need of that; adrenaline was already making his heart pound faster and harder than it ever had before.

He held onto the rail to steady himself as the ships collided with a jolt and a loud scrape. The grappling hooks immediately flew through the air and the men hauled on them, tightly binding the two ships together.

'Come on, lads! Follow me!' Sam snatched a rope from a surprised sailor and used it to swing across the still narrowing gap. He landed on the main deck of the French ship and stumbled a little, but quickly found his feet.

When the ships had crashed together the French sailors had finally realised what was happening and given up trying to clear the debris and they were frantically trying to arm themselves when he landed on their deck.

'Aha!' Sam cried, pulling out his cutlass and dropping into a fighting stance, like he'd learnt from so many fencing lessons and Errol Flynn films.

The fifty or so sailors near him on the main deck had turned in fright when he had first thumped to the ground behind them, but now, against his expectations, they actually grinned and laughed menacingly as they pulled wicked looking knives from their belts or picked up long wooden boards from the wreckage and started advancing threateningly on him.

Sam glanced to either side and found out why the French sailors seemed so confident; in his haste to get into the fight he hadn't noticed that his men hadn't been armed yet and none of them had followed him.

Despite the fact that he was alone facing so many enemies, he gritted his teeth and stood his ground. He'd always believed that it was right to stand up to bullies, like he tried to do to Rafa, and these rough-looking men certainly looked like bullies, especially with the way they were looking at him. He just wasn't sure that it was still the right thing to do when coming up against fifty of them at the same time.

Somehow, though, he wasn't nearly as nervous facing the French as he was before a fencing bout with Rafa, even though these weapons were capable of doing much more damage than the practice swords he used in fencing class. He grinned; it was probably because this was a dream and as such there was no way he wasn't going to come out victorious, or get hurt.

However, just as the French sailors were about to leap to the attack, they stopped and their faces fell as they looked up over Sam's head.

The crew of the Mermaid were finally getting into the fight, and a wave of them was swinging and jumping across to the French frigate.

The two forces immediately leapt to engage each other and a chaotic melee ensued.

Sam glanced to one side as Smith landed nimbly beside him, perfectly balanced on the gently rolling deck. He gave the man a scathing look. 'You took your time, Mr Smith.'

'Sorry, Captain, I couldn't find the key to the sword locker.' The first mate gestured to his waist where dozens of keys of all different sizes jangled together.

Sam shook his head in exasperation. 'Maybe you should label them?'

Smithy lunged forward to block the swing of a French sailor and barely managed to halt a wooden belaying pin scant inches from impacting with Sam's head. He sighed in relief, straining slightly as the French sailor tried to force the pin down, and shook his head. 'I would if I could read, Captain, and believe me, I will do what I can to rectify the problem. But for now, perhaps you'd care to turn your attention to the fight?'

Sam cringed at the sight of the belaying pin, inches from his head. 'Thank you, Mr Smith. I think that would be a good idea, what would I do without you?'

Before they could say anything more they were separated from each other by the melee as they both waded into the fight.

While battles like this usually meant two rough lines forming and the two groups of people hacking at each other until one of them gave up, Sam knew that he lacked the strength to fight like that. Instead, he knew that his best way of making a meaningful contribution meant relying on his superior skill and agility.

He forged ahead, dancing through the enemy pack while laying about himself with his sword, knocking people out with blows to the head, blocking strikes meant for his men, or tripping enemies up with a quick thrust between their knees, essentially making a nuisance of himself. He closed his ears to the swearing and cursing that followed him from downed French sailors, thanking his mother for not signing him up for French classes at school, although he probably wouldn't have been taught most of the words that they were using - not by the teacher anyway.

He had thought that the cutlass would have been too unwieldy for him to use properly, it was much heavier than any of the swords he was used to and the curve made its balance interesting to say the least, but he found that he was having no problems at all, in fact it felt right in his hand, as if he'd had years of practice with it, to the extent that it seemed to be simply an extension of his arm.

Sam grinned as he spun and thrust and eventually broke through the pack of ordinary sailors. He found himself at the foot of the stairs up to the quarterdeck and he glanced around at the battle to make sure that his men were doing fine without his help before nimbly leaping up to the deck above. He hoped that that was where he would find the officers, because the quickest, least bloody way of ending the fight would be to force them to surrender.

He got to the top of the stairs and came face to face with what he assumed was the captain of the French ship.

He was a large, overweight, ugly brute of a man with a squashed nose and he reminded Sam of a French actor he had seen in a film once, Gerald, or Gerard, or something. He glared angrily at Sam from under hugely bushy eyebrows and a slow, evil grin spread across his face that reminded Sam instantly of Rafa.

'Well, come on zen, leetle man!'

Sam barely understood what the French Captain had said; his accent was so thick, but his intentions were perfectly clear as he immediately pulled out his sword and charged headlong at Sam, brandishing it wildly over his head.

'Another Rafa...' thought Sam, and he would have sighed in disappointment, but he didn't want to be too overconfident; it could be a feint after all.

It wasn't.

As the French Captain's sword started to descend towards his head, Sam sidestepped, almost casually, and the sword swished past him with inches to spare.

The man was taken by surprise and he overbalanced, ending up sprawled on the deck, quite lucky not to impale himself on his own sword. He rolled over, but before he could get up Sam stepped forward and placed the tip of his cutlass gently on his chest. The captain immediately let go of his sword, which clanged to the deck, and put his hands up. He most likely would have given the order for the French flag to come down if it hadn't already been shot down earlier, but instead he had to make do with pulling a white handkerchief out of his pocket, waving it as a sign of surrender and then handing it to Sam.

Sam took it and put it in his pocket with a smile. He offered his hand, helped the captain to stand and then firmly guided him to the rail overlooking the main deck. He stood by with his sword held ready as the Frenchman shouted out to his men to put down their weapons. In truth there weren't many of them still fighting anyway; Sam's men had taken them so completely by surprise.

The crew of the Mermaid cheered wildly and started the job of rounding up the remaining French crew and herding them below decks, making sure that were safely locked away where they couldn't start fighting again.

'Captain, you did it!' cried Smithy, bounding up the quarterdeck stairs, 'and with scarcely any bloodshed whatsoever, I've never heard of such a thing! The French will think twice before trying to hurt our families again, especially now that we have two ships to defend our homes!'

'It wasn't too hard, actually; we have a good bunch of men. Now I suppose we should do something about all this.' They looked around at the ship, taking in the damage. It was mainly superficial; thanks to Sam's order to aim high, the hull itself hadn't taken much damage, but the ship wasn't going to go anywhere until its rigging was put to rights.

Apparently, Smithy knew exactly what needed to be done and he stroked his short beard as he considered the men that had gathered beneath them on the main deck. 'With your permission, I'll leave one of the more sober bosuns in command with enough men to guard the captives and effect some repairs - they'll need to clear the damage and jury-rig a mast before they can set a course for home. And I'll give them orders to drop the Frogs off in a neutral port on the way; they can spread the tale of how handily they were beaten. That should help to deter any further mischief, on the part of the French anyway.'

Sam couldn't stop himself from yawning; the adrenaline from the fight was wearing off and he was suddenly more exhausted than he'd ever been before.

'That sounds good to me, thank you, Mr Smith. I'm going to go to my cabin to rest for a while, I'll leave everything in your more than capable hands.'

With the battle over and the day won Sam was eager to get to bed; he thought that maybe if he fell asleep he would wake up at home. He went to the side of the ship, jumped easily back over to the deck of the Mermaid and headed towards the stern, where he knew the captain's cabin usually was on a ship. He had to make his way along the entire length of the ship to get there, though, and as he did so his sailors stopped what they were doing and cheered him, patting him on the back and shaking his hand - he was obviously very well-liked by his crew.

Bosun Brown in particular was vociferous in his praise and he latched onto Sam and escorted him across the deck, as if he were a manager leading a boxer to the ring. 'Didya see that, mateys? Captain went up against the whole of the French ship on his own he did! Beat them all single-handed and then took down the Frog Captain with one blow!'

Sam blushed and tried to deny the man's wild claims, but he was drowned out by the cheers of the jubilant seamen. He gave up with a wry chuckle, figuring that he might as well let them have their victory and it wasn't going to hurt if they thought of him as an invincible captain. He told himself that it was for morale purposes only - it certainly wasn't because he liked being everybody's hero for once in his life.

Eventually, he managed to get to his cabin and Brown opened the door for him with a bow. He turned and waved one last time to his cheering crew before going in, closing the door and leaning against it.

'This must be how famous people feel when they get mobbed by fans.' His face lit up in a huge smile and he laughed to himself. 'This really is the best dream ever!'

Sam peered into the cool semi-darkness of the cabin, a stark contrast with the bright sunshine and stifling heat outside.

The cabin had a low roof that was only a couple of feet or so over Sam's head, but was very wide and deep. It took up the whole of the space underneath the quarterdeck at the stern of the ship and it was much larger than his bedroom at home. Against the wall at the back under the large stern window was a huge, four-poster bed hung with white mosquito netting and covered with mismatched cushions of all shapes and sizes.

The rest of the room was dominated by large rectangular table, as big, if not bigger, than the one that Sam's family ate dinner at. His stomach growled at the sight of a large bowl of fruit and he realised that he hadn't eaten anything since lunch, however long ago that had been.

He stepped further into the room and was able to pick out more details as his eyes continued to adjust to the light streaming through the window.

He was delighted to see that there were swords of all types hanging on the walls around the room - along with a few large, strategically-placed pieces of silk and a couple of mirrors, they were almost the only decorations apart from the furniture. He grabbed a banana from the table and started to peel it as he went to the nearest wall and peered at the swords displayed there. Each of them had a little wooden plaque underneath inscribed with the sword's story and he leaned forward to read the inscription under an ornate straight sword with a basket hilt.

Royal Navy. Sword of the value of one hundred guineas, taken from the captain of the HMS Sutherland, 74 gun ship of the line.

He reached out to touch the sword, feeling the edge.

'Ouch!'

Sam alternately took bites out of the banana and sucked his cut finger as he wandered around the rest of the room. His gaze moved across the other swords, before taking in the various other pieces of furniture. Aside from the six mismatched chairs gathered around the table there was a large cabinet full of clothing, a wash stand with a cloudy and cracked mirror and a couple of small sideboards. His eyes finally came to rest on a very large iron-bound chest sitting on the floor by the bed and, curious, he knelt down in front of it and tugged at the lid, but he couldn't get it to budge; it was locked.

He almost gave up and moved on, but something told him that he really should have the key to a chest in his own room. He patted down his pockets and sure enough, in the breast pocket of his jacket, he found a large brass key. He inserted it into the lock of the chest and turned it with some difficulty; the salt air hadn't done it any favours and it desperately needed some oil. Eventually, it sprang open with a clunk and Sam heaved up the heavy lid of the chest.

His face was lit up with a soft yellow glow as the contents of the chest were revealed - piles of gold coins, gems, silver bars and other assorted treasures filled the chest almost to the brim.

'Oh, boy.' Sam was impressed and he reached in to pick up a gold coin. It was huge, easily the size of his palm, and whatever picture had been on it was now long gone, rubbed away by use, and the coin was now not much more than a smooth metal disk. Just like the one that he had rescued from Violeta in Andrew's flat only an hour or so ago, it was far heavier than it looked.

He put the coin back into the chest and took a quick look through the rest of the treasure. There were enough necklaces, tiaras from so many different places as to make a collector weep as well as thousands of coins made of all sorts of precious metals. Sam quickly lost interest, though; despite the fact that he knew that the contents of the chest could buy him enough games and games consoles to be the envy of all his friends, he wasn't the kind of boy to be obsessed over money. He closed the lid of the chest and locked it, putting the key back into his pocket.

He stood up and brushed off his knees.

'Well, I think I'm ready to go home now, please, I have a lot of homework to do.' He spoke out loud to the world at large, announcing his wishes, just in case anyone was listening. He waited for something to happen but it didn't seem that anything was going to.

An idea occurred to him and he looked down at his feet.

'There's no place like home?' He clicked the heels of his boots together and again waited, looking around the room and watching for something to happen, but still nothing did. He tried pinching himself on the arm, but that didn't do anything except make him feel even more foolish. He shrugged; he hadn't really expected any of those things to work, but it had been worth a shot.

He was at a loss; it didn't seem that he had any control over waking up or getting home or whatever he needed to do.

With nothing else to do, he resolved to go back to his original plan; hopefully if he went to sleep he'd wake up back in the real world.

He unbuckled his sword belt and put it, along with his hat, on the table, then hung his jacket from one of the chair backs. With a yawn went over to sit on the bed and started to take off his boots. They were tight and high, coming up almost to his knees, and he had to struggle with them for a while before they finally came off. He used so much force to get them loose that the second one actually flew out of his hands as it came free and bounced off the wall, knocking a sword flying, before ricocheting off of a table and landing with a thunk, somewhere out of sight.

'Oops!' He giggled and laid back on the bed, feeling very lightheaded all of a sudden with tiredness. He found a comfortable position amongst the cushions and settled down.

'Well, this has been a fantastic dream, I hope I have another one like it soon!' He closed his eyes and fell instantly asleep.

CHAPTER 4
PORT ROYAL

'Sam! Sam!' the voice was very faint and he could barely make out his mother calling to him from up the street where she stood in the door of his flat.

He turned his head up to the sky. It had stopped raining and the clouds were clearing up. There was a rainbow floating there now, brilliant in the early evening Spanish sun, the colours so bright they almost hurt his eyes. It was beautiful. He sighed and dropped his head, returning his gaze to the grey city and the dirty streets.

'I'm coming!'

He started to run but there was something wrong; no matter how fast he went he couldn't get any closer to where Violeta and his mother were waiting for him in the darkness of the doorway.

He slipped and slid uncontrollably on the rain-slicked pavement; it was like trying to run on ice. Puzzled, he looked down.

Why were his shoes red? And why was the pavement a bright yellow colour?

There was a rumble of thunder and heavy dark clouds passed in front of the sun. The rain came flooding back and the colours faded from the city around him, as if someone had flicked a switch and turned the world into black and white.

'Sam, it's dangerous out there! Please hurry!' From up ahead his mother beckoned urgently while Violeta looked on in fear, half hidden behind her skirts. Suddenly, they stiffened and Violeta pointed at something over his shoulder.

Sam turned and froze in horror.

Rafa was coming up the road behind him, stalking him, walking with no problems on the slippery concrete. For some reason he was wearing a black, pointed hat and had a green face, but Sam had no time to wonder why, he just turned and tried to run, slipping, sliding, falling, unable to escape...

'Run, Sam! Run!'

He could feel Rafa's fetid breath on his neck, hear him panting, coming closer and closer.

'SAM! SAM!' his mother was almost screaming now, calling out in fear.

Strangely though, his mother's voice was becoming far deeper than usual, more gravelly, more masculine.

And what was that she was calling him?

'Captain, Captain!'

Sam opened his eyes to find Smithy leaning over him, shaking him gently by the shoulder, waking him from the nightmare. He sat up and looked around at the dimly lit ship's cabin, blinking sleepily.

'This isn't Kansas.'

'Kansas? Er... No, Captain.' Smithy's brow wrinkled slowly in confusion, but he continued with his report anyway. 'Port Royal is in sight off the starboard bow.'

'Already? How long was I sleeping for?'

'Nearly two days.'

At this Sam came wide awake and stared up at the first mate in shock. 'Two days? No wonder I'm so hungry!' That and his parents would be worried sick about him as well, he thought.

He rolled out of bed and splashed water over his face from the nearby bowl, spilling much of it on the floor and the rest on his shirt, before stumbling across to the fruit on the dining table. It was all a little bit wilted, but still edible, especially for a teenage boy, and Sam was so hungry that he didn't care for a few black spots. He picked up an apple and bit into it as he looked around the room for his boots. One of them was near the bed where he had dropped it, but the one that had gone flying across the room was proving to be more elusive. Dropping down to all fours, he crawled across the floor, the apple hanging out of his mouth, and searched under the furniture for the missing piece of footwear.

'Er, excuse me, Captain, but we received a signal from the shore a few minutes ago. You have been summoned to a parlay with Captain Teach in half an hour.'

'Uh-huh.' Sam mumbled his assent around the apple, but he wasn't really listening - he had spotted his missing boot and was lying on the floor with his head underneath the cabinet in the corner of the room. It was in reach, barely, but somehow it had gotten wedged in firmly and was resisting all of his grunting efforts to pull it out.

'If you don't mind my saying, Captain, you should probably not dawdle; you know how, er, well... *violent*, Teach can get if anyone is late to an appointment with him.'

At last, Sam managed to tease the boot free and was backing out from under the table when what his first mate was saying finally got through to him. He froze where he was, with his arse sticking up in the air and an apple in his mouth, unconcerned about his dignity, while he ran over the man's words in his mind.

The information took a while to sink in, but when it did he shot up onto his knees and twisted to face Smithy, spitting the apple out in shock. 'Hang on a second. Captain *Teach* you said?'

'Yes, sir.'

'*Edward* Teach?'

'Uh... yes, sir?'

Sam suddenly went white and swallowed nervously. 'Captain Edward Teach?'

'Yes, sir.'

'Oh, boy.'

Suddenly it was very important that he got a move on. He pulled his boots and jacket on as quickly as he could, took his hat and sword from the table, and was about to run out the door when it occurred to him that it might be a good idea to have some money with him when he went into town, just in case. He unlocked the chest, grabbed a few coins at random and stuffed a couple of the big ones and a few of the smaller ones into his pockets, not really having any idea whether that was a lot or not. He closed and locked the chest and hurried out after Smithy into the brilliant sunshine on deck.

Bosun Brown and five other sailors rowed their captain and first mate in a ship's boat to Port Royal, the small town on the island of Jamaica that was home to the community of pirates. The place had been featured in so many books and films that it had taken on an almost romantic status and Sam was excited to see it in all its glory at the height of pirate culture in the Caribbean.

The reality was quite disappointing; it turned out to be not much more than a collection of a few dozen solid-looking buildings surrounded by numerous wooden shacks, all grouped haphazardly around the harbour and a large town square.

As they made their way across the bay, Smithy told Sam that the town had once been a lot larger and grander, with three forts, a church and English style brick buildings. Then, almost twenty years ago, there had been a severe earthquake that had destroyed almost all of the town and caused two of the forts to just sink right into the sea. The people had rebuilt, but had been understandably reluctant to expend too much effort just in case there was another disaster. It was a fear that proved to be justified when a fire burned most of the new buildings to the ground again only ten years later. Since then a couple of hurricanes had passed by, each time causing even more destruction, so most of the buildings had a very temporary feeling to them. The only people who had bothered to build properly, according to Smithy, were the ones that could afford to keep up with the almost constant repairs that were needed. Like Captain Teach for example.

They landed at a wooden jetty that served as the docks, directly in front of the square where a market was usually held selling the fish and goods that were unloaded directly from the ships in the harbour.

Sam climbed up the wooden stairs that led from the water to the square and turned to look back out into the harbour. There were about a dozen ships of various sizes anchored in a rough extended line just offshore. Most were small sloops or barges belonging to traders, but there were five other warships that were about the same size as the Mermaid. One of them in particular caught his eye; it was bigger than the rest, darker and just exuded menace, but before he could remark on it, Smithy patted Sam on the shoulder and gently but urgently pulled him away, reminding him that Captain Teach was waiting. He followed his first mate and they made their way across the square through the busy market and into the town itself.

Walking through Port Royal was a unique experience.

Sam's senses were assaulted from every side. Whatever way he turned there was something to turn his still mostly empty stomach; the sights, the smells, even some of the sounds were more disgusting than anything he'd ever come across. He was also extremely glad he had big boots on and didn't have to touch anything. Or anyone.

Compared to the cities that Sam was accustomed to, Port Royal was a tiny little place, more like the little village his Catalan grandmother had grown up in and that he visited a couple of times a year for local holidays. There were only a few streets, lined with closely packed wooden houses, some of which were little more than a shed such as you'd find at the end of a garden. The streets themselves were dirt mixed with sand mixed with all kinds of stuff that Sam didn't really want to think about.

However, Port Royal made up for its small size by the sheer number of people it managed to pack in and Smithy and the group of Sam's sailors had to all but force their way through the crowds so that their captain wouldn't be late.

All sizes and shapes of people were moving about the streets, from men missing limbs to women in colourful dresses and questionable make-up, to hard looking sailors with a stony glare in their eyes. One thing they all had in common though was the smell; obviously deodorant didn't exist here. Nor baths, probably.

Sam didn't see much of the people though, he was too busy concentrating on where he put his feet, or rather where he didn't want to put them. He shuddered when he noticed that none of the people around them, including his sailors, had shoes on. Most of the time you couldn't tell, though; their feet and legs were so caked with filth it looked like they were all wearing boots. His attention was so fixed on the floor that he jumped, startled, when he was narrowly missed by a stream of stinking liquid that was thrown from an open door next to him.

'Aargh! Haven't these people ever heard of a toilet?'

Smithy overheard Sam's complaint. 'Aye, Captain, they have, it's just sewers we don't have.'

'But we're right by the sea! Can't they just, you know, dump it over a cliff or something? Or even better, do their business in the sea in the first place?'

Smithy turned up his nose in disgust. 'In the sea? That's where we get our food from, that would be revolting! At least in the street all we get are dirty shoes that we can clean later.'

'I guess.' Sam shrugged before looking back down at the street and continuing to try to pick his way around the worst of the mess.

'Captain!' Smithy's voice alerted Sam.

He lifted his head in alarm and found that his nose was about an inch from an extremely hairy chest, he recoiled and stumbled backwards, only just avoiding a collision. 'Oh, I'm sorry, I wasn't looking where I was going.'

He tried to move around the man, but found his way obstructed by another hulking figure.

Sam stepped back again so that he could assess the situation. Five massive men, taller even than Bosun Brown, were standing side by side in front of them, completely blocking the road. They had their arms crossed across broad chests, were glaring down at Sam and his crew and looked like they weren't going to move out of the way any time soon. The locals couldn't pass either and were hurrying to find alternate routes, not wanting to be anywhere near what was obviously going to be trouble.

Smithy moved up to stand beside his captain and addressed the men in a threatening voice. 'We're on our way to meet Captain Teach, lads, at his invitation, mind you, so if you deny our passage then you are going against his express wishes.'

The biggest brute in the middle of the group, the hairy man who Sam had been about to walk into, spoke up. 'You are not wanted at the meeting.' Although "speaking" was a strong way of putting it; it was more like a sustained grunt that could barely be understood as words. He was obviously the leader though and, by the looks of the other men, possessed of the most brains of the bunch.

Sam turned to Smithy. 'Can't we get to the meeting another way?'

'No, sir.' Smithy pointed with his chin. 'The tavern is just beyond them and the route around them would take us more than fifteen minutes - Captain Teach would never forgive you for being so late and there's no guarantee that there won't be more of them waiting for us on the other side anyway.'

Smithy turned back to the men blocking their way. He was determined to get his captain to the meeting, but was not yet willing to try to force his way through. 'Who, exactly, doesn't want us at the meeting?'

It almost looked as if the man was going to panic as he realised that Sam and his men weren't going to just leave as expected. Even worse they were asking him questions that required him to use his brain, albeit only slightly, to answer. He looked around, seeking help among his friends, but found none and was forced to respond himself.

'Um... You are not wanted at the meeting.'

Smithy had completely lost his patience and he waved imperiously at the thugs. 'Clear the way immediately! Captain Teach will not be happy if we are delayed and will be looking for someone to blame. He will not have to look very hard to find you and undoubtedly you will very quickly find yourselves rotting in his cage.'

Strangely, far from being cowed by Smithy's mention of the pirate lord's anger, the man was seemingly gaining in confidence. Sam watched, fascinated - he could almost see the cogs turning in the man's head and nearly laughed at the look of almost mindless content that came over the man's face when he stuck with his decision to use the reply he'd been instructed to give, comfortable in the thought that it was the only thing he needed to cover all eventualities.

'You are not wanted at the meeting.'

Smithy was getting very annoyed. He turned to Sam, 'I'm sorry, Captain, this is useless, we'll have to force our way through.'

'I'd prefer not to resort to violence if we don't have to. Let me try something first.'

Sam had had enough. He recognised the man as being one of the, thankfully rare, breed of men who had completely ignored the development of his brain in favour of the development of his muscles and knew that there was a much better way of dealing with the problem than playing into his hands by fighting.

He stepped forward to confront the brute, even though it made him crane his neck to look up.

The man looked down at him with a sneer of disdain, 'you are not...'

Sam cut him off before he could finish. 'Yes, I know. You've already said that. Now tell us something we don't know. Who sent you? Why are you blocking our way? Does Captain Teach know you are doing this? Are you part of his crew or do you belong to the crew of one of the other captains? Are you here to stop just us or everyone who comes to the meeting?'

The man was getting more and more bewildered as Sam continued to bombard him with questions and his confusion quickly spread to the men around him. They started looking at each other uncertainly, getting more and more worried. The leader opened his mouth to speak, but evidently something had short circuited in his head and nothing came out except for a brief grunt.

'Uh....'

The big brute turned to the men at his side and they huddled together to try to work out exactly what to do. There was a brief discussion composed mostly of grunts and hand gestures that increased in violence as it continued, with much pushing and shoving. Finally, after about a minute of this, the leader punched one of the others in the face, signalling that some kind of conclusion had been reached. They broke from the huddle and turned to obstruct the street again and the leader answered Sam with a look on his face that spoke of absolute confidence in himself and pride in his understanding of his orders.

'You are not wanted at the meeting!'

However, instead of the young captain that he'd been expecting, the man found himself eye to eye with a passing donkey that gave him a funny look but otherwise didn't seem too worried about not being able to go to a meeting of any kind. The donkey didn't bother to stop walking either and just pushed the huge pirate out of the way. He fell on his arse with a squawk and a squish and rolled away, barely avoiding being trampled on; the locals had taken full advantage of the momentary absence of the blockade to start using the street again.

Sam and his escort had watched all this from further up the road - he had deliberately overloaded the man's mind with questions and then used the distraction resulting from his indecision to just stroll right past with his men. They hadn't even had to be particularly sneaky about it.

Smithy was trying very hard not to laugh. 'I'm not sure, Captain, but I believe that someone wants us to think we're not wanted at the meeting.'

'Very droll, Smithy.'

Sam shook his head and smiled wryly as he turned and led the group away. He was really beginning to like his first mate; he had a sense of humour that he could really appreciate and a knowledge of the world that Sam suddenly found himself in that he was sure was going to prove invaluable.

Smith grinned back at him, cheekily. 'Sorry, I just couldn't resist, sir. But still, if someone is trying to keep us from turning up, then this meeting must be very important for them.' He stopped walking and indicated that they had arrived at their destination, a building near what passed for the centre of town. 'Well, here we are, Captain. This is Edward Teach's headquarters when he's not on board the Queen Anne's Revenge.'

Sam looked up at what was apparently a tavern. It was far better constructed than the majority of the rest of the structures in the town and had every appearance of having been put together by someone who knew a little bit about what they were doing, or at least wasn't too drunk to knock in a nail straight while he was doing it. It was a wide, two story wooden building made of thick, solid looking planks of wood which looked like they had come from a ship, indeed some of them still had dried up barnacles clinging to them. The weather-faded sign above the door read "The Bloated Lobster" and Sam could just about make out a picture depicting a man dressed in a red jacket face down in the sand on a beach while the sun beat down on him. He frowned, not quite getting the reference and not quite sure that he wanted to either.

There were a few tattered wanted posters pinned to the side of the tavern showing sketches of some very rough looking men. One of them looked vaguely like Uncle Andrew and Sam laughed. He started to go and take a closer look, thinking that he could take it with him as a joke to show his uncle if he ever got home, but Smithy called him back with an exasperated voice.

'Captain? If you please? You're late enough already.' The first mate was holding the door open for him with an expectant look on his face.

Sam looked around at his men and his smile disappeared instantly; they all looked very nervous and most of them had their hands on the hilts of the cutlasses in their belts. They looked far more nervous now than they had before going into battle against the French, which wasn't very reassuring.

'Don't worry, Captain, he doesn't bite. Not often, anyway.' Smithy laughed, but it was forced and Sam could hear the note of fear in it.

Sam took a deep breath for courage, which was a mistake, and he coughed as the smoke coming from a nearby fire hit the back of his throat. It looked like someone was burning a pile of rotten vegetables to try to get rid of it, but for some reason the stuff in the metal bucket seemed to be moving.

Sam's eyes started watering and he gasped for breath. 'Oh wow, what I wouldn't give for a mint...'

He pulled the French Captain's handkerchief out of his pocket and held it over his mouth and nose; he'd noticed before that it was fairly heavily perfumed and he was hoping that it would do something to block the stench of, well, everything.

He took another deep breath, as much for luck and courage as for air, and moved past Smithy into the darkness of the tavern.

It took a while for Sam's eyes to adapt to the dim light in the single, large, smoky room. There weren't any real windows to speak of, just a couple of small holes in the walls, mostly blocked with shutters, and the only light was coming from a few scattered lanterns and a huge fire in the middle of the room over which was cooking what Sam hoped was a whole pig, but like most things in Port Royal he didn't want to look too closely at it to make sure. Consequently, there was no air in the room and it was stifling hot. Sam was finding it hard to breath, something that his nervousness and the continuing bad smells weren't exactly helping with.

They crossed the room towards the back of the tavern, stepping over the occasional snoring seaman who was passed out drunk, even this early in the afternoon. The benches of the long tables were filled with sailors laughing and playing cards or dangerous-looking games with knives. They were also drinking heavily. Everyone in the room was drinking, in fact, even the barmaids and the cooks. Sam didn't particularly take offence at this, though; he wasn't so young and innocent as to not know what a tavern was for and some of the boys in his year had even boasted of drinking in the park on weekends, something that he thought was much worse than what the adults around him were doing.

Smithy halted at a door at the back of the room and gave Sam a worried look. 'The invitation was just for you, Captain, we'll have to wait for you in here. Sorry. Give a shout if you need us.' He leant down to whisper in Sam's ear. 'I'll make sure the men stay sober, sir, just in case.'

'Good idea and keep a weather eye out for troublemakers. If what happened outside is any indication, then somebody might try to provoke them into something.'

Sam looked around the room at the sailors scattered about the tavern. They were a rough lot, but his men were tough and had the confidence of having just successfully come through a battle, plus if a fight broke out they would have the distinct advantage of being sober.

He gave Smithy a smile and steeled himself. 'Wish me luck.'

'Good luck, Captain.'

Sam turned and went through the door.

CHAPTER 5
BLACKBEARD

Sam stepped through the door and into the back garden of the tavern. There weren't many back gardens in Barcelona, but he'd been in quite a few in England and they all had grass, were green and pleasant, and usually had somewhere for children to play, like roundabouts or swings.

This one was quite a bit different, though.

For a start there was no grass, just sand with a few worn and dirty wooden boards thrown haphazardly onto it. There was a swing of sorts, but it certainly wasn't very typical and Sam hoped that it wasn't meant for children - in the back corner of the garden, swaying gently from side to side in the breeze, was a tall, thin cage hanging from a gallows-like stand. There was a skeleton with an eye patch standing in it, picked clean and bleached white by the sun, and as Sam stood just inside the door, it seemed to be looking right at him and grinning.

He tore his eyes away from the skeleton with some difficulty and took in the rest of the garden. It was large, easily as big as the tavern itself, and was surrounded by a high fence made of the same boards as the building. The fence blocked out much of the noise from the town, making the garden almost peaceful after the chaos outside, but unfortunately most of the breeze as well, making it stiflingly hot.

In the middle of this space was a long table piled high with food and drink. The chairs around the table were occupied by about half a dozen men and women of different shapes, sizes and races, but Sam hardly registered any of them as his eyes slid straight past, drawn directly to the huge man who was lounging in an enormous gold leaf covered throne at the end of the table.

This was Captain Edward Teach, better known to history as "Blackbeard" - one of the most feared pirates to ever sail the Caribbean seas and leader of the "Brethren of the Coast", the group of pirates based in Port Royal.

The pirate lord was dressed in a black jacket and black breeches with a white shirt and long black boots. On his head, partially covering his wild black hair, was a large black tricorn hat which was pulled low, obscuring his face and hiding his eyes. Poking out from under the brim of the hat was his trademark beard. Long and bushy, it looked like he could use it to hide food, or maybe nest a few small animals if he chose to do so, and he had what looked like small red firecrackers each with tiny white fuses woven into it. Somewhat incongruously for his fierce reputation, however, he was sitting in the shade of a large frilly pink parasol being held above him by a boy who looked only a few years younger than Sam.

He was paying no attention to the conversation around the table, instead he was using a curved sword that was at least a couple of times larger than Sam's cutlass to trim his fingernails. The huge blade somehow looked small in the man's gigantic hands and Sam swallowed as he had a sudden vision of them wrapping around his throat.

Sam pushed away his fear and forced himself to leave the concealing shadows of the door. He walked out into the sunlight, but his steps faltered and he came to a halt again as the pirates around the table fell silent, paused in their eating and, in unison, turned to look at him.

Noting the change in his guests, Blackbeard stopped his manicure and lifted his head slightly. Two fiery eyes looked out at Sam from underneath the hat and he shuddered when he got the feeling that his very soul was being inspected.

'Aargh, good! Finally we are all here. Nice of you to join us at last, Captain Vives.'

Sam swallowed nervously. 'Er... I... I'm sorry I'm late, Captain Teach.'

'Only fashionably so,' rumbled Blackbeard with a chuckle. 'I will forgive you, but only because I saw you drop anchor barely half an hour ago and know you could not have got here very much quicker. Just this once, though, mind you.'

Sam found that his anxiety was not in any way lessened by Blackbeard's "forgiveness", but he forced a smile and nodded, trying to appear unperturbed at being the centre of so much attention. 'Thank you, sir.'

'Don't mention it, Vives, don't mention it. Now, please, sit and enjoy my hospitality! Eat, drink, converse, and when everyone is well-satisfied we will begin.'

With that, Blackbeard lowered his head, which hid his eyes once more, and went back to trimming his nails with his unfeasibly large sword.

The rest of the pirates followed his example and returned to their food and conversations.

For the moment, Sam found himself largely ignored but, despite no longer being the centre of attention, he discovered that he was still feeling distinctly uneasy and there was a strange tingling at the back of his mind that he had never felt before. He couldn't quite pin down the source of the feeling, or even whether it was his mind's natural reaction to its first encounter with real danger or just the beginnings of a headache from having slept too long. Thankfully, though, it was only a momentary distraction and he found that he could ignore the sensation easily enough. He resolved to not let his apprehension get in the way of his enjoying himself, like it had so many times in the past, and he grinned at the thought that, even if he was in mortal danger, keeping the company of cut-throats and murderers who might turn on him at any moment, it was still a hell of a lot more fun than doing his maths homework.

And it wasn't as if anything could actually hurt him anyway, because none of this was actually real.

With his eternal internal debate out of the way, Sam looked for a spare seat and found that the only one left available to him was at the end of the table directly facing Blackbeard. It looked like none of the pirates already sitting around the table had been willing to be directly in the pirate lord's line of sight and Sam found some of his nervousness returning before he could force it back down again. He briefly wondered if he could drag the chair around to one side of the table so as to better remain unobtrusive, but he knew that he would just call even more attention to himself that way and he decided not to.

He made his way over to the chair, slipped quietly into it and inconspicuously filled his plate. He then tried to blend in by copying the other pirates, which essentially meant talking while chewing, eating with his hands, laughing with a mouth full of drink and generally scratching all those bits of his body that he had been told it was impolite to touch in public.

He probably should have been nauseated by the sounds the people were making and the general smell from the unwashed bodies sitting nearby, but he was far too hungry to worry about any of that, and he contented himself with filling his belly with the food, which was surprisingly delicious. He polished off a whole chicken on his own, most of a loaf of bread and followed it up with a couple of bananas for good measure, eating more in one sitting than he'd ever eaten in his life. One thing pirates did well, it seemed, was eat and drink, although he did stay clear of most of the drinks that were on offer and stuck to water instead of the alcohol that everyone else was drinking. It wasn't that he had anything against alcohol - he'd had sips of champagne at family dinners for toasts, but he wasn't quite ready to graduate to tankards full of beer and he certainly wasn't going anywhere near the hard spirit that was on offer here, even though the woman next to him looked like she was enjoying it immensely, swigging down glass after glass of it with no effect.

Aside from Sam and Blackbeard there were five other pirates sitting at the table and Sam inspected them curiously as he ate. Just as he himself was, the four men and one women were busy stuffing themselves as if they hadn't eaten in weeks, talking and laughing amiably for the most part, and he was content to stay silent, listening to them. At first the mode of address around the table was rather formal, so it was easy enough to learn their names.

The only woman present, Captain Bonny, sitting directly on Sam's left, was about thirty years old and very good looking. She was wearing tight brown leather trousers, a matching brown leather waistcoat over a white blouse, and had a pink silk sash wrapped tightly around her waist. Every so often she leant across the table to grab more food, which made her blouse gape revealingly and her knee brush against Sam's. This was understandably making him feel very uncomfortable, a feeling that persisted right up until she turned and smiled at him - the smile was distinctly lacking in teeth and those that she had were an unhealthy brown colour. He shuddered and from then on had no problem ignoring her close proximity.

Next to Bonny was a Chinese man, Captain Wong, who had an incredibly long and very thin droopy white moustache. He looked to be in his sixties and was wearing a little black hat with a tassel and what, to Sam, looked like red silk pyjamas that had most probably plundered from a noblewoman whose ship he had captured. He was holding his chicken with both hands and nibbling at it rapidly, rotating it as if it were corn on the cob.

On Sam's right hand was a big man, Captain Caesar, who had the darkest skin that Sam had ever seen. He was wearing loose beige trousers and a tight black waistcoat over a bare chest. The sun was gleaming off of his shaved head and his face was covered with tattoos that were almost invisible against his skin and looked like they extended down over his entire body. He was a very cheerful, friendly man, who laughed very often, revealing brilliant white teeth that were in stark contrast to his colouring.

The third man, Captain Fitzhume, sitting next to Caesar, was drinking from a huge tankard with his little finger sticking up, like Sam had caught his mother doing sometimes, and, if he hadn't already heard the man's clipped accent, that would have instantly told him that he was English. He was rather overweight and wearing what looked very much like a Royal Navy uniform - a dark blue jacket with gold buttons and gold epaulets that didn't make it even half-way around his body, as well as trousers that had somehow remained clean and white under the difficult conditions of the town. During the conversation Sam's suspicions that he had been an officer in the Royal Navy were confirmed, but he unfortunately didn't elaborate on how he left the service, whether it had been his choice or whether he'd been drummed out of the service. His manners at the table were impeccable, in sharp contrast to everyone else's, although he had the most annoying laugh that Sam had ever heard, akin to the braying of a donkey.

Even though each of the pirate captains was vastly different from the others, it was the final member of the party, sitting between Fitzhume and Blackbeard himself, who stood out most in Sam's mind.

He didn't seem to be a captain and the others certainly weren't treating him as one of them. He didn't attempt to join in with the conversation around the table, but just sat and watched, as if biding his time for something, and Sam wondered what he was doing there. He looked like he was probably around twenty years old, but the way he was hunched over his food as he ate made him seem almost like an old man. His face and hands were dirty and bronzed from the sun and his greyish-blue eyes were constantly roving around, almost hidden behind a curtain of long, lank, brown hair.

Unlike the rest of the pirates around the table, he wasn't dressed flamboyantly or richly, but rather he wore the same kind of rough clothing that Sam had seen on many of the pirates and locals around town. He did make one bizarre concession to individuality, though; there was a green parrot sitting on the shoulder of his long brown coat.

Sam was fairly sure that the bird was dead and stuffed because it was leaning at a bit of a drunken angle and wasn't moving in the slightest.

All in all, he was a very shifty looking character and Sam took an instant dislike to him. He was well aware that trouble often came from where you least expected it, and when it did, it was usually a lot more serious than when it came, say, from someone who was very obviously a bully, like Rafa. This man looked like trouble of the very worst kind and whenever their eyes met the man's gaze was filled with such intense hatred, as if Sam had done something to harm him, that he had to look away again almost instantly. It also didn't help that the uneasy feeling that Sam had had before came back twice as strong every time that he even glanced at him.

However, despite the animosity of the man sitting at Blackbeard's left hand, Sam found that he was really beginning to enjoy himself. The food was good and the company wasn't bad either, once you got past the smell and the table manners, and as the drink flowed and tongues loosened, they moved on from talking about polite matters like the weather and the sea.

Sam expected the captains to start competing with each other to see who could impress their audience with the most bloodthirsty tales of their heroism and daring, but, to his bewilderment, Wong and Fitzhume somehow got into an in-depth discussion about tea, of all things, and began debating the relative merits of Indian and Chinese varieties.

As a Spanish boy who was only partly English, tea didn't hold the same fascination for Sam as it did for people like his mother or Uncle Andrew, who never seemed to be without a cup in their hands, and the Chinese captain's reedy voice, totally in keeping with his bird-like table manners, added to the Englishman's nasal whine, matching his awful laugh, didn't make it a conversation that could hold his attention for long.

Fortunately, Wong and Fitzhume were at the other end of the table from him, so it was easy enough for Sam to blank them out and concentrate on the, thankfully, far more interesting things being said by the captains sitting on either side of him.

Sam didn't have any tales of his own to tell, beyond the attack on the French ship, so he contented himself with listening to Caesar and Bonny exchanging stories, asking the occasional questions and laughing at their jokes and anecdotes. The three of them became quite companionable during the course of the meal and he came to see that behind the ruthless exteriors of the pirates lurked funny and fun-loving people.

Sam was fascinated by Caesar; he was a powerful speaker with a rich deep voice and he told his stories with such passion that they almost seemed to come to life. It was his description of how he got into piracy after being kidnapped from his tribe in Africa that particularly caught Sam's imagination.

'My men and I stole a boat and escaped the slave ship bringing us to the new world during a hurricane off of the Florida reefs. We were the only survivors because, not long after that, the ship was driven onto the rocks of the same small island we had landed on. For a while we tried to live like farmers, just as we had back home, but it was impossible and we soon realised that our lives were now joined inextricably with the sea, so we pretended to be shipwrecked sailors. When ships passing by on the busy trading route stopped to rescue us, we would row out and board them, taking what we needed to survive by force. That wasn't enough for us though, so we eventually took one of the ships, which I renamed the African Queen, and left the island to come to Port Royal. And here I am, years later, with my own crew and ship.'

He paused, his story told, but not finished. 'I dream of going back to Africa and rejoining my tribe, but I know that is not possible; they will have chosen a new leader by now and will not accept me. But that is of no matter; I have grown so much since I left, seen so many wondrous things. My horizons have expanded so far and I love the sea too much to go back to the simple life I once had.'

Caesar gazed off into the distance, lost with his thoughts for a second, but then he shook himself and turned the full force of his smile on Sam. 'And you, Captain Vives, how did you get into our line of work?'

Sam couldn't answer straight away because he had just taken another large bite of chicken and his table manners were so deeply ingrained that he just wasn't able to speak with his mouth full. While Caesar patiently waited, he worked his mouth furiously, chewing as quickly as he could and trying to swallow the meat so that he could reply without too much delay. He was so occupied with his manners, however, that it never occurred to him that he had nothing to say.

He was saved from trying to make up something believable off the top of his head, something he'd never been very good at, when there was movement from the head of the table. Instantly everybody stopped what they were doing and turned to pay attention.

Blackbeard set his sword on the table with a loud clang, then cleared his throat and opened his mouth to talk.

Sam, however, was in mid swallow. Startled first by the sudden silence and then by the sound of the sword hitting the table, he swallowed badly.

He choked, then coughed. A pebble-sized piece of chicken breast was ejected forcibly from his mouth and flew across the table. It bounced a few times before coming to rest in front of Blackbeard.

Blackbeard closed his mouth with an audible *pop*. He glanced down at the half-chewed piece of meat glistening on the table in front of him and then slowly looked back up.

Sam coughed once more, behind his hand this time, his eyes watering. He smiled weakly. 'Excuse me!'

Blackbeard continued to stare at him for a second, but suddenly a broad grin broke out on his face and he roared with laughter, tossing his head back to the sky.

'I like you, Vives!' he said when his laughter eventually subsided. 'I hope I don't have to kill you!'

'That would be nice, thank you.' Sam put a brave face on and smiled back at Blackbeard. He was terrified but knew that the best way to stay safe in this kind of situation was to appear tough and carefree.

Blackbeard chuckled one more time, shaking his head in amusement, before suddenly his face changed, going back to its usual fierce expression.

He scowled at his guests and rapped his knuckles on the table three times, almost ceremoniously. 'I call to order this meeting of the Brethren of the Coast. For some of you it is your first time here in Port Royal and I bid you welcome.'

Blackbeard nodded first to Captain Fitzhume, who managed to bow elegantly in return, even though he was sitting down, and then to Sam, who contented himself with just nodding back, sure that he would just look silly if he tried to bow.

The giant pirate gave Sam a small smile and a considering look before he continued. 'Thank you all for taking time away from your busy lives to join me here today. I know that you all have legitimate business to take care of so I'll keep this short and then those of you that are in a hurry to leave may do so.'

As he spoke he looked around at the group assembled in front of him, his eyes boring into them one by one, and each of the pirates reacted in some way to his glare. Caesar and Fitzhume met it impassively while Wong and Bonny cringed slightly in fear, but Sam and, surprisingly, the shifty looking man with the parrot, met Blackbeard's eyes confidently, at least outwardly.

Blackbeard nodded, as if he had just had something confirmed, and went on with his speech. 'I have decided that I am going to retire soon. I have enough riches to last me more than one lifetime and now I want to be able to spend it without having to keep looking over my shoulder for the Royal Navy.

'I've gathered you here today because, of all the captains that are under my command, you are the strongest and best. And while some of you fall quite a way away from having my respect, I'm hoping that maybe at least one of you will prove capable enough to take over from me. However, that remains to be seen.'

There was quite a stir around the table as Blackbeard paused to let the words sink in. Most of the captains fidgeted in their seats or exclaimed to the person sitting next to them, but Sam saw that once again the man sitting at Blackbeard's left hand didn't react like everyone else; he remained silent and just watched the others. He had the same shifty expression as ever, but Sam saw that there was now a note of confidence and arrogance in his smirk; Blackbeard's revelation obviously wasn't new to him.

Blackbeard gave the group a fierce look, silencing the mutterings and freezing them in place. 'Do NOT think that I am going to just hand over my ships and men to one of you landlubbers without you proving yourself first!'

'So, what are you proposing, Captain?' Caesar asked, his deep voice posing the question that was on everybody's mind.

'I was just getting to that, Captain Caesar,' rumbled Blackbeard in a voice that was suddenly deeper and had a power behind it that struck straight to the soul of most of the captains, almost physically throwing them back in their seats. Sam, though, had to hide a laugh behind his hand with a discreet cough; he was reminded of the various Batman films and the silly voices that the actors put on while behind the mask to make them seem scarier.

'We are going to have a friendly little "contest" to see who is the best among you and therefore worthy enough to take over my empire.'

The pirate lord looked around the group, again meeting their eyes one by one. 'Captain Wong, Captain Bonny, Captain Vives, Captain Caesar, Captain Fitzhume, you will be joined by my first mate here, Jack Swallow, in contending for my soon to be vacated throne.'

Sam raised an eyebrow at the name of the first mate and caught the man laughing behind his hand. He wondered if that was his real name or whether he could possibly have chosen it for himself as some kind of joke, a reference to the *Pirates of the Caribbean* films. Of course, there was always the possibility that this was just Sam's subconscious giving someone a funny name to keep things interesting - after all, anything could happen in a dream. It would certainly explain the absurd parrot as well.

'Make sure you get some rest tonight because the festivities begin tomorrow at noon and you do not want to be too tired to put on a good show.' Blackbeard said this with an evil smile that made Sam think that there would not be much joy involved in these "festivities".

This was obviously a dismissal and the pirate captains downed the dregs of their drinks and stood up, a couple of them rather unsteadily on their feet. They started filing towards the door, all except for "Jack Swallow", who sat where he was and continued to study everyone else, sizing up his competition. He met Sam's eye and very deliberately reached out to pick up some breadcrumbs from the table. With a quick motion he threw them up at the parrot on his shoulder. The parrot didn't move, it was truly dead and stuffed - Sam could now see the wire that attached it by its feet to Swallow's coat. The action struck a chord with Sam, though, reminding him of something, but he couldn't quite remember exactly what it was. The moment was lost, however, as Swallow turned away to face Blackbeard.

Sam couldn't put his finger on it, but there was something wrong about Swallow, and it wasn't just the sensation he got every time he looked at the man. His train of thought was broken, though, by a sudden outbreak of cheering coming from inside the tavern. The door to the garden thumped closed, cutting off the brilliant sunlight along with the view of the grinning skeleton and Blackbeard leaning in to whisper with Swallow. He put them out of his mind and went to find out what his men were doing.

CHAPTER 6
NIGHT TERRORS

After the tension in the garden Sam found that he needed to relax a little and, at their invitation, he joined his crew around a table in the tavern. He bought a couple of rounds of drinks for them and some food from the coins he had brought from the ship and, to his surprise, one of the smaller gold ones paid for everything. His men toasted him, most of them downing their tankard of beer in one gulp, but Sam sipped cautiously at his, unsurprisingly finding that he didn't really like it. He guessed that it had to be an acquired taste, but it was one that he didn't really want to work on acquiring at that moment and he didn't drink any more beyond that first sip. Nobody seemed to notice that he wasn't drinking, though, and at the first opportunity he swapped it out for somebody else's empty tankard. Still, even if he wasn't getting drunk, he was enjoying just sitting there, laughing with the men and listening to them tell their tales; it was serving to calm him down considerably.

Smithy was as vigilant as ever and had declared that he wouldn't let the men have more than three tankards each, just in case there was trouble. When Sam asked whether that wasn't too much, Smithy claimed that three drinks weren't going to affect them in any noticeable way; they were used to having at least six or seven at a time and most of the men only really even started to get drunk after an even dozen. Sam found this hard to believe, until a quick glance around the large room showed him the sheer amount that both the men and women were drinking - everybody seemed to be emptying a tankard every few minutes and the beer never seemed to run out.

The men took much more time with their last permitted drink, savouring it while they talked and told tales of their lives before they had come to piracy. Bosun Brown was especially entertaining and he regaled everybody with a story about his first time at sea, as a boy in the Royal Navy. According to him, the captain had gotten drunk one night while on patrol off the Spanish coast near Cadiz and fallen overboard, unnoticed, most probably while using his private head at the stern. Apparently the man had washed up on shore and ridden a donkey back to Gibraltar to try to catch up with his ship. He'd then tried to blame his officers and get them court-martialled, but by then his crew had spread the story around the port and the man was laughed at by his fellow captains, who refused to convene the tribunal. He had apparently resigned his commission soon after and now ran an upmarket inn for officers in Portsmouth. The men were especially impressed by this story and applauded Brown for it; they loved hearing stories about officers getting their comeuppance. However, they made sure to let Sam and Smithy know that that didn't apply to them.

The men were having fun and Sam was enjoying himself immensely, but, in spite of the truce that ostensibly reigned between pirate crews while in Port Royal, the ever-watchful Smithy was not at all comfortable at being in a tavern owned by Blackbeard and surrounded by Blackbeard's men. They were constantly getting hostile looks from some of the men around them and when Swallow came in from the garden an hour or so later the atmosphere suddenly became so much more charged with repressed violence that Sam instantly agreed with his first mate's quiet suggestion that they should leave.

As they walked out, the now familiar feeling was making his stomach churn and he could feel the man's eyes burning into his back.

The streets were far less crowded now that the sun was going down; the people were going home and the shops and stalls were closing down. The smell wasn't quite as rank as before either, but Sam wasn't sure if that was because there were fewer people around to stir up the dust, dirt and other things or whether he was starting to get used to it. He hoped it was the latter; it would make his stay in Port Royal a bit more bearable if he didn't have to breathe through a perfumed handkerchief every day.

Now that there weren't the same crowds to contend with, or a blockade of hulking sailors, the walk to the sea front was accomplished much quicker than it had been that afternoon. However, when they reached the town square, they were confronted by a scene of such frantic activity that made them pause - the market had disappeared entirely, the stalls and the townspeople were gone, but their place had been taken by men from Blackbeard's crew, who were constructing something out of wood that, after what he had seen in Blackbeard's garden, Sam feared might be a gallows. He considered sticking around to find out what it was, but thought better of it; even though he'd just slept for almost two days straight, he knew that he still needed to rest so that he would be ready for whatever Blackbeard had in store for the next day.

He led his men down to the boat and they rowed him out towards the Mermaid. On the way Smithy pointed out the various ships anchored in the harbour, barely visible in the rapidly fading light. 'The ship on the end there is the Shin Chang, twenty six guns, she's Captain Wong's ship.'

Sam looked over at the curious ship that was swaying gently just beyond the Mermaid. It was a "Junk", one of the peculiarly shaped and sailed Chinese ships. She was strangely proportioned compared to the other ships in the harbour - high at the front and the back, low in the middle - and she was seemingly too long for her width, giving her a skinny appearance. She was painted red and black and had all manner of carvings and designs on her hull that just added to her strange appearance.

'Wong's a bit of a rum devil, very sly and untrustworthy; he never fights straight up, instead he ambushes his victims at night or in bad weather. Most of his crew is Chinese and it's commonly believed around Port Royal that they worship demons. I don't believe a word of it myself, but if the wind is right you can hear strange noises coming from the ship, like cats being tortured.' Smithy shuddered and made a sign that Sam knew was to ward off the "evil eye"; however, he was fairly sure that Smithy was describing the noise of Chinese music, something that often sounded like wailing cats to Sam's ear as well, and which, he guessed, was an acquired taste, just like the beer.

'That one there is the African Queen, Captain Caesar's ship of thirty two guns. Caesar's not the best sailor in the world, but he's a decent man and fair in his dealings.' Smithy called Sam's attention to the ship on the other side of the Mermaid. She was a dull brown colour, unpainted and unadorned wood, and was the shabbiest-looking of the ships at anchor. Sam frowned as he took her in; aside from her uncared-for look, her weight was also badly distributed - the stern of the ship was sitting too low in the water and the bows were too high. For Sam it was confirmation that Caesar had only come to the sea recently and hadn't fully learnt his trade yet.

'He has a few of his fellow tribesmen in the crew, but they're as civilised as you or I, which is to say not very! They're a good bunch, though; they don't kill or maroon their prey, but always try to find a way to get them safely home and they're more than willing to give a helping hand to a fellow pirate in trouble.' Or bite the hand that fed them, according to Caesar's story, thought Sam, but he kept his opinion to himself.

'Next to her is Captain Bonny's ship, the Vengeance, twenty guns. She's the fastest ship here.'

Bonny's ship was a beautiful, sleek vessel, pleasingly proportioned to Sam's eye and with obviously extremely well taken care of rigging that told of the emphasis her captain placed on being quicker than her prey.

'Bonny's crew love to create mischief, although it's usually only a bit of harmless fun, but when the fighting starts they are as fierce as the next man or woman. Speaking of which - you'd be surprised how many women want to be on board a ship and have an adventure and most of them gravitate to the Vengeance and Captain Bonny.'

Smithy next pointed to a large two decker ship that looked far neater than the other ships. She had her hull painted black, with the gun decks picked out in yellow and the gun ports themselves painted red. Gold leaf shone on her red-haired figurehead and on the large name plate at her stern.

'Just beyond the Vengeance is Captain Fitzhume's ship, the Good Queen Bess. She's an old thing, been patched up, repaired and renewed so much that probably not a single part of her is as the shipbuilders laid down. At fifty guns she has the heaviest weight of metal that she can throw with each broadside, but she's so slow and unhandy that something like the Vengeance, or even the Mermaid herself could run rings around her, but Fitzhume handles her so well that he more than makes up for most of her deficiencies.'

The last ship in the rough line was the ship that had caught Sam's eye when he'd looked out from the docks earlier. She was painted completely black, with none of the embellishments that the other ships had, and as the last of the day's light left she all but disappeared against the dark ocean.

Just as there had been with her crew members in the tavern, there was a sense from her of aggression that was barely being kept in check, as if she desired nothing less than to pounce on the other ships at anchor with her for invading her territory.

Smithy noticed the direction of Sam's gaze and nodded. 'That would be the Queen Anne's Revenge, Captain. She's Blackbeard's flagship - a frigate of forty guns. She was captured last year from the French, who were using her as a slave ship, but originally she was British, which is why her lines are so clean.' There was clear admiration on Smithy's face as he gazed at the ship, but he suddenly shivered as if someone had walked on his grave and he turned deadly serious. 'You never, ever want to get in a fight with that ship, or the men who crew it; they are the worst of the worst, the most vicious men you've ever laid eyes on. Most of them are escaped convicts - murderers, rapists and such, yet even so Blackbeard easily manages to keep control of them, which tells you just what kind of a monster he must be.'

Sam shivered as he remembered the way that the huge man's eyes had bored into him when he had spat his chicken across the table. There had been a moment, just before Blackbeard had broken out into laughter, when Sam had been sure he was a dead man.

He pushed the uncomfortable thought aside quickly, though, when something else occurred to him. 'Hang on, that's three Queens, a Vengeance and a Revenge in just four ships. Doesn't anyone have any imagination? Or get confused?'

Smithy shrugged. 'Pirates have simple tastes, Captain - we have our ideal women, like our own beloved Mermaid, and we like violence.'

Sam chuckled and gestured at the fascinating junk that was the closest ship to his own. 'And I suppose you're going to tell me that Shin Chang means something like "Queen of Retribution", right?'

'Actually, Captain, there were rumours going around that the name meant "Annoying Little Boy" but I wouldn't be surprised if you were right.'

They were now at the Mermaid and Sam nimbly climbed up the side, closely followed by Smithy.

Sam stood at the rail with his first mate beside him and looked around the bay. The sun had gone down fully and it was too dark to see the ships themselves now, just their lights.

'So, all these captains and crews work together and look out for each other and the town?'

'There is a code, the Pirate's Code, which says that yes, in theory they should, as part of the "Brethren of the Coast". The town and the people here give us a certain amount of security, without them we'd have to look a lot further for food and a safe harbour, so we're encouraged to take care of them. Also there is safety in numbers, so supporting each other is good - the more pirate ships there are the harder it is for the British and French to destroy us. Having said that, you'd be surprised how many times the code is conveniently forgotten when plunder or power is at stake.'

Sam nodded. 'That's what I was afraid of. So we can't count on everybody to be civilised and obey the rules of this little game of Blackbeard's.'

Smithy laughed at this. 'Some pirates are more civilised than others! But no, Captain, you can be assured that they'll all do what they have to do in order to win the prize. Not all of them will kill for it, though.'

'Swallow strikes me as the kind of person that wouldn't hesitate to kill if it served his own interests.'

Smithy considered briefly then nodded, 'yes, I think you're right, Captain.'

Smithy waited patiently at his side as Sam stood there, staring out over the bay, trying to organise his thoughts and work out a plan. Eventually, he realised that there was nothing he could do to influence the outcome of tomorrow's "contest", especially seeing as he didn't know what form it was going to take, so he decided that he might as well try to get some rest.

He pushed himself away from the rail and nodded at Smithy. 'I'll be in my cabin if you need me. Thank you, Mr Smith.'

'Sleep well, Captain.'

A few hours later Sam was lying on his bed in his cabin, still awake, staring up at the deck above him and trying to take in the events of the day.

He still didn't have a clue what was going on and how he had suddenly become a pirate, but he was determined to have as much fun as he could while the adventure lasted and he had already decided that he was definitely going to go all out to win Blackbeard's competition. If he could avoid getting hurt too much or dying while he was doing that, then that would be good too. Although, now he came to think about it, maybe dying would end the dream - he'd heard that people woke up if they died in a dream, so it would probably be worth a shot if he got fed up with being here.

The thing was that, while his common sense was telling him that it had to be a dream, he couldn't help but feel that something else was going on and that somehow what he was going through was real. But at the same time he still couldn't quite bring himself to believe that he was actually in Port Royal, that he had met Blackbeard, and that he was a pirate captain; it was impossible.

'Aargh!' He slapped the bed beside him, suddenly angry with himself. His mind was stuck in a kind of loop and he was getting very tired of trying to work out if he was dreaming or not.

Right then and there, he made a decision. People were always telling each other to live in the moment and seize the day and that was exactly what he was going to do - he would take things seriously, stop wondering if he was going to wake up at some point and treat it as if this was his life from now on. For all he knew, that was a distinct possibility anyway.

It was a relief and a weight off his mind and he smiled, suddenly feeling so much happier, but sleep still wouldn't come. He knew he should stay in bed and get some rest for the morning, but he was too excited, so he leapt out of bed and struggled into his boots then went back out on deck and walked up the stairs to the quarterdeck, nodding to the officer of the watch before going to the rail and looking out across the bay.

It was a warm night and Sam marvelled at the sheer number of stars overhead. He'd never seen so many - even in the nights when he'd been out in the Catalan countryside on camping trips there had still been so much light pollution from nearby cities that most of the stars were hidden, but here... Sam could see how the astronomers of old had been able to name so many different constellations; it seemed like you could almost reach up and touch them.

Suddenly, there was a huge bang and a bright light hid the stars from Sam's view. A heartbeat later a shock wave hit him, throwing him back from the rail and knocking him to the deck. The ship heeled sharply as a wave, this time of water, hit it.

Sam lay on his back, wondering what had happened and feeling the ship slowly settling back beneath him. His head eventually cleared and he struggled back to his feet and raced back to the rail.

Only a couple of hundred metres away one of the ships was burning. It was barely recognisable as a ship anymore, though; the explosion had flattened her masts and blown away a large part of her hull.

'It's the Shin Chang, Captain Wong's ship.' Smithy had joined Sam at the rail in a rush along with the rest of the sailors who were on duty.

'What the hell happened?'

'It looks like a spark got into the powder magazine, Captain. By accident or design, who knows?'

Sam gritted his teeth, 'I'm sure that somebody knows. Actually, I think that we all do. Send a boat please, Mr Smith, to see if there are any survivors. Maybe if someone is still alive they can tell us something definite.'

'Aye aye, Captain. But whether there are any survivors or not, it looks like you'll have one less competitor to deal with tomorrow,' Smithy said with an ironic grin and a shake of his head. He turned and quickly gave instructions to launch a boat before turning back to the rail with his captain. They watched as a boat was lowered into the water and quickly rowed out towards the stricken ship.

Sam looked away from the burning ship and over to the other side of the Mermaid where the ships of the competing captains were anchored in a rough line. Blackbeard's flagship, The Queen Anne's Revenge, was on one end of the line and the Shin Chang was at the other. The Mermaid was the closest ship to the burning Chinese ship, so if anyone else was going to be attacked tonight it would most probably be them.

'Make sure the men stay on the alert tonight, please, Smithy. I don't want the same kind of "accident" happening to us.'

'Aye aye, Captain.'

Smithy marched away to see to the security of the ship, giving orders to double the watch as he went, and threatening to do all sorts of things to the men as a punishment for not staying alert, using terms that Sam didn't understand and wasn't sure that he wanted to either.

More and more of Sam's men were coming up on deck; they had been woken by the explosion and wanted to see what was going on. At Sam's signal, the officer of the watch came over and handed him a telescope and he trained it out over the water.

There was very little left of Captain Wong's junk now, just a sliver of hull and half a mast that was tilted at a steep angle to one side, but flames were still shooting into the sky from it. The Mermaid's boat approached cautiously, avoiding burning pieces of wood, moving slowly and searching for anyone still alive. Occasionally one of the members of the boat crew would reach down into the water to check something, but they never hauled anything on-board.

Sam was straining to watch the boat, hoping that they would find someone, when he heard a noise coming from below him.

He looked down.

Against the hull was a tiny boat with three men in it and one of them was in the process of prying open a gun port. They had gone unnoticed so far because there was nobody left below to hear them; everybody was up on deck watching the show.

'Smithy!' Sam hissed urgently and waved for help.

'Captain?' Smithy wandered back over, a puzzled look on his face.

'Look! Down there, against the waterline!' He pointed over the rail at the boat.

The men in the boat heard him and their faces turned upwards to catch the moonlight. They panicked and fumbled with the oars, trying desperately to row away.

Smithy had other ideas, though, and he reacted immediately and aggressively. 'Come on, men!'

He and about a dozen of the Mermaid's crew leapt past Sam over the rail and dropped the short distance into the sea. They splashed feet first into the water and quickly surfaced on all sides of the boat. While some of them caught hold of the oars to halt its progress, the others fought with the men themselves, swarming over the gunwales of the boat. By this time the saboteurs had abandoned their attempt to get away and grabbed belaying pins. They were wildly lashing about in an attempt to beat off their attackers, but they were so outnumbered that they were very quickly overcome. The crew of the Mermaid bound their hands behind their backs and brought them back to the ship, bundling them roughly up the side.

Sam looked down at the saboteurs from the quarterdeck. Now that they had been brought into the light of the lamps on the main deck he could see them much better - they were dressed in nondescript dark clothing and had black faces and hands; they had covered themselves in something like soot or shoe polish so as to avoid being seen at night, and the sailors holding them had black patches on their hands and clothing where they had come into contact with them.

Smithy climbed up the stairs and joined Sam on the quarterdeck. He was dripping water and breathing heavily, but was smiling grimly at his small victory.

Sam looked him up and down. 'Did anyone get hurt?'

'Nothing life threatening, just a few bumps and a couple of scratches that'll leave a scar the men will be proud of getting.'

Sam nodded, relieved. 'Who sent them, Smithy? Where did they come from?'

'They were in a skiff from the town, but if they're townspeople then I'm a singing squid. They had a small chest full of these.'

Smithy handed Sam a metal ball. It was a bit larger than a tennis ball, with what looked like a long piece of string hanging out of it and

Sam almost laughed; it looked like something straight out of a roadrunner cartoon. However, the serious look on Smithy's face and the care he was taking in not dropping it told him that it wasn't a laughing matter.

'Did they use those to blow up the Shin Chang?'

'Without a doubt, Captain. One of these anywhere near the powder magazine would do the trick, no problem.'

'So, who are they then?'

'They're not saying nothing, but some of the men say they recognise them from the Queen Anne - they're Blackbeard's men, without a doubt.'

'So Swallow sent them to get rid of his rivals.'

'Aye, Captain, that's my thinking too.' Smithy leaned in close and spoke in a hushed voice so that nobody else could hear. 'The men are in favour of stringing them up for what they've done tonight, and I can't say that I don't agree with them. Sorry, Captain.'

'I understand completely, Smithy.'

'Would you like me to get them to talk? It shouldn't be too hard to get a confession out of them that'll condemn Swallow and satisfy Pirate Law enough for us to see them dangling come morning.'

Sam dismissed the idea straight away and shook his head, 'no, we're not going to do that.'

He looked down at the three men. Sam could see in their faces that they fully expected to be executed in the next few minutes, but even so they were merely glaring up at him with defiant looks.

Sam wanted nothing more than to mete out punishment for their crimes; they were murderers and if they had had their way then the Mermaid would have joined the Shin Chang at the bottom of the ocean, but he knew that he couldn't condemn them out of hand and he really wasn't sure that he had it in him to order them hanged. However, looking around his crew, he knew that they would find it hard to accept anything other than a death sentence and the bloodthirsty looks on all of their faces, including Smithy's, was frightening.

Sam realised he was seeing a side of his men that he hadn't seen before, even when in battle against the French. It was what he had actually expected when he had first found himself in the company of pirates and he wondered if this was their true face - whether they were only "playing nice" for their Captain the rest of the time.

It was a dilemma, then; he couldn't look weak in front of his men or disappoint them enough for them to doubt him and think of mutineering, but he also had to appease them and stop them from taking justice into their own hands. After a brief consideration he realised that there was only one course available to him and he put on a show of reluctance and a rough growl to soften what he knew would be a bitter pill for his crew to swallow.

'Clap them in irons; they can be our guests on board for the night. In the morning we'll take them to see Blackbeard and I'm sure he'll know exactly what to do with them.'

'Aye aye, Captain.' Smithy nodded reluctantly and went back down the stairs to organise things.

As the prisoners were taken away, Sam turned to the rail and looked out across the bay. The Shin Chang was no longer burning, but only because it had sunk, and the rescue party had given up and were on their way back.

He peered down into the boat when it arrived, but the sailors just looked up at him and shook their heads gravely; they hadn't found anyone.

Sam gritted his teeth and slapped the rail in frustration. 'Damn them, they'll pay.'

He walked across the quarterdeck to the opposite rail and looked towards the other ships anchored in the harbour. It was too dark to see whether there was still any activity on them, but no boats had come to see if there was anything they could help with and any alarms that had been sounded in the initial excitement were quiet now.

Smithy came back and stood by Sam. 'There might be other saboteurs out there looking to destroy the other ships, shouldn't we warn them?'

'I think that if there was anybody else, they would have struck at the same time as they did the Shin Chang.'

Smithy considered this and nodded. 'You're probably right, Captain, but we could still send a boat out to make sure everyone knows that we have the perpetrators in custody.'

Sam chuckled and smiled wryly. 'I don't think that's a very good idea. If I were one of the captains of those ships I'd be standing by the cannons, ready to blow anything that got too close, and wasn't mine, out of the water. I'm not going to risk losing a boat crew just to warn them, especially seeing as it was almost certainly one of them that was behind the attack anyway. I think they'll survive fine without us.'

They stood in silence, looking out at the harbour and the town beyond it.

Despite his calm exterior Sam was furious inside. He couldn't imagine how the honour of inheriting Blackbeard's position when he retired could possibly be worth such a loss of life, especially seeing as he knew that traditionally pirates didn't tend to live very long, and it was highly unlikely that the winner would even be able to enjoy his reign for much more than a few months, a year or two at the most.

He suddenly realised that most of the people here most likely knew that. They accepted it and dealt with it in their own way, living life as fully as they could, knowing that disease, war, storm, shipwreck or so many other things could kill them at any time. Consequently, just a chance at such glory and power, for even a short time, would be enough motivation for many of the pirates to try to snatch the prize at whatever cost. And after seeing how Smithy and the Mermaid's crew had hungered for the saboteurs' blood, it was probably more of them than he'd previously thought.

That didn't make such tactics right, though, and he would make sure to see that justice was done in the morning.

Sam bade Smithy goodnight and then shoved himself angrily away from the rail. He stomped off to his cabin and slammed the door behind him. He stalked across the room and threw himself onto the bed.

He was fairly sure that he wouldn't be able to sleep with all the excitement, anticipation and worry, but as soon as he'd fought his boots off and turned down the lantern, he fell into such a deep sleep that he wasn't woken by the ship's bell tolling the hours throughout the night, or the stomp of the extra guards he'd ordered as they marched across the deck over his head every minute or so.

CHAPTER 7
BLACKBEARD'S JUSTICE

Sam was woken up early the next morning by a knock at the door and a ray of sunlight shining straight into his eyes through the glass window at the stern of his ship. He squinted against the light and for a moment he wasn't sure where he was; despite his resolution of the night before to treat this situation as real, he had still half expected to wake up back in Barcelona, in the street, his bed, or possibly the hospital with a huge lump on his head.

He propped himself up on his elbows and looked around the cabin with bleary eyes. Everything was just as it had been and his ship hadn't exploded. Which was nice. Outside on deck he could hear the normal sounds of a ship at anchor and he assumed that, since he hadn't been woken up, there hadn't been any other attacks or panics during the night.

'Come in!' He swung his feet out over the side of the bed and rubbed his eyes. He wasn't used to not showering every night and the accumulation of sleep stuff in his eyes was amazing. An unpleasant odour came to his nose and he realised that that wasn't the only result of his not having washed.

All this was forgotten as the cabin door opened and in came Smithy bringing with him a delicious smell. He was accompanied by a sailor carrying a huge wooden tray piled high with food, which he put down on the table, then left.

Sam stood up and padded over, barefoot, scratching his head and running his hand across his itchy scalp; it felt like something was crawling in his hair.

He sat down and looked at the food hungrily. There were rashers of bacon, huge chunks of bread, a whole pot of butter, eggs and not a single piece of muesli in sight; it was all the kinds of stuff that his mother was always telling him were bad for him, but that tasted so good. He hadn't been given any cutlery, so he just shrugged and started picking at the food with his fingers like he had done in the inn. He tucked in, sampling something of everything, stuffing his face as if this were his last meal on Earth.

Smithy was standing opposite him, waiting patiently for orders, and Sam looked up between bites and blushed; his first mate had been able to hear all of his moans of pleasure and belches, and all without a napkin to cover them. The first mate, however, just smiled, seemingly happy that his captain was enjoying himself.

Sam motioned to a free chair. 'Why don't you help me with all this?'

Smithy grinned. 'Don't mind if I do, Captain.' He sat and started digging in, tearing off a moderate chunk of bread and folding it around some bacon. He took a knife out of his belt, used it to spread butter thickly on top of all of that and then took a huge bite.

Sam watched him, incredulous, then did the same thing, all the while wondering how long it would be before they both had a heart attack.

The two of them ate without speaking for a while, both of them now groaning and moaning in pleasure as the greasy, but tasty food filled them. They smiled at each other, content to just enjoy themselves for a while.

Eventually, though, Sam had had enough and he pushed himself back from the table slightly to give his suddenly swollen belly a bit more room. He belched, loud and long then quickly covered his mouth with his hand in shame. However, Smithy just laughed and then belched himself.

'Tea, Captain?'

'Please.'

Smithy poured two mugs of hot tea from a large pewter jug and handed one of them to Sam. They saluted each other, then sat nursing them.

'So, Mr Smith. Tell me - how did you get into piracy? You seem too, well, *decent* to me, not at all like the usual kind of person who decides to embark on a life of crime.' Sam smiled, expecting some kind of amusing anecdote, but Smithy's reaction surprised him.

The smile slowly fell from his first mate's face and his chin dropped onto his chest. He stared into his tea.

'I'm sorry, I shouldn't have pried,' said Sam, too late realising that most people didn't turn to piracy because of some romantic notion of adventure like films loved to portray, he was coming to see that the reality was very different and there was evidently something in Smithy's past that was difficult for him to talk about.

'No, it's alright, Captain.' The voice that came from Smithy was quiet and filled with emotion and he was suddenly a far cry from the merry young man that Sam had come to like and admire.

Sam watched the man struggle with his emotions. He waited patiently, curious as to what could be troubling him so much.

When next Smithy spoke it was with a voice that cracked momentarily with sorrow for a painful past. 'I was born in Nassau, in the Bahamas. It is a place not much different to Port Royal, just smaller, cleaner, with less people. My father was a baker, my mother sold the bread and I was apprenticed to my father, just like he had been to his father before him. I was raised good; my parents were god-fearing and we were in church every Sunday, regular as clockwork. We were happy.' He paused and took a sip of tea while he composed himself.

'I was fourteen in 1703 when the town was sacked by a combined French and Spanish force. There were only a couple of hundred souls in the town and they killed half of us, including my mother and father. They took most of the survivors prisoner and sailed away with them to who knows where.' Despite the horror of the events his voice was matter of fact as if he were just recounting something he had read in a history book.

'Our house was destroyed in the opening cannon barrage and the raiders didn't find me because I was buried in the rubble, unconscious. It took me almost two days to dig my way out and when I did everything was different; quiet, empty. I stayed around the town for a while, living wild and doing what I had to do to survive, but it was no life and there was barely anybody left to live it with. So when Samuel Bellamy came along and asked me to join his crew I signed on without a second thought.' Another shadow crossed Smithy's brow. 'I swore that I would take my revenge, one ship, one day at a time. No matter how long it took.'

Smithy paused briefly and Sam thought that he was perhaps renewing his vow to himself, but then the darkness passed and he smiled slightly. 'I spent a few wonderful years with Black Bellamy as we sailed the seas in partnership with Captain Hornigold. I got to know ships and the sea and eventually worked my way up to be his mate. But then a year ago he died and the crew drifted apart; I was again left with nothing. And that's when you came along and offered me a job. I knew your reputation so I jumped at the chance.' Smithy looked up finally and shrugged before dropping his gaze back to his tea. 'And here we are, drinking tea and thinking about the possibility of you becoming Blackbeard's heir. My hope is that, if you are successful, you will deem me worthy of commanding one of your ships and I might be able to finally begin to carry out my vow to scrape this ocean clean of the French and Spanish scourge that plagues it.'

Smithy's tragic story really put Sam's bullying problem at school into perspective a bit and for a moment he was lost for words. He was also very surprised to find out that he had a backstory of his own here and was desperate to find out more, but he knew that it would be a bit strange if he started to ask questions about it, so he changed the subject, getting back onto more familiar ground, and turning Smithy away from his reflection on his past losses.

'So, what do you think Blackbeard has in store for us, Smithy?'

Smithy smiled, and Sam could see he was glad to get back onto a more comfortable subject. 'I don't know, Captain, but I wouldn't worry too much; if he tries something treacherous then we and the other crews have more than enough strength to take him down if we band together.'

'There's one less of us now, though.'

'Aye, that there is...' Smithy considered this briefly, then nodded. 'It would be a close fight, but I reckon we'd still come off on top.'

They sat in silence for a few seconds, each lost in their own thoughts.

'Do you think Blackbeard is really trying to find a successor, Captain? Or has he got something up his sleeve?'

Sam thought about this. 'I really don't know, maybe both...'

Sam was interrupted by the ringing of the ship's bell sounding the hour, and the shouts and noise of running feet as the watch changed on deck.

'I guess we'll just have to wait and find out.'

'We won't have to wait too long, Captain, there's only half an hour until we're due to meet him on the docks.'

'Oof!' said Sam, patting his belly and groaning. 'I guess I'd better put my boots on and start getting ready then.'

Half an hour later, Sam stepped into the heat and glare of the Caribbean sun and he squinted against it, holding his hand over his eyes to shade them. Despite being just an hour or so after sunrise, the heat and humidity were already oppressive. It was like summer in Barcelona; always moving quickly from utter darkness to blinding light and back again - a world of sharp contrasts.

When he could finally see the world around him he noticed that the French ship he had captured was just coming into view as it rounded the point, past the only intact fort that remained defending the harbour. He was pleased to see that the prize crew had been busy, that repairs were well underway and she was sailing easily under a jury-rigged mast. This wasn't what had caught his crew's attention, though; a large group of sailors were crowding around the rail that faced the town, pointing and commenting animatedly. Instead of fighting through them to see what the fuss was about, Sam climbed up to the empty quarterdeck and went to the side.

A small two-masted ship, which he knew was called a brig, had been moored just off the shore, about a hundred metres from the docks. It was flying Blackbeard's flag: a skeleton spearing a red heart on a black background. Beyond it, the construction work that had been taking place the night before in the square was revealed to be stands, what were called "bleachers" in American films, much like what would be found beside a football pitch, and not the gallows that Sam had feared it was going to be. They had evidently set up to allow the people from the village to watch whatever Blackbeard had in mind for his contest.

It looked like a party atmosphere was already springing up around the town square, with enterprising salesmen setting up stalls and the seats in the stands already filling with townspeople.

Smithy came up to the rail next to Sam. 'Well, if Blackbeard does plan to betray us, at least there'll be an audience to his treachery.'

'And we will have an audience to our success or failure.'

Smithy shrugged and grinned. 'Stage fright, Captain?'

Sam grinned back at him. 'Not even a bit, I sing in the choir.'

Smithy looked really puzzled at this. 'Sorry?'

'Oh, uh, nothing.' Sam looked away hurriedly and gestured at the shore in an attempt to cover his mistake. 'Shall we go?'

'I'll call for your boat, Captain.' Smithy moved off to organise a boat and crew to take Sam to the dock.

Sam was left alone and he tried to take the opportunity to try to calm his nerves, but wasn't quite able to. It certainly wasn't stage fright, as Smithy had suggested, it was more a fear of the unknown and of disappointing his men.

He sighed, then made his way to the main deck, went over the side and climbed down into the waiting boat.

The three saboteurs were in the boat already, heavily chained. He was glad to see that they were essentially in one piece, even though they did have a few more cuts and bruises than Sam had seen the night before. He was puzzled to note, however, that they all had a slight smile on their faces and were smirking at each other, as if they knew something that Sam and his crew didn't. This did nothing to put him any more at ease and he became more and more worried as he was rowed to shore, so much so that he barely heard the cheers of his crew as they lined the side of the ship to wish him luck.

Sam found the other captains and Blackbeard gathered in front of the stands, in an empty space left by the townspeople, who didn't seem to want to get too close to the pirate crews after the events of the night before.

There was an extremely heated argument going on and it looked like things were on the verge of breaking out into violence - the combined crews of Bonny and Caesar were faced off against Blackbeard's thugs, just like their captains were confronting each other. The atmosphere was oppressive and it seemed that they were all just waiting for an excuse to fight. However, it was a fight that wouldn't go well for Caesar, Fitzhume and Bonny because Blackbeard's crew had them heavily outnumbered, and even if Sam's men joined in they still probably wouldn't win because it seemed that Blackbeard had been expecting trouble and had come prepared, bringing almost his entire crew with him.

Blackbeard was presiding over the meeting, sitting on his golden throne under his pink parasol, both items having been moved out here and placed in front of the stands on a small raised platform. The cage that had been in the garden was also there, hanging from the same macabre stand with the same skeleton grinning mirthlessly inside. It seemed that Blackbeard took this everywhere with him and Sam had to admit that it served as a pretty potent and effective reminder of his power and ruthlessness, although he did wonder how many people had ended up in there after laughing at Blackbeard's pink umbrella.

The three surviving captains were shouting accusations at Blackbeard and he wasn't taking it very well. He was glowering at them, his hand curled tightly around the hilt of his sword, and Sam could see his knuckles whitening with his desire to pull it out and draw blood.

Sam wasn't surprised to see Swallow standing off to one side and not taking part in the argument; the man had struck him as being the kind of person who delights in causing trouble, but never got his own hands dirty. He was the first to see Sam coming and he winked, provoking a twinge in Sam's gut that made him wish he hadn't eaten quite so much for breakfast.

Blackbeard looked up as Sam approached and his face lit up with a large grin, evidently glad of at least a momentary distraction to calm the brewing storm. 'Ah! Captain Vives! Punctual as ever! I take it that is your prize dropping anchor in the bay?'

Sam nodded, grinning. 'Yes, the Medusa, a French forty-gunner. Her captain thought that we were easy prey. We weren't.'

Blackbeard frowned. 'I didn't see any damage to the Mermaid, how did you manage to take her down in a fair fight?'

Sam shrugged. 'Anything is possible with a bit of straight shooting, a fair amount of luck and an excellent crew.'

'Well said, Captain! Very well said indeed!' Blackbeard laughed. 'I'm sure she will be a valuable addition to the pirate fleet.'

The pirate lord smiled at Sam, but then he turned back to his accusers and suddenly the thunderous scowl was back on his face, his mood changing like the weather.

'Before you arrived, Captains Bonny, Fitzhume and Caesar here were trying to tell me what my duty is with regards to the events of last night and I would be interested to hear where you stand on the matter, Captain Vives.' Blackbeard scowled angrily at the three captains, who quailed slightly under his glare.

Captain Bonny turned to address Sam. She was clearly furious and her cheeks were a not completely unattractive crimson colour. 'We were merely saying that the attack on one of our own last night must be punished under Pirate Law and the culprit brought to justice - we are all perfectly aware of who was responsible and he must be dealt with accordingly.'

She turned to stare accusingly at Swallow, but if anything the man's smirk widened under her glare; for some reason he seemed absolutely unafraid of suffering any consequences.

'What do you say to that, Captain Vives?' asked Blackbeard.

'I agree with Captain Bonny,' Sam said, 'and to that end may I introduce you to the three men directly responsible for last night's tragic events. They're refusing to say anything, but it's obvious who sent them, seeing as they are members of your crew.' Sam waved at his sailors who shoved the prisoners forward roughly and forced them to their knees. 'My men were all for dealing with these murderers on their own, but I thought that it would be better to see justice done, both to them and the man who gave them their orders, here, in front of the everybody.'

Blackbeard's scowl deepened, but he nodded in acceptance. 'It seems that I am outvoted, so let us take a closer look at these captives of yours and see if they really are mine.' He stood up from his chair and stepped down from the platform with a great show of reluctance.

This was the first time that Sam had seen Blackbeard standing up and he was a fearsome sight. He was tall, broad-shouldered and powerful-looking, and he moved easily despite his bulk. If he really was planning on retiring it certainly wasn't because of age or weakness, he looked to be in the prime of his life.

The other captains stood aside and he stalked past them, bearing down on the three prisoners. He stopped and glared down at them, his legs spread wide and his hand still wrapped tightly around his sword hilt.

There was a sudden hush as everybody present held their breath, wondering if the men were going to meet a sudden and very bloody death at the end of Blackbeard's sword. Sam was certain that there were many in the crowd who were secretly urging him on, willing him to draw his weapon and strike their heads from them. He himself didn't think that was going to happen - he was actually wondering if all three men would fit into Blackbeard's cage at the same time.

The saboteurs looked up at Blackbeard. Against all odds they seemed unafraid and to Sam it appeared that, far from being terrified in the face of almost certain death, they seemed to be waiting for something, like the punchline to a joke that only they were a party to.

Suddenly a huge grin broke out on Blackbeard's face. 'Well done, my boys! Tom, Dick, good job! Harry, good job indeed! I couldn't have done much better myself,' he waggled his thick finger at them, telling them off jokingly, 'although you did get caught, so you still have a lot to learn before you can even think of challenging me!' He laughed and the three men joined in. 'Now strike those chains off 'em and bring 'em some grog!'

Sam and the other captains were flabbergasted. They were forced to stand by and watch as Blackbeard's men helped the prisoners to their feet and took them from Sam's sailors. Their chains were removed and then they disappeared as a group into the crowd in search of drink, cheering and laughing loudly.

Sam was disgusted with Blackbeard's perfidy, but stayed silent, keeping his feelings inside; he didn't want to be the one to confront Blackbeard, he knew a losing battle when he saw one - there were some kinds of bullies you just didn't stand up to and people in positions of absolute power, like Blackbeard, were a prime example.

Captain Caesar, however, was too angry to keep his tongue and he stepped forward to confront the pirate lord. Sam could see that he wasn't the kind of person to take what he saw as a grave insult without answering, no matter the size or importance of the opponent. 'Just what do you think you are doing, Captain Teach?'

The big African was the only one of the captains who came even close to being the same size as Blackbeard, but even so he wasn't quite nose to nose with him, more nose to beard, and the impression that Sam got, as Caesar looked up at Teach, was that of a petulant teenager talking back to his father.

Blackbeard didn't back down or step back and he answered Caesar with a voice that carried to all corners of the square. 'I am enforcing the rules of the contest, and they will take precedence over Pirate Law until I have chosen my heir. Those men are undeniably mine, and they were indeed acting under the orders of Mr Swallow. However, he was merely getting a jump on the game by trying to eliminate his opponents, and should be congratulated on accomplishing the first success of the day! I feel no pity for Captain Wong; last night's shenanigans were only to be expected and it was his unworthiness and lack of foresight that caused him to fall victim to such an obvious tactic. There are to be no recriminations and no punishments handed out because none are deserved.'

'That is completely unacceptable! Those men have murdered an entire crew with their skulduggery, *here*, in Port Royal, which is supposedly a safe haven for our kind. And you, as their *captain*, with your precious *contest* as an excuse, is going to allow them to walk away without punishment? Under what circumstances do you think that is fair and just?'

'Under the ones that state that while I am in charge I make the rules here and if you don't accept them then you will never become my successor. And furthermore, if you defy me you will no longer be welcome here.'

Blackbeard said this last in a very quiet voice that could barely be heard, but it was far more threatening than when he had shouted before and Caesar was rocked back on his heels slightly by the almost physical threat emanating from the pirate leader. The African captain's hand strayed almost unconsciously to the handle of the huge curved sword at his side, as if expecting to have to defend himself.

The sailors gathered around the captains were getting increasingly restless - hands were going to weapons and threatening looks were being exchanged on both sides. It would take very little to spark off a very deadly encounter and Sam could see that Caesar wanted nothing more than to draw and damn the consequences, but thankfully his common sense won out and he stayed his hand.

Blackbeard nodded, pleased at Caesar's restraint. 'Are you satisfied, Captain Caesar? Or would you like to leave now?'

Caesar fumed, but nodded curtly, saying nothing. He was obviously unwilling to press his luck or lose his chance at winning the prize. He signalled to his men to back down and then stalked away to go and stand by the other captains.

There was a collective sigh as hands relaxed from weapons, and the danger dissipated somewhat, although the tension remained.

Blackbeard went back to his throne and sat down, accepting a tankard of ale from a busty barmaid, one of several serving drinks from a temporary bar set to one side of the stands. He drained the tankard in one go and accepted another from the girl. He slapped her behind with a laugh as she walked away and received a coy smile in return.

With Blackbeard distracted, Sam took the opportunity to wander over to his fellow captains, who were leaning together and whispering animatedly. They stopped talking and glanced up as he arrived, giving him a wary look.

Fitzhume turned to confront him, elegantly raising an eyebrow despite the sweat pouring down his face. 'And what do you say about all this, Captain Vives?'

'I think that it is right not to punish those men.'

The three captains began to turn away from Sam in disgust, astounded that he could say such a thing.

'But...' Sam halted them with a word and they turned back. 'Only because ultimately they are not to blame for this betrayal; Blackbeard and that snake of his, Swallow, are.'

'So what do you suggest?' asked Captain Bonny, looking at Sam frankly in a way that was making him slightly uncomfortable.

Sam knew that the four of them were going to have to be very careful if they were going to outfox the two men - he got the feeling that Swallow was far smarter than he looked and he was positive that

Blackbeard would not have survived in charge for very long if he wasn't extremely clever, or at least cunning enough to manipulate the people around him into doing what he wanted. It was probably going to take their combined efforts to ensure that they stayed safe during the contest.

'I propose that we play Blackbeard's game for now as best as we can. We make it look as if we were hostile rivals, doing what we can to take the prize, while in fact we make a pact and promise not to do anything underhanded to each other. That way we are free to keep an eye out for any further trickery they have planned and we can also watch out for each other. And then, when we get the chance, we take Swallow down hard.'

'That sounds like a good idea to me,' said Bonny, nodding. She turned to Caesar, 'do you agree?'

Caesar smiled at Sam. He nodded. 'I'm not sure that I fully trust you, but I do like the way you think. I want nothing more than to see Swallow brought to task for what he did to Wong and Blackbeard must be shown that he cannot flout Pirate Law whenever it is convenient for him. So for now I agree and I will do what you say. Fitzhume?'

The large English captain nodded and waved his hand regally. 'It is by far the best course of action that I have heard so far and I say aye.'

'Thank you, Captains. Now, they mustn't know that we're working together, otherwise this won't work, so we should really stop looking like we're plotting something. I'm going back to my men and I suggest you do the same.'

With this, Sam gave the captains a nod and walked back over to Smithy and his sailors, who were still grumbling and complaining amongst themselves about the prisoners having gotten away scot-free.

'What's happening, Captain? Are we really going to let them get away with this farce?'

Sam made sure he got up close to Smithy and the men before he answered, huddling them together; he didn't want anybody overhearing. 'Of course not. We are going to act as if we've accepted Blackbeard's decision and are playing along with this damn game of his. Later? Who knows? For now just act normal, don't look like we're up to anything and above all keep an eye out for each other.'

Sam's men cheered up considerably at this, but tried not to show it too much.

They really were a good bunch of men, Sam reflected, there certainly wasn't the same amount of drunkenness and misbehaviour that all of the other crews seemed to be plagued with. Looking around the square Sam could spot at least a dozen men who were already well on their way to unconsciousness, including the three saboteurs, who were still being plied with food and drink by their celebrating crew-mates. Perhaps that could be useful later.

All in all the mood in the square was that of a party, with Blackbeard's crew and the locals making most of the noise. The crews of the four captains, though, were oases of calm, as they stood around in somewhat morose groups, mourning their comrades and waiting for Blackbeard to get his contest under way.

CHAPTER 8
WHITTLING DOWN THE COMPETITION

They didn't have long to wait.

All of a sudden Blackbeard jumped up onto the seat of his throne, pulled a pistol out of his belt and shot it in the air. The loud bang served to gain the attention of the townspeople in the square and they quickly settled on seats in the stand or crowded around the crews of the five ships. When everything was quiet again the pirate lord addressed them with a loud voice that easily carried to everyone.

'Welcome, my friends! Welcome, one and all, and thank you for coming! I'm sure you're all wondering what this is all about and don't worry, I'll get to that in due course!' His voice suddenly took on a sombre tone as he continued. 'However, before I start I'd like you all to join me in a moment of silence to mourn the passing of Captain Wong and his brave crew.'

With a flourish, Blackbeard took his hat off and held it over his heart while simultaneously dropping his chin onto his chest.

The crowd fell into an uneasy silence. Some of them bowed their heads and a few of them even looked like they were somewhat saddened by the events, but they were in a minority. Most of the crowd didn't seem to give a damn; death was as much a part of pirate life as the sea was. However, even if they didn't agree with him, they didn't want to go against Blackbeard's wishes and at least stayed silent.

After about ten seconds Blackbeard peeked out from under his bushy eyebrows and looked around at the crowd. He caught the eye of Sam and winked, grinning from ear to ear. Suddenly he threw his head back and his arms wide. 'Well, that's quite enough of that! Those worthless lubbers don't deserve a full minute! Let's get on with the show!' He stuffed his hat back on his head and flopped into his throne with a laugh.

The crowd laughed with him and cheered wildly at this. They didn't seem to have particularly liked either Wong or his crew, probably more due to the rumours of devil worship and such than anything else.

Sam looked to his fellow captains, expecting trouble. Caesar was fuming, his sword already pulled a couple of inches out of its scabbard. The big man was only just being restrained by one of his sailors, probably his first mate, who had his arms wrapped around him and was holding him back, talking insistently in his ear.

Sam managed to catch Caesar's eye and gave him a short shake of the head. It was this more than anything that brought Caesar back from the brink of violence and he angrily thrust his sword fully back in its sheath.

Relieved, Sam turned back to Blackbeard, but not before he had caught sight of Swallow standing in the crowd - he was watching Caesar's reaction and laughing to himself. Sam tried his best to ignore him, but the man was infuriating; there was just something about him that rubbed Sam the wrong way and made him want to wipe the smile off of his face, more than almost anyone else he'd ever met, and it went far beyond the sheer evil of the man in killing an entire crew and laughing about it later.

For now, though, Sam put him out of his mind to concentrate on what Blackbeard was saying.

'My friends! It is my sad duty to inform you that I have decided to go into retirement and step down from my role as your leader and protector.'

This drew calls of denial and disappointment from the crowd, many of whom genuinely didn't want him to retire. He was popular not only because of his personality, but also because of the protection he provided for the community.

Blackbeard smiled indulgently and held up his hands to forestall their protests. 'Now, now, don't worry; I'll still come and visit you every so often to make sure you're all behaving yourselves.'

This brought a few laughs and he paused to let them die down naturally, smiling avuncularly.

'Rest assured, I'm not going to leave you without a leader to protect you and while they may not be as strong or competent or as good-looking as I am, they will be the best available!'

There were more cheers and laughter at this and Sam was astounded that this killer, a man whose reputation for barbarous deeds preceded him, who took a dead man in a cage with him wherever he went, who harboured murderers who killed their fellow pirates and allowed them to avoid punishment, could be so well loved by people who knew how cruel he could be.

'So, we're going to have a little friendly competition to decide which of the fine captains you see gathered here today is worthy of taking over from me.'

Blackbeard was mostly playing up to the crowd, but he was also talking to the captains and he started meeting their eyes one by one as he spoke.

'Well, we're going to put on a show for you today! Each of these brave captains are going to take it in turns to show us what they are made of. They're going to demonstrate their leadership and organisational skills, as well as their fighting prowess, and the winner will take my throne! Well, not literally, I'm going to keep this one; it's too comfy to give away.'

Blackbeard patted his golden chair and grinned at the people, pausing again to allow the crowd time to laugh.

Sam had to give it to him; he was certainly charismatic and knew how to use that charisma to his best advantage. Obviously being a pirate lord meant more than just being the strongest and holding onto the crown by force - in order to stay in charge you had to win and keep the loyalty of the people, or, failing that, rule through fear. Blackbeard managed to tick all those boxes in Sam's opinion.

'No, instead the winner will get *this* as a symbol of his victory and new status as my heir.' From out of his pocket Blackbeard pulled a gem. It was an uncut diamond, almost the size of his palm and it refracted the light of the sun, dazzling the crowd. He rotated it in the sunlight, making its rainbow beams dance around the square.

For a few moments, every one of the hundreds of people in the square were transfixed by the beauty of it and there was an awed silence. Quickly though, thoughts of greed and desire took over and, looking around, Sam could see written plainly on most people's faces the lengths to which they would go to obtain that stone. Caesar, already consumed by thoughts of revenge, had a strange look on his face as he gazed at it, and the rest of the captains weren't much better.

Eventually, Blackbeard broke the spell by closing his fist around the gem and tucking it back into his pocket.

The crowd sighed as one and woke up as if from a dream, so mesmerised had they been by the sight of it. An excited murmuring started up as the crowd discussed the stone.

Sam fully believed that given enough time they might work up the courage to swamp Blackbeard and his men in an attempt to take it away, such avarice had it aspired.

Blackbeard seemed to be perfectly aware of this and he quickly distracted the crowd by going back to the matter at hand, reminding them of the coming entertainment.

'Enough of that! It's time to start seeing which of our captains has the mettle to be our new leader. However, with the sad loss of Wong, there are five crews now, an unfortunately odd number, and we're going to have to whittle down the field a little. So, before we get down to what I originally had planned, we're going to have to have ourselves a little race.

Blackbeard dropped his voice slightly and spoke directly to the captains. 'I've stationed two boats in the harbour, one by Salt Pond Reef and the other to the seaward of Drunkenmans Cay. Round them both, then come back here. The last man, or woman, to return and drop anchor where they started is eliminated, while the winner gets a hundredweight of gold from my own private hoard. It's about a six mile round trip so you should be back in an hour or so.'

Blackbeard grinned at them, looking from one captain to the other. He met Sam's eyes last and when he did he raised an eyebrow. 'Well?'

The captains looked at him for a couple of seconds more, dumbly, not quite understanding that the race was already under way.

Sam was the first to react, followed almost instantly by Swallow, then by the other captains and they all raced towards the dock.

Sam tried to force his way through the crowds, but it was hard going; at every turn there was a civilian or a drunken sailor to dodge. Out of the corner of his eye he saw Swallow making good progress. He didn't see Swallow himself, of course, just the heads and shoulders of half a dozen large men moving as a group, forcing their way through, their progress punctuated more often than not by screams and cries of pain as some innocent or other was hurt in the resulting scrum.

Suddenly, Smithy was by his side, accompanied by several of the crew.

'Come on, sir, this way.'

'Thank you, Mr Smith.'

Bosun Brown led the way as the tip of a spearhead of five big men from the Mermaid and he started to push his way through the crowd.

Sam was excited about the prospect of the race and his blood was up with the need to get to the ship as soon as possible, but he still kept his head about him enough to worry about the civilians; winning wasn't worth death or injury. 'Easy there, Bosun, try not to hurt anyone.'

'Aye aye, Cap'n.'

The crowds were thinning out now, partly because they were scrambling to get out of the way of the ships' crews, but also because they were searching out vantage points from which to see the race. A glance over his shoulder showed Sam that Blackbeard himself was leading a large procession up to the fort on the top of the hill where even now several large brass telescopes were being set up on tripods.

In a matter of seconds they arrived at the docks and jumped down into the boats.

'Shove off, there! Oars!' Smithy's shout had a note of panic in it and Sam saw why - Swallow's crew had a good head start on them. In addition, Sam's order not to use too much force on the people in the crowd had squandered any lead that Sam's quick reactions had gained them and the other crews were now level with them.

'Pull, damn your eyes, pull!' Smithy ground his teeth together and bellowed at the men, although Sam had no idea what he hoped to achieve; the men were already giving it their all.

'Mr Smith!'

Smithy turned to face Sam, his face red with his frustration. 'Yes, Captain?'

'The men are doing their best, so why don't you relax and join me in making it look like we are confident in our ability to win this race of Blackbeard's?'

Smithy grumbled under his breath, but sat down nonetheless. However, sitting still and doing nothing obviously didn't agree with the man - his hands were opening and closing almost continuously and his eyes were darting around without cease, going first towards the men at the oars, then to the Mermaid coming ever closer, finally searching out his inexplicably unconcerned captain, before starting all over again, making a circuit every few seconds.

Sam gave him a smile and casually leaned back against the side of the boat, but he wasn't feeling nearly as calm as he wanted to look like he was; inside he was in turmoil. His anger over the "justice" that Blackbeard had meted out warred with his nerves at the challenge ahead which were tying his stomach into knots. Those nerves were in turn made worse by the chaos that was reigning in his mind - his thoughts were twisting this way and that as he worried about how he, with no sailing experience whatsoever, was going to be able to navigate a course around the bay and back. He knew that the easiest thing to do would be to temporarily delegate command of the ship to Smithy during the race, but he really didn't want to do that; he wanted to have as much fun as he could and experience everything that he could while he was here, and if that meant losing a race because he didn't know how to sail, then that was what he would do. At least that way he would have tried. Besides, it wasn't as if the course was very long or particularly difficult; it was only a few miles inside a bay - he was fairly sure that even he couldn't mess that up too much.

For some reason Sam was a lot calmer now that the decision had been made and somehow he knew it was the right thing to do. He relaxed slightly and with the release of tension his mind cleared enough for him to be able to work on the problem of the coming race.

'Mr Smith?'

The first mate paused in his unceasing fidgeting at the question. 'Sir?'

'Do we have a chart of the bay?'

'Yes, sir.'

'Have it brought on deck, please, and I think we're in hailing range, now, so you may give the order to begin weighing the anchor and setting sails.'

Smithy grinned and let loose the breath he seemed to have been holding. 'Aye aye, sir.'

He stood up and, with a shout that almost deafened Sam, started bellowing orders over the waves.

A couple of minutes later Sam climbed, with as much dignity as he could muster, up the side of the ship to the clanking sound of the capstan bringing in the anchor and the snapping of canvas overhead as the sails unfurled.

Smithy had acrobatically leapt to the ship and run straight to the chart room, but Sam wanted to keep up his pretence at unconcern over the result of the race; it seemed like the Hornblower thing to do.

He strolled to the quarterdeck, acknowledging the greetings of his crew on the way and walked over to the man at the wheel. 'Hard to port as soon as the rudder bites and set course due west, please.'

'Due west, aye, sir.'

The order had come out naturally and easily, the words coming from somewhere in the back of his mind, but Sam spared only a second to wonder how that was possible before other concerns took over. He walked to the rail and one by one took in the sight of the other four ships that were also hastily preparing to make sail.

Predictably, the Queen Anne's Revenge had a head start on them all; not only had they gotten to the ship quicker, but also because they had been anchored at the end of the line closest to the start of the course and therefore they had a natural advantage over the other ships. However, the Mermaid had done good work in getting under way quickly and the gap to the Queen Anne wasn't as large as it might have been. In addition they were the first of the chasing ships to do so and had a clear run towards the open bay, whereas the others would have to fight for the same space and the same wind.

Smithy hurried up with a small roll of paper and laid it out flat on the box next to the wheel that held the ship's compass. He pointed out the course without comment, tapping his finger first on Port Royal, then on the two way points, describing a roughly isosceles triangle with the bottom side much shorter than the other two. Sam saw that the course would first take them around two miles to the southwest, where they would find Salt Pond Reef. The reef was large enough for them to then have to sail south alongside it for almost a mile before they could turn almost due east for the mile and a half run to Drunkenmans Cay, before lastly turning north for the almost two mile home journey.

On the map the course looked easy enough, but like all things to do with Blackbeard, Sam was coming to discover that appearances were almost always deceiving. In this case the simplest route, taking them directly from one way point to the next, was impossible, passing as it did over shoals and reefs and other unnavigable features that lay in wait to sink the unwary. The first leg was straightforward enough, though.

Sam looked up from the chart and quickly checked their position relative to Port Royal. The decision and words came to his mind as easily as before. 'I think we have enough sea room now. Helmsman, set course west-southwest, please.'

'West-sou'west, aye, sir.'

The helmsman turned the wheel, Smithy gave orders for the sails to be trimmed, and before long the Mermaid creaked and groaned happily as she settled smoothly onto her new course, flying over the waves, racing before the wind.

Sam closed his eyes and took a moment to appreciate the breeze on his face and the lively movement of the ship beneath his feet. It would have been a pleasant day for a sail if it weren't for the dangers lurking under the surface of the bay or the other ships scattered around them.

He swayed easily with the pitching and yawing of the ship, marvelling that he had what were called "sea legs", despite this being his first time at sea except for one time on a jet ski with his father, which obviously didn't count.

He opened his eyes again and looked around at the situation. All five ships were now on the same course and heading for the first way point. They were in a rough line with the Queen Anne's Revenge leading and the Mermaid following close behind. There was then a small gap to the African Queen and the Vengeance, who were neck and neck, and bringing up the rear was the Good Queen Bess. Each of the ships was carrying as much sail as it could carry and it was a beautiful sight, despite the dirtiness of most of the canvas on display.

It took only a quick glance for Sam to see that, true to her reputation, the Vengeance was by far the fastest ship of the five and as he watched she pulled ahead of the African Queen and started to gain rapidly on the Mermaid. Looking forward he saw that the Mermaid was in turn gaining slightly on Swallow's ship, but not by as much.

It was obvious that if the race had been in a straight line there would be clear winners and clear losers. However, this course around the bay would test seamanship and crews just as it would the speed of the ships.

The boat marking the turning point was still a mile or more away so Sam took the opportunity to study the chart with Smithy.

The first mate smoothed out the wrinkled and browned chart and propped it open with a few coins from his pocket. 'The wind is from the east-southeast at the moment and holding steady, as I'm sure you've already noticed, Captain, so for the first leg we'll be running easily before the wind, but for the second leg, between the two turning points, we'll be heading almost directly into it, and that's where we'll have the most difficulty. That's also where the most hazards lie.'

Smithy tapped a pair of points on the map.

'These shallows for example are on the direct route between Salt Pond Reef and Drunkenmans Cay. There is a narrow channel between them that would cut down the distance we have to travel, but it's extremely risky trying to run it, especially against the wind, so you'll have to decide whether to pass the shallows to the north or south. Then after Drunkenmans we have a fairly straight run through this channel to home.'

Smithy ran his finger along the chart, passing a few shallow points, before stabbing it back on Port Royal.

Sam nodded. 'It's a simple enough course for anyone with an ounce of seamanship.' Seamanship was something that Sam knew that he didn't have, but he wasn't about to tell Smithy that. 'However, we'll have to factor in the other ships as well; we may well be fighting for the same course at times, and I don't know how fairly our friend Swallow is going to play.'

Smithy grimaced at that. 'We'll just have to be on the lookout for anything untoward, Captain.'

'Good, thank you. One last thing - whenever we get close to any of the reefs I want a hand at the lead just in case. We probably won't cut it very fine, but better safe than sorry.'

Smithy grinned. 'Already taken care of, sir.'

Sam chuckled and shook his head wryly. 'What ever would I do without you, Mr Smith?'

Smithy was saved from answering by a chorus of shouts from off of the ship and they both looked up.

Creeping past, close by on the starboard side, was the Vengeance, and the members of her crew that weren't engaged in handling the ship were lining the sides and jeering good-naturedly.

Sam laughed and made his way to the side. As the other ship drew level he spotted Captain Bonny on the quarterdeck, their eyes met and he lifted his hat in salute with a wide grin. She put her hand to the brim of hers and then threw her head back in laughter. Sam was glad to see that at least one of the other captains was having as much fun as he was; it took some of the seriousness out of the situation and it meant that, at least for a while, Blackbeard and Swallow's treachery had been forgotten.

'Captain, the Queen Anne is changing course.'

Sam looked forward to where Swallow's ship was turning slightly to the south in order to round Salt Pond Reef. They had been gaining steadily on her and were less than a hundred metres behind now.

'Very good, we'll follow in her wake. Give the order please, Mr Smith.'

'Aye aye, sir.'

Sam watched as the crew efficiently went about turning the ship onto its new course. Because the Vengeance had had to go around the outside of them as they made the shallow turn, they had overtaken her again and Sam's crew took the opportunity to show their derision. Their joy was short lived, though, as the Vengeance soon drew up to them again. However, it was all part of the game and they didn't resent the speed advantage the other ship had; they knew that their own beloved Mermaid had its own strengths that more than compensated.

The channel between mainland Jamaica and the reef narrowed considerably here as the land jutted out. There would normally be no danger of running aground on either the reef or the beach, but with three ships in such tight quarters it became a risk and Sam had no doubt that Swallow would try to make the possibility a certainty for at least one of his competitors.

The Vengeance was now almost nose to tail with the Queen Anne's Revenge and Bonny obviously didn't have the patience to wait for open water to pass Swallow safely. Sam watched as she let her ship fall off slightly, aiming to pass the Queen Anne on the mainland side of her, but Swallow had been waiting for her to make her move and he let his ship fall off slightly as well, hoping to drive Bonny onto the beach.

Sam gritted his teeth and clenched his fists, but the expected disaster never came. With a neat change of course and sails, Bonny put her tiller over and turned into the wind, barely missing the stern of the Queen Anne's Revenge with her bowsprit and surging down her side. Too late, Swallow tried to compensate and turned the Queen Anne back into the wind, but the Vengeance was past.

'This is our chance!' Sam turned to the helmsman. 'Steer for the gap, we'll pass her.'

The channel was opening up now and there was plenty of room for the Mermaid to draw up alongside the Queen Anne's Revenge.

Sam could almost picture the calculations that had to be going on in Swallow's mind - he could let his ship fall off again and push the Mermaid towards the shore, which would undoubtedly force Sam to fall back again, but that would send the Queen Anne far from the optimum course and give the other three ships in the race the chance to overtake. Sam suspected that he wouldn't do it, it wouldn't be worth it, but Swallow was unpredictable and might well try it just to spite him.

In the end, Swallow held his course and the Mermaid drew level and nudged slightly ahead.

This time the crew of the Mermaid didn't line the side to taunt the rival crew; it wasn't wise to poke a crew like the Queen Anne's; you never knew when they would turn and bite.

The Mermaid forged slowly ahead, but they now had the same problem that the Vengeance had had with them earlier. The boat marking the way point came and the Mermaid didn't have enough of a lead to be able to turn in front of the Queen Anne so Sam was forced to order the steersman to veer wide while Swallow's ship had free rein to heel over and take the inside line.

The manoeuvre cost them dearly and they came onto the new course a good fifty metres behind. However, the situation was now vastly different; it was impossible to take a direct route from this way point to the next because the wind was almost directly in their faces, so everyone was going to have to plot a zigzag course. That meant that there were now many more choices to be made in handling the ship and seamanship was going to start counting far more than just sheer speed.

Swallow had come onto a new heading towards the southeast, but it was too early to tell if that meant he was going to pass the shallows to the south. Sam would have liked to have laid on the opposite tack so as to get as far away from the Queen Anne as possible, but, unfortunately, because of the reef close by on the port bow, the Mermaid was going to have to follow in her wake and try to pass her again.

This was where things really got interesting. As they rounded the boat each of the ships set a course as close to the wind as possible in order to get as far to windward as they could and the differences between the types of ships in the race gave them advantages where before they had been disadvantaged and vice versa. Bonny's ship, for example, was the fastest, but it was also the lightest, which meant that it didn't grip the sea as well as the other ships and the wind had more of an effect on it, pushing it backwards almost as much as it clawed its way to windward. The Queen Anne's Revenge on the other hand was much heavier and didn't have that problem, but it was still slower, so it was only slightly reducing the lead that the Vengeance had over it.

The Mermaid, of all the ships there, had the best time of it. She wasn't quite as heavy as Swallow's ship, but was heavy enough to be able to resist the wind. She was also able to steer closer into the wind than the Queen Anne, which was a distinct advantage.

Somehow, Sam knew this and he turned to the helmsman. 'Luff up a point. She can take it.'

The man struggled to turn the wheel to force the ship a little bit more into the face of the wind. The Mermaid was reluctant but obeyed and settled on her new course. For some reason it had felt like the most natural thing in the world to give the order and it was very satisfying to see the helmsman nodding in obvious approval of his captain's seamanship.

Smithy was jumping up and down with excitement. 'We're headreaching on her!'

Sam gave his first mate a small smile and a nod before turning back to watching the race; he was still trying to do his best Hornblower impression and stay as stoic as possible.

The Mermaid was indeed "headreaching" on the Queen Anne's Revenge - gaining distance to windward over the other ship. In a race like this the actual speed of the boat wasn't so important, compared to the distance it was travelling into the wind, and the Mermaid was doing it better than all of the other ships, including Bonny's, and especially Swallow's.

The Queen Anne was close enough now for Sam to clearly see Swallow at the stern of the ship, gazing back at them. His face was beetroot red and his knuckles were white on the rail with his frustration and anger. Sam gave him a lazy salute and chuckled as the man turned his back.

'If he stays on this tack we'll pass him with room to spare, Captain.'

Sam nodded. Again, somehow, he'd already come to the same conclusion - the shallows were fast approaching, only a couple of hundred metres ahead, and he could see the lighter coloured water where the sandy bottom lurked only a few feet below the surface. If the Mermaid kept to her present course she would clear the danger narrowly, but safely.

While Sam had been looking forward they had been creeping up on the Queen Anne and were now drawing almost level. He looked across to the rival ship's quarterdeck, wanting to watch what happened to Swallow's face as they passed him, but instead of the anger or despair that he'd expected, there was a look of cunning and sheer viciousness.

In a flash, Sam realised what the man was planning and just as the sails of the other ship started to shiver he was already bellowing his own orders.

'Hands to tack ship!'

There was no time to let Smithy know what he wanted; Sam knew he had to do it himself if he was to save his ship and the race.

'Wheel down.' The first order went to the helmsman. 'Slowly, handsomely there...'

The Mermaid turned slowly into the wind.

'Helm's a-lee!' The bellow sent the men to handling the sails and lines. 'Tacks and sheets!'

Sam turned to the helmsman. 'Hard over!'

The helmsman spun the wheel, turning the ship sharply now.

'Haul on the mainsail!' Sam gave the shout and the yardarms turned round exactly when the Mermaid was pointing directly into the wind.

'Now, helmsman! Meet her, hard over!'

The helmsman spun the wheel back the other way, stopping the Mermaid's turn as she tried to fall away from the wind.

'Haul off all!'

It was done, they were on the other tack, and just in time as the Queen Anne's Revenge was less than ten metres away. If they hadn't turned when they had, there would have been a collision, and the Queen Anne, as the far heavier ship, would have come off much the better for it, quite likely turning the Mermaid into a wreck that would even now be sinking to the bottom of the bay.

The danger wasn't over yet, though; since the Mermaid could sail closer to the wind than the Queen Anne, the ships were still on a collision course.

Sam made some quick calculations and came up with answers that he didn't like. On this tack it wasn't possible to weather the shallows, so they couldn't just keep going as they were. However, while they were almost in front of their rival, they weren't going fast enough to get clear of the Queen Anne before her bows made contact with the Mermaid's side, which meant that they couldn't go back onto the other tack in time to get past the shallows. The only choice that was left to him, then, was to change course entirely and go the long way around to the north, but that meant the Mermaid would give the other ships so much time to overtake that they wouldn't possibly be able to catch up again and the race would be lost.

'Let her fall off a point.'

The order put the Mermaid on a parallel course to the Queen Anne, out of immediate danger, and gave Sam an additional few seconds to think.

He glanced over to the Queen Anne and saw that Swallow had left his quarterdeck and was now in their bows, grinning cruelly, obviously unwilling to miss a moment of Sam's defeat.

'We're not done yet.' Sam's growl wasn't so much for Swallow as for himself; there had to be something he could do.

There was.

'Mr Smith! Get the lead swinging! Helmsman, let her fall off another point and head for the channel there!'

Involuntarily, the helmsman glanced at the thin channel between the shallows. His look of shock and fear lasted only a second before discipline and trust in his captain took over again. 'Aye aye, sir.' To his credit there was barely a hitch in his voice as he gave the only reply he could.

Sam turned to Smithy, but before he could say a word, Smithy preempted him. 'Sir, we can't get through the gap! It's almost dead into the wind - it's impossible!'

'It's going to be difficult and dangerous, yes, but hopefully not as impossible as you say, Mr Smith. We're going to run straight for the northernmost shallow, gather as much speed as she'll make and getting as close as we can before coming about on the other tack.' Sam ran his finger through the gap. 'Like you say, under normal conditions we wouldn't be able to hold a course between the shallows, but I'm going to sacrifice some of our speed for leeway, and by the time we come around on the other tack we should be almost clear.'

Smithy's mouth opened and closed a few times in such a good impression of a fish that Sam would have laughed if there had been time. Instead he just patted the man on the shoulder. 'I'm going to be in the bow, I want you to handle the ship from here. When I give the signal to turn, I want you to put the helm up and bring in all sails. On my second signal put her on the other tack and set the sails again. Can you do that, Smithy?'

Again, there was only one reply that a member of Sam's crew could give him and Smithy did as good a job as the helmsman had done before him. 'Aye aye, Captain.'

There was only time to give him a nod of acknowledgement, then Sam was flying down the steps and racing towards the bows. He reached it in what felt like record time and climbed up onto the rail to give him the best view, hanging on to the mermaid figurehead for safety. He ignored where his hands were on the incredibly realistic carving and looked back towards the quarterdeck. Satisfied that Smithy could see him he turned back to the sea.

The Queen Anne's Revenge was still following them, but she had fallen behind now and Sam knew that he could safely disregard her, so instead he turned his full attention to the fast approaching shallows.

They weren't quite on the course that he wanted so Sam motioned to Smithy, sticking his hand out to the side as if he were on a bike, to indicate his wishes.

This was the trickiest part of all; the ship would take some time to turn onto its new course, so Sam couldn't leave it too late or they would run aground, but if he gave the order too soon then they would never make it through the short channel.

He could feel the eyes of the men swinging the lead burning into him, could feel them shifting nervously as they did their job, but he spared them no notice; all his attention was on the patch of lighter sea that was almost underneath them.

'Now!' He accompanied his shout with a frantic wave and felt the ship lurch beneath him as the helmsman reacted to Smithy's order and put the helm over.

'Four! I have four fathoms on this line!'

That was the port side lead. Even as the ship swung to starboard the seabed was shelving fast beneath them.

The sails were brought in and they were now pointing directly into the wind. There was complete silence on board the ship now except for the men at the lead calling out the depth of water beneath them.

'Three and a half fathoms!'

The panic in the man's voice was evident, and it was probably what every man on the ship was feeling. Sam included himself in that and the confident smile that he gave the man wasn't anywhere close to being genuine.

The ship was slowing noticeably now as its inertia fought and lost the battle with the wind pushing against its timbers and the drag of the water, and Sam knew that if he left it very much longer they wouldn't have enough way to turn onto the new tack and would be stranded. He glanced to his right, to starboard, where the light patch of water marking the southern shallows stretched out in front of them.

He thought he saw a darker patch in the water just ahead, marking the end of the shallow, but he wasn't sure. He squinted, shading his eyes from the sun. He couldn't be certain if it was, but neither could he leave his decision any longer. He was going to have to risk it.

He waved his hand frantically and felt the sluggishness of the ship beneath him as the wheel was put over. For a second he thought that the Mermaid was going to refuse the demand of the rudder, but finally her bows came round and there was an almighty snap as her sails unfurled overhead.

There were a nervous few seconds as Sam watched the shallows approaching the starboard bow and he held his breath, expecting any second the ship to grind to a halt, cracking the masts, tearing a hole in the hull and sending them all to disaster, but the shock never came and they shot out of the channel, hard on the port tack with the wind on the left side of his face.

There was a wild cheer, but Sam hardly heard it as he sagged against the figurehead with relief. It was a relief that was short-lived, though, as he realised just what part of the mermaid he had his face pressed up against.

He hastily jumped down into the ship and received the congratulations of the men around him. He knew that it was the moment when Hornblower would have said a few words or made a joke so that the men would remember the situation fondly, but he couldn't bring himself to do that; he'd never been very quick with words, instead the men who were still swinging the lead gave him the perfect excuse to immediately get back to the business of running the ship.

'Avast there, you men! And thank you! Thank you all.'

As he looked around at the men he noticed something beyond them that made him grin and gave him at least something to say that would stick in his men's minds.

'Without a crew like this one, that pass through the channel wouldn't have been possible and right now we would be like them, or worse, aground.'

Sam pointed over the stern to where they had left behind the Queen Anne's Revenge. Swallow had been so intent on trying to put the Mermaid out of the race that he hadn't had a thought for his own situation. He'd taken his ship so close to the shallows that he'd had to painstakingly turn in a complete circle to be able to get back on the course that he'd originally been on, which had given everybody else, even the unhandy Good Queen Bess, the chance to overtake him.

'Have you ever seen anything so lubberly?'

It wasn't a joke, or even close to being funny, but the crew laughed nonetheless, although Sam told himself that it probably wasn't his words, but the sight of the rival ship being forced to sail away from them that they found so amusing. No doubt they were delighted with the knowledge that they had been able to thumb their noses at the crew that had drawn their ire so recently and contribute towards their possible downfall.

Sam let them have some time to relish the moment, but there was much left to do and the race still to be run and he quickly sent them back to work.

With the ship clear of obstacles for a while, his return journey to the quarterdeck could be rather more leisurely than his leaving it had been and he took the time to chat with a few of the men on the way, trying to learn more of their names and getting to know them a bit better.

Smithy was all smiles when Sam hopped up the stairs to the quarterdeck a few minutes later.

'Very well done, Captain, very well done!'

'Thank you, Smithy.'

'What would we do without you?'

Sam laughed as he had his own words turned back on him, but then blushed as he saw the admiration in his first mate's eyes. Not used to having anyone look up to him, except Violeta, he found himself suddenly uncomfortable and turned away to see how the race was developing so that he wouldn't have to awkwardly try to answer.

The situation had changed vastly since he had last had a chance to take it in fully. They were more than half way to the second turning point at Drunkenmans Cay and, as Sam had known would happen, the tougher conditions were showing who were the better sailors amongst the captains.

Captain Fitzhume was making a very creditable showing, despite having the slowest ship, and he was close on the heels of Caesar's African Queen. Sam suspected that it wasn't only because Fitzhume had handled his ship well, but also because Caesar wasn't the best seaman, even though, considering his background, he was doing better than would be expected. Both ships were a long way past the Queen Anne's Revenge and, unless either of them made an error, they would most likely finish that way.

Sam put the three following ships out of his mind, they were so far behind as to no longer be of concern to him, and looked to starboard.

The Vengeance had rounded the south side of the shallows and was now on the starboard tack, heading almost directly to the Cay and Blackbeard's second boat. The Mermaid on the other hand was on the port tack on an intersecting course. Sam would have to tack the ship at some point in order to reach the Cay and the only question was whether he would do so in front of Bonny or behind her. If the Mermaid was behind, then the race was lost. However, if they could squeeze in front of her then they were in with a chance, in spite of the fact that, with a more favourable wind, the Vengeance would be the faster ship on the return leg to Port Royal.

Smithy joined Sam at the starboard rail and they both stared out at the other ship, watching the angle between the two magnificent vessels changing minutely.

'I think...' Smithy started, but then stopped, unsure.

Sam was positive, though, and he grinned. 'You're right, Mr Smith, we're going to be able to tack in front of her. Please make all the necessary preparations.'

Smithy returned Sam's smile and went off to stand by the helmsman.

This time the distance between the two ships when they passed the Vengeance was far greater, but it was still possible to make out Bonny's lithe figure on the quarterdeck. She waved and Sam took off his hat, with the absurd red feather, and used it to return the friendly gesture. He was struck by the contrast between the different ways the competitors were behaving; everyone wanted to win, but how they went about it said much about their characters.

Swallow would do, and had so far done, everything he could to win, including kill. He was evil, Sam thought that he could recognise that now and he wondered whether the feeling he got whenever he was with the man was an indication of that, of something within him reacting to that fact.

Bonny, however, was at the other end of the scale. If this had been one of the role playing games that some of the boys at school played at lunch she would be "chaotic good" as opposed to Swallow's "chaotic evil". She would more often than not do the right thing, but she would have fun and create mischief while she was doing it.

Caesar struck Sam as being more neutral. He was self-serving, yes, but he had yet to do anything truly selfish, and if anything he seemed to have a sense of right and wrong that put Sam's own to shame.

Fitzhume was a bit of a mystery still - while his manners were flawless, and his speech was refine, he must have done something bad to be forced to become a pirate and leave the Royal Navy, or, if it had been his own choice, that in itself would say much about the man.

Lastly, Sam's thoughts turned to Blackbeard. Until now the man had shown himself to be a bit of a tyrant, but there was evidently something in him that loved fun as well, otherwise he wouldn't be having this kind of competition to find his successor.

A loud cough brought Sam out of his thoughts and back to the task at hand. He looked around to find Smithy at the wheel staring tactfully towards the Cay and the boat that they had to round - it was time to tack and if Sam had continued daydreaming he might well have handed the advantage back to the Vengeance.

'Ha - h'm.' Sam cleared his throat to cover his embarrassment and smiled shamefacedly at his first mate before giving the necessary order. 'Lay her on the starboard tack, please, Mr Smith.'

Smithy returned Sam's grin with a lopsided one of his own. 'Aye aye, Captain.'

The ship turned easily and was soon on its new course, heading north with the wind almost directly from the side. Bonny's ship was almost directly behind them now, just off to the seaward side of their wake and about fifty metres from the Mermaid's stern. It was a good lead, but Sam wasn't entirely sure that it would be sufficient to give them the win because the Vengeance's superior speed would start to tell again on this final leg. It would be a close run thing, but in his opinion the Mermaid would lose, although perhaps by only a matter of seconds.

Sam looked around the ship, noting how heeled over she was, noting the strain being put on the masts.

'Mr Smith, I want the guns run out on the windward side and have the hands sit on the rail please.'

'Aye aye, Captain.' The frown on Smithy's face showed clearly that he wasn't quite sure about Sam's order, but he carried it out anyway.

Sam knew that changing the weight distribution wouldn't make much of a difference, however it would serve two purposes, one would be to perhaps coax enough speed for them to be able to hold off the Vengeance for a few seconds more, but more importantly it would give the entire crew a sense that they were doing all that they could to win the race, instead of standing by and helplessly watching Bonny's ship overtake them for the third time.

Sam stood at the stern of the ship and looked back at the Vengeance slowly creeping up on them.

It was frustrating, not being able to affect the outcome of the race, and Sam wondered if this was something that he was going to have to get used to in the future when he became an adult. And if he didn't like not being in control of the outcome of a race, how was he going to feel not being in control of his life?

However, even though there was nothing more he could do, he kept his eyes roaming about the ship, constantly assessing whether he could set more sail, making sure that everything was as it should be and praying for a change in the wind that would allow him to outpace the Vengeance.

In the end the two ships reached their original anchorage at almost exactly the same time and the noise of both of their anchors dropping blended into one sound.

'A tie, by god!'

This came from Bosun Brown, who was one of the men who had been sitting on the quarterdeck rail and Sam smiled wryly as he replied.

'We may see it as a tie, Mr Brown, but it is Blackbeard's opinion that counts, and we all know how fickle he can be.'

There were groans and grumbles of agreement at that from the members of the gun crews on the quarterdeck.

Sam gave them a laugh, trying to appear unconcerned. 'Well, at least we didn't come last, that honour will go to our friend Swallow!'

As one, the crew turned to watch the other ships entering the harbour.

First came Caesar's African Queen, closely followed by the Good Queen Bess, and each turned smartly into the wind before dropping anchor.

Almost a minute later, Swallow's ship rounded the point and entered the bay.

Sam frowned; there was something about her that looked wrong but he couldn't quite put his finger on it.

The Queen Anne's Revenge glided slowly forwards, but instead of rounding into the wind and dropping anchor where she had started the race from, she bore down on the Good Queen Bess, like the predator she was.

Sam's gasp was echoed by the crew around him as they all realised the significance of the altered appearance of the ship - her gun ports were open.

As they watched, horrified, cannon poked from the holes and her strange behaviour took on sinister meaning.

The crew of the English captain's ship had no idea of the danger that was approaching; they were too busy jumping up and down on their decks and waving their hats in the air, celebrating having advanced to the next round in the contest and beaten a despised rival.

The sound of the broadside was deafening and the two ships all but disappeared in the smoke of the discharge.

Every cannon had been depressed to fire into her hull below the water line, and at such close range the heavy balls must have torn through her, because it was as if the bottom fell out of the Good Queen Bess - she heeled over at the weight of the water entering her and in moments had disappeared beneath the water.

In less than twenty seconds nothing remained of the once proud and beautiful vessel. Unlike the Shin Chang, which had literally blown apart, there was barely any debris from the destruction of the old ship - the only sign that she had ever existed were the waves, caused by her violent demise, that gently rocked the rest of the anchored shipping and slowly dissipated into nothing.

Sam shouted his orders into the shocked silence that fell after the thunder of the guns had faded. 'Hands to quarters! Clear for action!'

As the men ran past him, Sam turned to Smithy. 'Smithy, slip the anchor cable and get us under way, bring in the starboard guns and run out the port guns, we'll give her a broadside as we pass. Signal the other ships and ask them to stand with us - together we might have a chance of destroying the Queen Anne before she sinks us all.'

'Aye aye...'

Smithy was cut off when a cannon fired from the shore and they both spun to look, wondering at the target of the shot, but they quickly realised that it was just Blackbeard calling attention to a signal that he had hoisted over the fort.

'It's "all captains", sir. Blackbeard wants us ashore.'

Another gun went off, insisting on obedience, and Sam turned away from the signal in frustration to look at the enemy ship. Amazed, he watched as the Queen Anne's Revenge placidly ran in her guns and closed her gun ports. Her sails furled and she dropped her anchor, coming to a smooth halt. It seemed that Swallow was finished. His job was done; he'd eliminated another one of his rivals and perhaps ensured that he would remain in the competition, even though he had lost the race. Now, just like the bully and coward he was, he wasn't going to fire on the rest of the ships; it was one thing attacking an unsuspecting victim, quite another to take on crews that had been forewarned and had time to prepare for him.

'Acknowledge the signal please, Mr Smith.' Sam said through clenched teeth. 'We won't be needing the guns after all, so dismiss the gun crews. Send out men to search for survivors, and call away the boats, please - let's all of us go and see what Blackbeard makes of this.'

CHAPTER 9
THE CONTEST

A quarter of an hour later, the remaining captains were once again gathered in front of Blackbeard's throne and once again the atmosphere was charged with violence and hatred.

Despite the size of the town square, it was completely filled with sailors; this time Sam, Bonny and Caesar had left only a skeleton crew to guard their ships and brought as many men and women as they could instead of just one boatful. Every single one of them was armed to the teeth and the crews of the three surviving captains were eyeing the unrepentant Swallow's men with open animosity.

Survivors from the Good Queen Bess had been fished out of the bay and were standing huddled to one side. Captain Fitzhume had tragically not been found, and their thirst for revenge for their lost leader was adding greatly to the oppressive atmosphere.

It seemed like it would only need one person to cough at the wrong time for an all-out battle to commence.

The townspeople could feel the tension and, unlike the previous occasions where they had merrily mingled with the crews, now there was a hushed silence. To Sam, however, it seemed that half of them were scared of fighting breaking out while the other half were actively willing it to do so, just for the "fun" of it.

'Gentlemen.'

The word was softly spoken, but its deep bass rumble nonetheless carried to everyone and all eyes turned towards the source of the voice.

Blackbeard was sitting hunched over in his throne in front of the viewing stands. His giant cutlass was across his knees and he was using a pistol in his left hand to scratch his chin underneath his beard.

His eyes bored into the captains one by one before finally settling on Swallow.

The scruffy man's confident grin faded under Blackbeard's glare and he shifted uneasily as the silence lengthened.

'It appears that, despite your ridiculous attempts at sailing my ship, your ruthless elimination of your competition means that you will be continuing in my contest. However, that will be quite enough of that, Mr Swallow - we'll have no more wanton destruction, otherwise there will be no fleet to lead. I forbid you to move against any other ship in this fleet. On pain of death.'

Swallow nodded. 'As you wish, Captain.' The corners of his mouth twitched upwards as he fought against a smile; he knew he had gotten away, quite literally, with murder. Again.

'Captain Blackbeard, I must protest!'

The words were out of Sam's mouth before he even knew they had formed and he gulped nervously as Blackbeard's full attention turned to him. He continued regardless; he had plotted his course and now he had to sail it as best he could.

'When Swallow destroyed the Shin Chang you excused him, saying that he was just playing the game, but surely you must admit that this time Swallow has gone too far; his behaviour has nothing to do with the rules of your contest and everything to do with being a sore loser. He has destroyed two ships now and that is two too many, in my opinion, for him to be forgiven.'

'But it is my opinion that matters, Captain Vives.'

Blackbeard's voice was still calm, but there was a note of menace in it that made even Sam sway back in trepidation. However, the eyes under the brim of his hat didn't hold the same note, instead Sam thought he detected a hint of sympathy, perhaps of sorrow in them, before Blackbeard hid his feelings behind his usual ferocious mask.

'My decision is made, the matter is settled, *and I will hear no more on it*. Understood, Captain Vives?'

For some reason, Blackbeard's growl didn't have the same power behind it that it usually had. Sam looked at him speculatively and saw what he thought was an appeal in his dark eyes, as if he didn't quite believe his own words, as if he were frightened of the matter going further and the possible consequences of things getting out of control.

Sam suddenly came to the realisation that there was more behind Blackbeard's decision than the simple desire to have his own man remain in the contest and that if he pushed and forced the pirate lord to demonstrate his dominance then war between the crews might well break out. The pirate lord knew that, despite the injustice of Swallow's continuation in the contest, it was most probably the only way to avoid violence, bloodshed, death and the probable dissolution of the "Brethren of the Coast", the association of pirates that protected them all - the crew of the Queen Anne's Revenge were only going to be satisfied if Swallow were allowed to continue in the competition, so that was what Blackbeard had to make happen. However, that meant angering the other crews, so the pirate lord needed at least one of the opposing captains to openly accept his decision and lead the way in keeping the peace. Hence his silent appeal.

Sam clenched his teeth, chewing off the harsh retort that was bubbling up. He could feel the disbelieving eyes of Bonny and Caesar on him as he reluctantly swallowed his pride and forced himself to nod in acceptance. 'Understood, Captain.'

Sam definitely saw the glimmer of relief and gratitude in Blackbeard's eyes this time, but it was only there for a second before the big pirate grinned and turned his gaze back to the crowd of townspeople silently watching from the edges of the square and the stands.

He stood up and climbed onto his throne, once again the showman, and raised his voice so that it carried to his entire audience. 'Now that we have our four final aspirants, we can get on with the show, but, before that, there is one last insignificant, inconsequential, trivial thing left to deal with.'

He made an ostentatious motion and two burly men came out from underneath the bleachers behind him, struggling to carry a small, iron bound chest between them.

They set the chest on the ground in front of the throne and flipped the lid open.

As one, the crowd gasped at the sight of the glittering gold coins within.

Blackbeard jumped down and walked forwards.

Sam was watching him, rather than staring at the gold like everybody else, so he caught the sad look and the small shake of the head as the pirate lord took in the universal greed of the people around him. Their eyes met briefly, and again it was like an understanding passed between them, but once more, it was just a brief impression,

quickly gone, and Sam wasn't entirely sure that it had been there at all
- perhaps he was just assigning too much humanity to the callous cut-
throat.

Blackbeard bent down and dipped his hand into the chest, pulling
out a huge handful of the coins. He let them slip slowly from his fist
and this time even Sam was mesmerised by the flash of light upon
them. When every coin had tumbled with a heavy clink back into the
chest, Blackbeard kicked the top closed with a thud.

The entire crowd, including the crews and captains, sighed as the
sight of the fortune was cut off.

'As promised, a hundredweight of gold for the victor of the race,
gold so fresh from a captured Spanish treasure galleon that it has never
known the touch of human hand... apart from my own greedy mitts,
of course!'

He showed his huge hands to his audience and received the laugh
that he had been expecting. It was a feeble joke, but most of the people
in the square were already so drunk that their sense of humour wasn't
as refined as usual - not that it normally was anyway, from what Sam
had seen.

When the laughter faded Blackbeard dramatically put his hand to
his beard and stroked it thoughtfully. 'But the question is - who should
the prize go to?'

Sam exchanged a glance with Bonny and received a shrug in reply;
they both suspected that Blackbeard would give the victory to her, just
to spite Sam for his continuing defiance, but the pirate captain
surprised them both.

A group of Blackbeard's crew appeared from the direction of the
town, jogging along, drawing a small handcart between them.

'Ah, here it comes now!' Blackbeard waved his men over. 'Just in
time, lads, set it right there, next to the other one.'

Two of the men lifted an almost identical chest down from the cart
to sit next to the one already in the square and Blackbeard opened it
briefly to show that it too was filled to the brim with golden coins.

He looked up from his bent over position and winked at Sam before
closing the chest again and straightening up.

'I declare the race a tie! One chest each to the salient men and
women of the Vengeance and the Mermaid!' He flung his arms wide in
invitation and the crowd roared in delight.

While the chests were being taken to the boats in order to be safely
conveyed to the ships, Sam looked around at the crowd and the crews,
noting the smiling faces where before there had been resentment and

fear, and Blackbeard's motives for his generosity became clear - Sam had helped him diffuse the dangerous situation and now, at the price of only a small chest of gold, he had managed to win back the love of the people and of two of the three ship's crews that Swallow had squandered. Now they were all firmly back on Blackbeard's side and the demise of poor Captain Fitzhume had been all but forgotten.

Once the commotion had subsided, all eyes turned expectantly back to Blackbeard, whose full attention once again fell upon Sam.

'Handy piece of seamanship, taking your ship through that channel against the wind, Captain Vives.'

'Thank you, Captain.'

Blackbeard waited, obviously expecting Sam to say more, to boast of his achievement or elaborate on the tale of how he had gotten the better of Swallow and the crew of the Queen Anne's Revenge, but Sam just remained silent. He wasn't one to blow his own horn, and besides; everybody already knew what he had done because he had done it in full view of them only a few miles across the bay.

Blackbeard nodded imperceptibly, his eyes glinting with amusement and something like respect. He grinned, covering for the awkward silence. 'Of course, I could have done it a lot better.'

The pirate lord's words brought laughs from the crowd and some gentle, well-meant heckling, but they had a vastly different effect on Sam himself. He only now grasped just what he had just done - he had handled a ship as if he truly were its captain, using knowledge he shouldn't have and instincts that weren't his own and done so better than colleagues with years of experience. It was impossible, he shouldn't have been able to do any of that, even in a dream; his mind shouldn't have known where to begin.

There wasn't time to wonder about it, though, as Blackbeard leapt up on his throne and faced the crowd, throwing his arms wide. He was grandstanding again and the crowd was loving it. 'Right then! With all that out of the way we can finally get back to my contest! What say you? Are you up for a bit of fun, my hearties?'

The response was a deafening and unanimous "aye!" that came from townspeople and seamen alike. Only three people in the crowd didn't share in the enthusiasm, instead Sam, Captain Bonny and Captain Caesar shared worried glances, concerned that their own murder might well go equally unpunished in the near future.

When the noise died down again, Blackbeard pointed out into the bay where the small, two-masted ship was still waiting.

'Now, the more eagle-eyed among you may have noticed my little brig moored just off shore...'

There were more laughs at this; it was a bit hard to miss, anchored as it was right off of the docks in front of the square.

'We've tested their seamanship and now, for the next part of my contest, our intrepid captains are going to show us their fighting prowess and prize-taking skills by either defending that ship or attacking it with a boarding party. It's going to be one hell of a scrap! But don't worry; nobody's going to get hurt, at least not too badly.'

There was disappointment from many in the crowd, who had obviously been looking forward to a healthy bit of blood with their violence, but Blackbeard ignored them and continued straight on. He reached out a hand and a sailor gave him a padded stick the size of a sword. 'The crews are going to be using these instead of steel. But, believe me, this will just make the battle much more fun for those of us watching!'

He swung the stick and whacked the sailor who had handed him it on the arse. The sailor comically jumped into the air and ran howling into the crowd, clutching himself.

Even though it had obviously been rehearsed and planned, there was laughter at the man's clowning and when it died down Blackbeard continued, but now he spoke directly to the captains. 'Right, then, you lot! Here's how this is going to work. You'll be in pairs and a coin toss will decide who attacks and who defends. The attackers get a force of fifty men, but because the defenders have the advantage they only have thirty. Up there, flying from the top of the mainmast you can see my flag. All the boarding team has to do is capture that to win, it doesn't matter how long it takes and I don't care how you do it... just don't burn down my ship or I'll string up the lot of you! The defenders on the other hand just have to beat back the opposition enough to make them give up, and we all know what happens to a man's will to attack when he's thrown off a ship a couple of times, so that shouldn't be too hard. You lubbers got all that?'

Blackbeard glared at them all and received nods in reply.

'Good. First up we'll have Caesar and Swallow, followed by Vives and Bonny. The winners of those initial bouts will then fight each other in a final round and whoever wins that one will take the prize. So, good luck to you all, fight well, and may the best man, or woman, win!'

At this last, Blackbeard shared a grin with Swallow, who had been looking very smug throughout, and Sam wondered what the two had planned to swing this contest in Swallow's favour, because he had no doubt they had something up their sleeves to make it a little less fair.

Swallow and Caesar stood together while Blackbeard tossed a coin. Sam thought it looked very civilised, like the start of a football match, but he knew how often football matches could devolve into all-out war.

Swallow called heads, won the toss and elected to attack.

The formalities over, the two men shook hands like boxers at a weigh in. Caesar tried to psyche out his opponent by snarling at him and squeezing his hand far too hard but, to Sam's surprise, Swallow was giving as good as he got - he met Caesar's glare with a dead-eyed stare of his own and returned the handshake without problem, something that such a scrawny-looking man shouldn't be able to do. Eventually, Caesar gave up on his intimidation tactics and both men backed away to their crews to choose their men.

Swallow had very obviously had prior knowledge of the contest because all he did was whistle and fifty of Blackbeard's biggest and toughest men stepped out of the crowd. They were already armed with the padded weapons, a lot of which looked suspiciously under-padded to Sam's eye. Sam was also unsurprised to see among them the thugs who had blocked the road when he had gone to the inn to meet with Blackbeard and he shared a wry smile with Smithy, who had also spotted them; that little mystery was now solved.

Caesar took somewhat longer to choose his thirty men, but eventually he and his crew went down to the water and got into the boats to go out to the ship.

As the big African captain was being rowed away, Blackbeard called out. 'You have ten minutes to prepare your defences, Captain Caesar! We start at my pistol shot!'

Sam glanced sideways at Smithy. 'Have you got a watch, Mr Smith?'

'Yes, Captain.'

'See how long Blackbeard thinks ten minutes are, please.'

'Aye aye, Captain.' Smithy grinned ironically and took out an expensive looking silver pocket watch, most probably plunder from some raid or other. He flipped the lid open and made a note of the time.

'Have you got some men in mind to help us with this?' asked Sam.

Smithy looked up from the Swatch. 'Yes, Captain. I have some strong deckhands already picked out for defence and we have some very good, experienced men for a boarding party. We're in good shape, whatever side we get.'

'Good.' Sam paused, thoughtful. 'Keep an eye on the men and make sure they watch out for each other. I wouldn't put it past Blackbeard, or Swallow for that matter, to try to make sure as many of our men are out of action as possible, any way they can, before the contest begins.'

'Already taken care of, Captain... And already tried by them. We've had to refuse quite a lot of suspiciously free grog already this morning.' Smithy grinned at Sam.

Sam returned the grin. 'Well done. What would I do without you? Remind me why I'm the captain and not you, would you?'

'Because we all owe you our lives and besides, you continually do things that surprise us all.'

'As long as they surprise the enemy as well.'

They chuckled companionably, but were interrupted by the sound of a shot as Blackbeard started the first round of the contest.

Smithy looked down at the watch. 'Barely six minutes.'

'As expected.' Sam sighed and shook his head.

Swallow's men swarmed down to the boats, five men going to each of them, and they quickly rowed out towards the ship. As they reached the brig they spread out. Some of the boats made their way behind the ship, while others went to the stern and prow ends, and in short order they had surrounded it completely. It was all very disciplined, far too disciplined in fact; it was clear that Swallow had not only had time to think about his strategy, but had also been able to rehearse it thoroughly with his men.

When all of the boats were in position, Swallow stood up. He was in the one closest to the stern of the ship and so he was in full view of everyone, townspeople and sailors alike. He struck a heroic pose, with his foot up on the prow of the boat, and looked around, checking to see that his men were ready and not very subtle making sure that all eyes in the audience were on him. Apparently satisfied, he held his arm up in the air and waved it around in a wide circle a few times. He then gave an ostentatious forward motion as if he were conducting a cavalry charge.

In unison the boats surged towards the ship as the oars bit deep into the sea.

Sam was amused to see that, in making his grand gesture, Swallow had forgotten to brace himself and was thrown headlong into the bottom of the boat, landing on one of his sailors and causing the oarsmen to break rhythm and the boat to slew round out of control.

The crowd, that Swallow had wanted to watch him so closely, laughed hard, seeing a lubber who couldn't keep his balance in a boat rather than the heroic figure he'd tried to appear.

It took his crew a few moments to pick Swallow up out of the bottom of the boat and he immediately started striking out at his men with his padded stick, shouting at them to start rowing again, his face beetroot red.

'Got a bit of a temper that one, Captain.'

'Indeed.'

He had a temper, yes, but it seemed that he also had a bit of a brain and his tactic of spreading his men around the ship had Caesar scrambling frantically to reposition his men around the brig. The big African had obviously expected a head-on assault and had grouped his men to face it, which meant that he was still disorganised when the attackers arrived. Because of this, some of Swallow's five man teams were met with more force than was necessary, while others were met with less, or none at all. This allowed a couple of the attacking teams to gain the deck easily and those men were then able to run to help the other teams that were hardest pressed. They leaped on the defenders from the side and in seconds the entire ship was one mess of fighting.

The crowd had the entertainment they had been promised. They laughed and cheered as men from both sides were thrown off the deck and into the water. Swallow's men were being dragged off of the ropes whenever they attempted to climb up to the flag and Sam saw at least one sailor being thrown through the air to crash into a group of his companions.

It was complete chaos and Sam would have enjoyed the spectacle immensely if it wasn't for the screams of pain ringing out across the water from men with broken bones or other injuries.

Caesar was in the middle of everything by the ship's main mast, surrounded by the remaining defenders. His arm rose and fell time after time as he laid about himself with his stick, never seeming to tire. His men were faltering and outnumbered, though, and they couldn't be everywhere at once, so one of Swallow's men had gotten almost to the top of the mast before they spotted him - the man had climbed one of the ratlines out of reach of Caesar's stand around the base of the mast. Caesar desperately sent men climbing to try to stop him, but the man had too much of a head start and before they were even halfway up he had the flag in his hands.

Blackbeard's pistol went off and the fighting stopped. Swallow's men grouped around the sailor who had captured the flag, lifting him onto their shoulders, cheering and celebrating, while Caesar and his men dejectedly made their way down the sides of the ship and into their boats.

Sam frowned. 'That was too easy; Swallow has obviously been preparing this for a long time.'

Smithy grunted in agreement. 'It is indeed a little bit of an advantage, being first mate to the man who came up with this whole thing, Captain.'

Sam glanced over at Captain Bonny, she looked like she was as worried as he was and didn't seem at all happy about Swallow's victory. 'We won't have the same problem with Bonny, but whoever wins will have to take on Swallow and I have a feeling he hasn't shown all his cards yet.'

Soon, both Caesar and Swallow were back on the docks accompanied by their men.

Caesar's men had gotten by far the worse of the combat; there didn't seem to be a single one of them that wasn't bleeding and three or four of them were completely unconscious and laid out on the dock being seen to by a doctor. Still, nobody had died. The padded swords had ensured that at least.

A few of Blackbeard's sailors busied about the brig. They repaired what little damage there was and put the flag back in its place high on the main mast then abandoned the ship, ready for the next round.

While Sam was waiting for Smithy to arm and prepare the men, he looked around the square.

Caesar and Bonny were talking together quietly and it looked like she was commiserating him after his loss, although he didn't seem to be taking it too badly; after all, they had known that Swallow was going to be given unfair advantages over them.

The crowd were having a great time; this was probably the most excitement that some of them had had in their lives and they were using the occasion to its fullest - it was like a giant street party now, with music, food, drink and various street entertainers, who had seemingly sprung out of nowhere and were now causing a nuisance of themselves.

Blackbeard and Swallow were likewise having a good time, laughing and joking, surrounded by their victorious sailors. They looked happy and confident, thick as thieves, like two people who were sure of an outcome.

The one thing that Sam just couldn't figure out was, if Blackbeard wanted Swallow to win so badly, why would he even bother with this contest? Why not just hand the reins over to him? It had to be that something else was going on, that Blackbeard had some kind of hidden agenda that nobody, not even Swallow was aware of. Or maybe Blackbeard just wasn't really sure of Swallow and wanted him to prove himself, even here in a contest heavily weighted in his favour - the environment had been contrived by Blackbeard himself and he had made it so that it would be impossible for Swallow to do anything stupid enough that it would cause any permanent damage to the pirate lord or his crew. Sam thought that that was probably it; Swallow was the favoured candidate, but still needed to convince Blackbeard - perhaps this contest wasn't going to be so fixed that there wouldn't be a chance of winning after all.

Finally, everything was ready and Blackbeard called Sam and Bonny over for the next round. 'Right, then! Who's going to call the coin toss?'

'Captain Bonny can do the honours.'

Blackbeard grinned. 'Ever the gentleman, Captain Vives. Watch she doesn't take advantage of you for that because many a woman would... But perhaps that's what you're hoping for!' He laughed and winked at Sam, who coloured slightly. Blackbeard grinned at his discomfort and turned to Bonny, who was smiling sweetly at Sam, making him decidedly hot under the collar. 'So, what'll it be then, darlin'?'

Bonny took a second to consider. 'Heads.'

Blackbeard tossed the coin, slapped it into his hand and revealed it. It was heads. 'Good choice. What's your pleasure?'

'I'll attack.'

Blackbeard stuffed the coin back in his pocket and turned to address the crowd. 'Captain Bonny is going to attack. Captain Vives will defend!'

The crowd cheered, even though they probably didn't care who was doing what as long as they got a good show.

'Off to your boats then, laddie, you've got ten minutes. Good fortune to the both of yer.' Blackbeard touched the brim of his hat in salute then walked away and sat down on his throne, accompanied by the slimy Swallow.

Sam held out his hand to Bonny. 'Good luck, Captain.'

She looked down at his hand in surprise. After a second she took it and looked up at him. Sam had to admit she was good looking... then she smiled and Sam caught a glimpse of her teeth. He suppressed a slight shudder as they shook hands.

'Thank you, you too.'

Sam turned away and rushed to his sailors. Smithy had been busy after the announcement and Sam found the defensive team ready and waiting - twenty eight of some of the biggest men he'd ever seen.

'Let's get to the boats then, shall we? Lead on please, Smithy.'

They trooped down to the boats, clambered in and rowed out towards the ship. Sam got into the same boat as Smithy, who immediately looked to him for instructions.

'What's the plan, Captain?'

'I want you to spread the men equally around the ship in teams of three, so that we're prepared for an attack on all fronts, like Swallow just did. However, make sure that the men know what to do if another team needs help; I don't want them running around like headless chickens if they find themselves without anyone to fight - I want one man assigned to go to the team to their left, one to the team on the right, and one to always stay at their post, unless you or I give the order to fall back or do otherwise.'

'Good thinking, sir.'

'Next, if I call for everyone to fall back I want every place where someone could climb up to the flag covered, not just the main mast. And I want one of your biggest men ready to go up the mast and defend it if we do have to fall back. He'll have to be a topman, obviously. Make sure that he knows that he is to defend as well as he can, but I don't want anyone falling to their deaths from up there - if one of Bonny's men tries to do something silly I'd rather see her win than anyone suffer casualties unnecessarily.'

Smithy seemed doubtful at this and raised a questioning eyebrow, 'if you insist, Captain.'

'I do, Mr Smith; this contest is not so important that lives should be lost trying to win it, especially not from Bonny or Caesar's crew. Later on, if we win and go to the next round, we will see whether we give the same consideration to Swallow and his men - if they go too far we will adjust our strategy to match.'

Smithy nodded, satisfied with this explanation.

They were now at the ship and Sam and his men scrambled up the side. Smithy quickly organised the sailors into three man teams, giving them Sam's instructions and then sending them to their posts. That left Smithy and Sam guarding the side of the ship closest to the shore, where they could keep an eye on Bonny's movements.

The man who Smithy had chosen to complete their three man team turned out to be the big bosun, Brown.

'Mr Brown! Good to have you with me today! I feel safe now, knowing that you have my back!'

The bosun touched his forehead and smiled sheepishly. 'I'll do my best, sir.'

'That is all I ever expect from any of my men, thank you, Mr Brown.' Sam smiled and nodded to the man, who beamed his pleasure at being so addressed by his captain.

Smithy looked at his watch. 'Seven minutes, Captain.'

Sam's plans had been put into action so quickly and efficiently that the men were standing around at their posts with a good few minutes to spare and nothing to do.

'We've still got time if you want to change the plan at all.'

Sam glanced around quickly, 'I don't think we can do much better than this, unless you can pull a few dozen men out of your hat, Mr Smith?'

'I'm afraid not, Captain,' Smithy said, grinning widely. 'Maybe you'd like to say something to the men, though? A few good words from you and they will fight like they've never fought before.'

Sam considered his first mate's suggestion. Hollywood liked to show over and over the supposed power that a rousing speech had before a battle and he'd seen *Braveheart* enough times to have a good idea of what he could say. He just didn't think that a tacky speech about freedom or some such was really going to do anything, especially seeing as there wouldn't be stirring music in the background to make it less boring.

He looked around the ship, assessing the mood of the men. They were standing at the posts that Smithy had given them but many of them were shifting anxiously from one foot to the other, frowns on some of their faces as hands toyed nervously with the hilts of their wooden swords. He realised that he probably should do something to settle them and when he replied to Smithy he raised his voice slightly so that they could all hear, while trying not to make it too obvious. 'They're good men, Smithy and I trust them to do me proud.'

His simple words had an instant effect on the men - they stilled as they puffed their chests out and stood up straighter, reassured by the confidence their captain had in them.

Smithy nodded at Sam, impressed.

Just then, Blackbeard's shot rang out to signal the start of the contest. Smithy checked his watch and chuckled. 'That was almost the whole ten minutes, Captain.'

'It seems that Blackbeard doesn't care as much about the outcome of this fight as he did the last one.'

Sam watched as boats swarmed away from the docks carrying Bonny and her sailors. They spread out across the water; predictably Bonny was trying the same thing as Swallow had and was sending boats to each point of the compass to surround them.

'Excuse me a second, Smithy, I'll be right back.' He ran to the mainmast of the ship and climbed up a bit so that he could see exactly what was going on.

Bonny hadn't organised things nearly as well as Swallow had; there were more men in some of the boats than in others and they weren't forming an exact circle around the ship. Sam realised immediately that he could restructure his defences slightly, committing more men to some places and taking them from others. He clambered down and then ran around the ship from crew to crew giving last minute instruction before ending back at his post with Smithy and Brown.

Bonny gave the signal to attack and Sam watched as the boats closed in. Once more, Bonny was showing her lack of preparation and the boats were arriving at the ship in dribs and drabs, not all at once. This meant that Sam's men were at leisure to reinforce the groups to either side of them, repel the attack with ease in seconds, then move back to their original positions with plenty of time to be there in overwhelming force for the next boat that arrived.

The attack went very badly for Bonny's men and after only a few minutes the vast majority of them were in the water, bruised and out of breath from their exertions. They clutched the sides of their boats in order to stay afloat, defeated and completely out of the fight.

Sam himself confronted the boat led by Bonny.

While Smithy, Brown and reinforcements from the groups on either side dealt with the four men accompanying her, Sam was left facing Captain Bonny herself. He deliberately allowed her to come up the side and over the rail.

She jumped lightly down onto the deck and lifted her padded stick into the en garde position, Sam did the same and the two captains stood there, sizing each other up. Her guard and stance were strong; she was lightly balanced on the balls of her feet and didn't have any immediately apparent openings or weaknesses. She looked like she knew what she was doing.

They stayed like that for a few seconds, eyeing each other, but then Sam slowly straightened up and lowered his stick to his side.

Bonny was puzzled, but stayed as she was, thinking it was a trick of some kind. 'What are you doing?'

In answer Sam just gestured around them at the rest of the boat. None of Bonny's men had made it to the deck and half a dozen of Sam's men had found themselves with no more opponents to repel and were advancing on Bonny and the crew of her last boat. They were the final threat to the ship and weren't going to last very long.

Bonny grinned and straightened up out of her fencing stance, 'I was quite looking forwards to crossing swords with you. It's a pity, but it seems like it's not going to happen.'

Sam smiled. 'I must admit I'm a bit disappointed myself, so how about this - concede defeat and then invite your men up on deck to dry off. We can have our fight and, now that it doesn't matter, it can just be for fun.'

The smile on Bonny's face widened considerably, which, unfortunately, showed her teeth to the maximum. Sam found he was getting used to them, though; after all, most of the people he had met here were exactly the same - even Smithy, who obviously took better care with his dental hygiene than most, looked like an ice hockey player.

Five minutes later, the men from both of the crews, half of them wet, half of them dry, all of them laughing and joking together, were lounging back against the rails around the main deck of the little brig.

Sam and Bonny stood in the middle of the deck near the mainmast in the space that had been left clear for them. Sam leant on his padded sword and smiled at the men around them. 'I'm glad to see there are no hard feelings between our men.'

'Of course not! They may not like losing, but they recognise when they have been beaten fairly by a superior foe. And now that you've shown them what you and your crew can do, they think you have a good chance of winning against Swallow. Which makes them almost glad that you won.'

'I'm not entirely sure that anyone has a chance, but we'll certainly do our best to wipe that smirk of his face.' He turned to face her and lifted his sword. 'Shall we?'

Bonny grinned and lifted her own sword in reply. 'Ready when you are.'

What followed was a contest that was talked about for a long while afterwards. Over time and under the influence of alcohol it became so embellished that the men there could have sworn that they saw Captain Vives somersaulting through the air and Captain Bonny leaping on high, lifted by angel's wings. One telling of the tale also mentioned that the two captains had to pause in order to fight off a sea monster that had somehow sneaked up on the ship, attracted by the sounds of battle, but the sailor telling it was a habitual liar and wasn't believed - not fully anyway and not by many people.

The reality, though not exactly like the retellings, was just as exciting, but almost impossible to satisfactorily describe, which was probably one reason why the tale changed so much over time. And while there was a certain amount of leaping involved it certainly wasn't quite as incredibly acrobatic as later described.

This was a very different contest to Sam's fight with the French Captain and it was especially different from his ones with Rafa. For a start, there were no rigid rules about touches or having to stay in bounds, which meant that they weren't limited to just the middle of the open deck. Then there was the vast difference in the quality of his opponent; Bonny was a very talented opponent who wouldn't dream of using intimidation as a tactic. In fact, when Sam thought back on the fight later, he was reminded most of the sword fight in *The Princess Bride,* a scene which he had watched many, many times.

Sam had the time of his life; he couldn't stop grinning as he clambered over wooden crates, hung from ropes and balanced on the thin rails, perilously close to the drop into the water. All the time he was matched by Bonny, who more than made up for a lack of physical strength with an agility that surpassed even Sam's own. The only thing that Sam felt the fight was missing were the ubiquitous strategically-placed candlesticks, there only to be impressively cut in half as a major part of any half-decent sword fight, although the padded poles certainly wouldn't have been up to the task.

In the end the contest came down to an exchange of thrusts, parries and ripostes in the centre of the deck between the masts that drew gasps of awe from the men watching them, even though they could barely follow the swords.

Neither of them could get a clear advantage and as the exchange went on they drew upon the reserves of their energy to power limp arms. As they tired, their swings lost the fine control that they'd had and started to get wilder and wilder; in return, the telegraphed blows were not so much parried as dodged outright. Finally, their reactions were so dulled by exhaustion that they both went for a strike at the precise same time, each thinking that they were quicker.

But neither was.

They stood panting, grinning from ear to ear, their swords held motionlessly at their opponent's neck.

'Shall we... call it... a draw?' Sam panted, barely able to get the words out.

'Unless... you feel like... going again?' Bonny gasped, her chest heaving, not unattractively.

Sam chuckled and withdrew his sword while Bonny did the same. They grinned and clasped their left arms together in respect for each other's abilities.

Suddenly, they were swamped by the sailors and the difficulty they were having in breathing was compounded by the congratulatory thumps on the back that they were forced to suffer. Sam didn't mind one bit, though; he'd never been this popular and wanted to savour every moment of it. He exchanged a smile and nod with Bonny then each turned away to receive the admiration of their men.

The jubilant mood didn't last long, however, as a familiar voice bellowed out across the deck, 'WHAT THE HELL IS GOING ON!'

Everyone went silent and turned towards the speaker.

Balancing easily on the rail at the side was Blackbeard, a furious look on his face. He was accompanied by Swallow and five of his men, armed with real swords.

Sam made his way through his sailors to stop in front of Blackbeard.

Blackbeard looked down at him. 'Captain Vives, please explain yourself. What is happening with my contest?'

Sam waved off Blackbeard's question casually. 'We finished that business a while ago, Captain. We were just having some fun before we came back to the dock.'

Blackbeard waited expectantly.

Sam looked up at him, fully conscious that Blackbeard wanted him to say more, but with his newfound confidence he was content to make him wait, just for the fun of it.

Eventually Blackbeard broke the silence, angrier than ever. 'Well?'

'Well what, Captain Teach?' Sam asked innocently, tilting his head to one side and feigning puzzlement.

'WHO WON!?!'

'Oh, of course, sorry! Well...' Sam made a show of screwing up his eyes and shading from the sun as he peered up at the masthead. 'The flag is still flying, so I guess I did.'

Sam turned away and returned to his men, leaving Blackbeard swearing and throwing insults at his back under his breath. He grinned; little victories like this made everything worthwhile and just a bit more fun.

Smithy was standing with a group of his men and he congratulated his captain by shaking his hand and patting him on the shoulder. He had a slightly worried look on his face, though.

'It's very dangerous to provoke him like that, Captain,' the concern was almost instantly replaced by a broad grin. 'But it was worth it to see the look on his face!'

'Wasn't it just?'

They shared a laugh.

'Well, I suppose we should get back to shore and prepare for the final round. Get the men to their boats, please, Mr Smith.'

'Aye aye, Captain.'

As the men started to swarm down the side of the ship, Sam turned and looked back at Blackbeard. The pirate lord had calmed down a little bit - he no longer looked like he wanted to murder someone, but he was still furious. He was talking to Swallow, well, talking was a delicate way of putting it; he had his face about an inch from Swallow's and was bellowing at him, gesticulating wildly and angrily. Sam couldn't quite make out everything that Blackbeard was saying but he caught his own name at least twice.

Swallow was flinching back every few seconds, both from the vehemence of the tirade and also because spittle from Blackbeard was hitting him in the face almost continuously.

Blackbeard ended his lecture by poking Swallow hard in the chest, knocking the small man back a step, he then turned and went down the side and into his boat and rowed away without saying a word. Swallow was left watching him go, open mouthed, from the rail.

By this time the only people left on board the ship were Sam and Swallow. Sam glanced over the side and saw that the only boat that remained, now that Blackbeard had abandoned Swallow, was his own.

He toyed with the idea of leaving Swallow, but realised that there was a more enjoyable way of dealing with the situation. He smiled to himself and sauntered over to him. 'Mr Swallow, may I offer you a ride back to the docks?'

Swallow hadn't noticed Sam approach and was somewhat startled by his appearance at his side. He looked around and his face fell as he finally realised that he was on his own with no way to get back to shore.

'Or would you prefer to swim?' Sam asked sweetly, taking a step away, as if to leave Swallow behind.

The slimy man looked at Sam with evident hate in his eyes, but was forced to swallow his pride. 'Thank you, I would appreciate it.' His lip kept trying to curl with a snarl as he replied, but he fought it back, probably realising that a little indignity at that moment would save him a lot more later if he had to try to get to shore on his own.

'After you, then.' Sam held out his hand, indicating the way to the rail where his boat was waiting. He let Swallow walk past him before allowing a huge grin onto his face. This time he was careful not to let his adversary see it; while he was fine with poking fun at Blackbeard to a certain extent, he was wary about doing the same with Swallow - he seemed very vindictive, like a man who couldn't take a joke, especially one at his own expense, and Sam would soon be facing him with a weapon in his hand, albeit a padded one. He didn't want to give Swallow any more reason than he already had to take his frustrations out on him or his men.

Swallow clambered over the rail and went straight down into the boat without asking permission or saying anything else. He immediately sat to one side and glared out over the bay towards the town, not meeting anyone's eye. Sam followed closely and sat in the stern at the tiller.

Smithy caught his eye and raised a questioning eyebrow, but Sam just shook his head and the first mate shrugged and gave the order to start rowing.

As Sam steered the boat back to the docks he watched Swallow closely, but unobtrusively. The man was calming down a bit now, but Sam could see that he was still seething. He wouldn't sit still and was tapping on the side of the boat, humming a tune that Sam couldn't quite make out, but was somehow familiar - possibly one of those pirate songs that everybody recognised, about bottles of rum or shivering timbers or something. Although, it did sound very much like a Taylor Swift song that was being played on the radio all the time back home.

As soon as they arrived at the dock Swallow leapt off the boat and scrambled up the wooden stairs, not even thanking them. He disappeared quickly into the crowd.

'What a rude man,' said Smithy drawing a hearty laugh from Sam and the boat crew.

'Come on, let's go and see whether Blackbeard has calmed down yet.'

Sam led the way into the square. He passed through the crowd, many of whom called out their congratulations, and wandered over to Blackbeard's throne, where Bonny, Caesar and Swallow were already waiting. He was surprised to see that Blackbeard was smiling and joking with Caesar and Bonny and he was very glad to notice that Swallow was standing on his own, sulking off to one side away from the group.

As he joined them he was welcomed with a smile by Bonny and Caesar, a cold glare by Swallow and a speculative look by Blackbeard.

'Very well done, Captain!' Caesar said, holding his hand out, and Sam could tell he meant it. He shook the offered hand and returned the smile, receiving a nod from Bonny as well.

'Well then, Captain Vives, if you've finished with your fun and games, would you mind if we continue with the business of the day?' Blackbeard's words were stern, but there was a mischievous glint in his eye as he said them. He seemed to be especially enjoying Swallow's suffering and Sam was surprised to realise that behind the fierce façade lurked a man who liked to have fun just as much as the next one.

He was starting to think that maybe Blackbeard wasn't such a bad person after all, but then he glimpsed the skeleton hanging in the cage out of the corner of his eye, swinging gently in the breeze - it was a stark reminder that Blackbeard had a reputation for extreme violence that was well deserved. He also remembered that he had warned himself never to let his guard down, even for a second, something that he had just been on the point of doing; this could be just another way for the pirate lord to put his first mate's opposition off balance. He needed to keep up his show of strength, not show any weakness, and make sure that he wasn't duped by Blackbeard or his mate. So, he decided to reply in kind, but not buy into the pirate lord's seeming change of heart.

He waved his hand graciously. 'Not at all. Please, go ahead, Captain.'

'Thank you so much.'

'You're welcome.'

The people around them were following the exchange closely and there were chuckles and admiring looks from some of them for Sam's courage in standing up to Blackbeard.

Blackbeard, however, had other ideas and immediately took back control of the situation. 'Actually, on second thoughts, I'm hungry, I think it's time for a spot of lunch! Why don't you all come back an hour before sunset, I think that would be an appropriate setting for the big finale, don't you?'

With a dismissing wave, the big pirate immediately spun on his heel and marched off in the direction of his tavern, leaving the captains and their men standing in the square watching him go.

Taken by surprise Swallow had to scurry to catch up with his captain. The despicable man was looking more ridiculous by the second.

Sam's stomach growled at the mention of food and he realised that it was hours since he had eaten anything. Breakfast had been so long ago, but, despite so much having happened, it was still not even midday. He made a spur of the moment decision and turned to Caesar and Bonny. 'Would you care to join me aboard my ship for lunch?'

The captains were somewhat surprised at the offer; hospitality like that was not very common among men and women such as they - most captains didn't allow anybody that wasn't one of their crew aboard their ships, preferring to jealously guard their secrets. However, both of them readily agreed and Sam arranged for them to come at one o'clock.

When the other two captains wandered away, Sam turned to Smithy. 'Er, Mr Smith, we do have enough food and drink to go around, don't we?'

'I've already got some men laying in a bullock, a few chickens and a couple of barrels of grog, Captain. On top of that we've got a good lot of stores that we captured from the Medusa; the Frenchies have no idea how to fight, but they certainly know how to eat!'

Sam chuckled. 'Excellent. Oh, and make sure that the men who come with them have plenty to eat as well, please.'

'Right you are, sir.'

'Well done, thank you. How did I ever manage...?'

'I don't know, Captain, I really don't know.'

They shared a grin and went down to board a boat for the return journey to the Mermaid.

CHAPTER 10
LUNCH WITH NEW FRIENDS

While he waited for lunch Sam lay on the bed in his cabin, resting, staring up at the ceiling, lost in his thoughts. He had more or less come to the definite conclusion that he wasn't in a dream and his principal worry was no longer what had put him in this situation, but had actually become how he would ever explain to his parents where he'd been for so long. And why he smelled so bad.

He was currently running through possible excuses in his head, wondering whether they would believe stories of abductions by aliens, the CIA, or some secret organisation, or whether it would be best to claim a sudden onset of amnesia that had caused him to live on the streets for a few days. He didn't think they'd believe he'd gone on a camping trip and forgotten to tell them, especially since he'd just disappeared from the pavement outside his house in plain sight of his mother and sister.

Nothing he came up with was entirely satisfactory, but before he could make himself too crazy there was a knock on the door and Smithy came in. 'With your permission, Captain?'

Behind the first mate were sailors carrying trays of food and jugs of drink.

'Of course, come on in, Mr Smith. What time is it?'

'It's about ten minutes short of one of the clock. Our guests will be on their way soon.'

'I'd better get ready to receive them then.'

Sam rolled off of the bed and put his boots on. He had asked for clean water for the bowl by the bed earlier and he used it now to wash his face and then scrub his armpits as best as he could. It didn't do much to get rid of the smell but he felt better at least. Maybe later he could go for a swim or get the crew to rig the pump, like Hornblower did, so that he could have a shower without the risk of getting attacked by sharks.

He put on a relatively clean shirt and made his way to the door past his sailors setting the table with the food. 'Looks wonderful, men, thank you.'

The sailors all muttered their gratitude at his noticing and Sam couldn't help but see the smiles that they exchanged. Maybe, like Hornblower, he could be truly popular with his men. Perhaps they would even come up with a nickname for him; he would like that.

Sam was walking a little bit taller as he came out of his cabin and into the midday sun. It was hot and humid and his armpits prickled with sweat, immediately soaking his fresh shirt.

He climbed the stairs to the quarterdeck and went to the stern rail, greeting the officer of the deck as he went past. From there he could see that the boats from the African Queen and the Vengeance were on their way to the Mermaid, but it would still be a good few minutes before his guests arrived.

Sam took the opportunity to look around his ship while he waited.

Everything looked to be in order - he didn't consider himself to be much of an expert, but for some reason he seemed to have an instinct about it. He also trusted his men and Smithy to do what was necessary to keep the ship running smoothly without too much input from him.

He walked down to the main deck and talked to the men who were working, cleaning or just resting, taking full advantage of this moment of peace while in port. He asked them how they were, whether they needed anything, and complemented them on the incredible wooden figures that some of them were whittling. An awning had been set up to provide some shade from the midday sun - it was just a sail stretched tight over the deck, but it was sufficient to make life just a bit more bearable, and most of the men were grouped under it. Sam helped them to raise another one so that their guests could also have some shade, and he hauled on a rope with them for a couple of minutes, earning a delighted grin from the men at his deigning to do menial work.

Overall, Sam discovered that the Mermaid was a happy ship with nobody having any real problems beyond the usual ones that a group of men at sea for long periods of time had.

He completed his tour of the deck just in time for the boats to arrive.

Smithy came jogging out of the cabin and joined Sam at the rail. 'Lunch is ready, Captain.'

'Thank you, Smithy, just in time.'

Sam motioned to the side, where Bonny was the first to appear. She leapt lightly over the rail onto the deck and strutted smiling towards them. She was dressed in tight brown breeches, long black boots, a frilly white shirt with a black waistcoat over the top and on her head was a large hat with a huge white feather in it, which was just as large as the red one in Sam's own hat. Sam had to admit she looked very striking and that her teeth were bothering him less and less each time she smiled at him.

'Thank you for the invitation, Captain Vives.'

'You're more than welcome, Captain Bonny, especially after that practice bout we had!'

'It was fun, wasn't it?'

They turned and looked back to the side of the ship as Caesar now appeared.

The crew of the Mermaid, who had gathered around to greet their guests, gasped at the sight of him.

The African pirate was already a large man, but the way he was dressed emphasized that fact and turned him into a giant. He was bare footed and wore his usual light and roomy trousers, but that was where all pretence of normalcy ended. Draped around his shoulders was the pelt of a fully grown lion, the head of which he had pulled forwards to cover his own bald scalp. To top it all off he kept his eyes wide open and staring to make the white of his eyeballs stand out even further against the blackness of his skin.

He stood, balancing perfectly on the rail with his hands on his hips, staring down at the men waiting for him.

Collectively the ship held its breath, transfixed by this mountain of a man.

Suddenly he broke into a grin. He jumped down onto the deck with a thud that reverberated through the ship, threw his head back and roared with laughter.

Sam couldn't help but grin. He was a showman, nearly the equal of Blackbeard, but, unlike the pirate lord, Sam could tell that behind Caesar's usually fierce mask was a good heart in a good man.

The big African padded catlike to the group, holding out his arms and grinning. He enveloped Sam in an enormous hug, crushing the breath out of him.

Just when Sam thought he was going to pass out, Caesar released him. Stepping back he held Sam's shoulders at arm's length and looked him in the eye.

'I know it is just an invitation to a meal, but this means a lot to me. Many times I have heard about this supposed brotherhood of pirates or the waves or whatever it is called, but I have never experienced it until now. Thank you, my friend.'

Sam was slightly embarrassed at the obvious emotion in Caesar's voice and if truth be told was feeling a bit teary-eyed himself. He covered quickly, though. 'You're welcome, Captain. Shall we eat?'

Caesar laughed, throwing back his head again. 'A man after my own heart!'

'Mr Smith, my first mate, has prepared some food for your boat crews as well. If you don't have any objections they can dine with my crew here on deck in the shade.'

Both captains nodded happily, glad that Sam had been so thoughtful.

'To my cabin then!' Sam led the way into the cool of his cabin.

The meal was a very enjoyable affair. The three captains were joined by their first mates, but there were no thoughts of rank or other such distinctions; they were friends, brothers in arms, allies against Blackbeard and Swallow, and they were there to have good food in good company.

Bonny's first mate was a large woman, Natalia, who reminded Sam very much of the Amazon warrior women that he had read about in his mythology books. She was not quite as big as Caesar, but Sam thought that an arm wrestle between the two of them would be very interesting indeed and considered proposing one. However, he thought better of it. For the time being, anyway.

Caesar's first mate, Charles, was a small man who looked very bookish, with slicked-down hair parted in the middle. He wore small round glasses, which he was constantly cleaning, and kept using big words in the conversation, some of which Sam had never even heard of before and wasn't entirely sure weren't made up. Caesar apparently used him as an adviser, wisely making up for his own nautical deficiencies by using the knowledge of others.

Smithy was there as well of course and he started off the conversation by regaling Caesar and his first mate, who were the only ones at the meal that hadn't witnessed the fight, with a blow by blow description of Sam and Bonny's fight. He was such an incredible storyteller that Sam found himself getting completely caught up in the tale, reliving the match as if he were watching it on television.

Halfway through the telling, Bonny leaned across the table towards Sam and grinned. 'It's almost like being there, isn't it? Although, I think I know who's going to win.'

Everybody laughed and Smithy faked being angry at her before continuing. 'Please! Don't spoil it for everyone else! Now, as I was saying before I was so rudely interrupted…'

After an hour or so, they had eaten their fill. They pushed themselves back from the table and relaxed, rubbing stuffed bellies and refilling tankards with drink. Their minds were no longer occupied by the food and the conversation had slowed and finally faltered into silence as the looming event made its presence felt.

Caesar broke the silence by putting into words what was on everyone's mind. 'Be careful this afternoon; you cannot believe everything that Blackbeard says, but, more than that, you *must not* trust that treacherous first mate of his. Please, do not turn your back on him in this coming fight.'

Bonny chimed in as well. 'Yes, he strikes me as the type of person who will do anything to get what he wants. And he wants to win this contest *very* much.'

'I think you're right,' Sam agreed. 'I'm fairly sure that we still haven't seen the worst of him because Blackbeard has been supporting him at every turn and he's confident of his victory. But if that has changed, then he might do something out of desperation, and we don't want a repeat of the Shin Chang or the Good Queen Bess.'

'What makes you think it has changed?' asked Caesar, frowning.

Sam grinned. 'Well, he was getting a real dressing down from Blackbeard on the brig after my wonderful bout with Bonny.'

Caesar chuckled. 'Oh, I wish I could have seen that! And I wish I'd been there to see your fight, too. After hearing Mr Smith's evocative account I'm sure that it was a spectacle that will be recounted in ballads.'

Sam laughed modestly. 'Oh, I wouldn't go that far. Maybe a limerick or two at most.'

'You're too modest, Captain,' Smithy said, 'those of us that were there know the truth of the matter and none of us have ever seen anybody fight so well or elegantly as the two of you did.'

'Thank you for your kindness, Mr Smith,' Bonny said and then blushed as she realised that Caesar was watching her every move. She quickly changed the subject to cover. 'So, Captain Vives, what is your plan for beating that snake?'

Sam actually wasn't quite sure what he was going to do, but he could see that the others were waiting, expecting something brilliant; such was their faith in him. He didn't want to disappoint them, but on the other hand he didn't want to betray their trust by feeding them some lie, so he considered his words carefully before replying. 'I think that it's going to be a hard match. I'd like to defend again because I know I can beat the strategy he used to defeat Captain Caesar,' he nodded at the big African in apology. 'No offence intended, Captain.'

Caesar huffed and waved away Sam's apology. 'None has been taken; I was caught totally unprepared and fairly beaten.'

'Although the lack of time to prepare didn't help...' put in Smithy, drawing a nod from Caesar and a wry smile.

'However,' continued Sam, 'I know that whether I attack or defend it won't matter; Swallow's desperation will cause him to make a mistake, I'm sure of it.'

Caesar looked gloomy. 'Whatever happens, just be careful. We already know he'll do whatever he can to win, but if he thinks he's going to lose, then that is when he will be the most dangerous.'

'And if he does lose I really don't think he'll just accept it like a man,' added Bonny.

Everyone around the table fell silent again, staring into nothing; a future where a man like Jack Swallow was lord and master of Port Royal wasn't one that they liked to contemplate.

Sam gazed around the group. While he was certainly having fun and enjoying the company of friends, he couldn't help but feel a little sad; he usually had meals like these with his extended family, joined by cousins, aunts and uncles, and, while they were by no means as boisterous or entertaining as this one had been - indeed, he usually complained about having to stay seated at the table for hours at a time - he nonetheless found that he was missing them and would rather be home with his parents. It had only been a few days and, admittedly, the time had flown by, but he still had grave doubts about whether he was ever going to be able to get home and this made his feeling of homesickness more poignant. He wasn't in danger of bursting into tears or anything, but there was that little note of bitterness always at the back of his mind. Still, this was an adventure and he had resolved to savour whatever time he had here, so he shoved his feelings to one side and dived back into his role as host.

He filled his tankard and stood up, holding it out in front of him. 'A toast!' He waited for the rest of the party to fill their drinks. 'To good friends and good companions.'

'A brotherhood of pirates!' Caesar added, to universal approval.

The rest of the company echoed his words and they all stood and toasted each other. Caesar and Bonny drank, looking each other in the eyes. Sam saw them and smiled inside; friendship was not the only thing that was being cultivated here it seemed.

They were interrupted by a knock at the door and it opened to reveal Bosun Brown. He stood in the doorway and touched his hand to his forehead in salute, bobbing his head slightly in nervousness as he eyed the group. 'Er, beg pardon, Captain, but the men would like to invite you and the other es… esty…' he paused and tilted his head to one side as someone out of sight behind the door jamb fed him the word he was looking for. 'Er… *esteemed* guests out on deck in order to parlate' a more urgent whisper caught his attention and he corrected himself, '*partake* in a little entertainment of our own making.' He let out a breath and deflated almost visibly in relief at having discharged his duty more or less intact.

'Well said, Mr Brown!' Sam smiled.

The bosun had probably rehearsed the speech quite a few times before coming and interrupting, but even so the words of the invitation had not been his, so he had stumbled over them. The wording had probably been arrived at by committee and then Brown nominated to deliver them as being the one most in favour with the captain.

Sam turned to his guests. 'Shall we adjourn to the deck and see what the men have in store for us?'

Bonny smiled broadly and nodded, 'I think that would be a wonderful idea.'

Caesar nodded as well, 'and a welcome distraction.'

Sam turned back to the bosun, 'thank you, Mr Brown. We would be delighted to take you up on your gracious invitation.'

Brown's face lit up with a wide grin. He bowed theatrically, indicating the door and the bright sunshine on deck, 'Well, in that case, if you'd kindly make your way to the quarterdeck, please, ladies and gentlemen, we will begin momentarily!'

Sam led the way past Brown and up the stairs to the quarterdeck where they found an awning set up to provide shade to the area next to the rail that overlooked the main deck.

Sailors brought chairs from Sam's cabin and the three captains and three mates sat down, exchanging amused glances and with wide grins on their faces, keen to see what the men had come up with. Below them on the main deck, men from the three crews were seated in neat files, smiling up at them like children on a playground. Each crew had a different colour handkerchief wrapped around their arms; Sam's crew had a red handkerchief while Caesar's crew had black ones and Bonny's had white.

Brown was now standing in front of the crews. He waited for the spectators to get settled and then spoke out in a loud voice. 'Blackbeard's not the only one that can have contests around here and we've organised a few little games of our own to show him how it's done.'

There were cheers and laughter at this from the men.

Bonny called down to him with a smile, 'I see a few more of my men down there than I brought with me, Mr Brown. Have you kidnapped my crew?'

'Begging your pardon ma'am, but as soon as we cooked up this idea we sent word to the other ships and they were more than eager to show their prowess. If we hadn't put a bit of a limit on how many of them could come, then your whole crew, and that of Captain Caesar, would be here on deck with us.'

'So, what do you have in store for us, Bosun?' rumbled Caesar, flashing his bright white teeth in a huge grin.

'Well, sir, we thought we'd have a few tests of skill and courage then finish off with something a bit more creative. All to be judged by your own worthy selves of course, if it pleases your worships.'

'I think we are all more than happy to stand as judge to whatever competition you care to propose, Bosun. Yes?' Sam looked around the captains, receiving nods of agreement and smiles from them. 'But the big question is: what shall we have as a prize for the winners?'

Caesar leaned forward in his seat. 'Silver? Gold?'

Sam shook his head, feigning sadness and regret, 'no, no, that won't do. This is a competition between friends, I wouldn't feel right seeing my men take *all* of your crews' money away from them after they have beaten them.'

This earned a laugh and some good-natured jeers from everyone and Sam waited for it to die down before continuing, 'no, I think that the winning crew should have the privilege and the pleasure of regaling us all with the entertainment of their choice.'

Sam could see that this was being well received; sailors always liked to have the opportunity to show off their talents and he could see them already making plans, nudging each other and excitedly making suggestions. Sam received the approval of the other captains and it was decided.

When the men had settled down again Sam asked, 'Mr Smith, how long until we have to be back in town?'

'Three hours, Captain.'

Sam thought quickly and then called down to the bosun, 'let us have two hours of competition, Mr Brown, then the winners will have an hour to entertain us.'

'Right you are, sir! Come on then, lads, you heard him! Get to your places!' The sailors shot to their feet and ran off, each team going to one of the three masts.

Brown came up the steps to the quarterdeck and stood in front of Bonny. He had a pistol cupped in his hands which he offered to her.

'If it please, your honours, we're going to start off with a little race around the ship. Captain Bonny, ma'am, would you care to give the signal to start? It's charged, but not loaded.'

'With pleasure, Mr Brown.' Bonny took the pistol from him delicately.

'Thankee kindly, ma'am.'

While Brown ran down the steps to join his team, Bonny went to the rail and surveyed the teams, who were looking up at her expectantly. She flourished the pistol, struck a very fetching pose and then discharged it with a bang.

Immediately, one man from each team started up their respective mast, all three of them ascending simultaneously towards the highest points of the ship. They touched the very tip of the mast and then returned to the deck, before running to the next mast in line and climbing again. Once they had scaled all three masts they raced back to their team and placed their armband on a nearby rope, freeing the next man in line to start his lap of the ship.

There was no chance of cheating; every eye on the ship was closely following each of the men, making sure that he touched the very top of the mast and that only one armband at a time was attached to the ropes.

Sam was astounded by the sheer speed with which the men went up the masts, but his breath was truly taken away by the way they came back down. They slid down the ropes so quickly that he was sure they would strip the skin from their hands, but incredibly they did no damage. Their agility was amazing, but he knew that the men regularly had to take in and set sails during storms at sea with the ship pitching and rolling wildly beneath them, so under these conditions it really was just a game to them.

He stood and went to the side rail to get a better view, trying to keep track of who was in the lead. He was joined by Caesar and Bonny and together they watched their men race up and down, cheering along with their combined crews.

Caesar put his arm around Sam's shoulders companionably, 'Captain Vives, the men will have their prize, but how about a little wager between the three of us?'

'What do you have in mind, Captain Caesar?'

'I think it would be appropriate if the victor won the privilege of hosting the next meal between friends.'

Sam smiled, delighted by the suggestion. 'Agreed, and with pleasure!'

Caesar turned to Bonny, 'and what do you say, ma'am?'

'A wonderful idea, Caesar, I accept your wager!'

The race was down to the last relay and it looked like it was between one of Caesar's men and one of Sam's. The two men raced up the masts, seeming to be neck and neck, going up at the same time and coming down at the same rate, and both crews were getting frantic, exhorting their man to greater efforts.

It was down to the last descent and it was still too close to call when Caesar's man did something that almost made Sam want to instantly call an end to the contest; instead of descending normally he ran towards the end of the spar and leapt. He must have been at least a hundred feet in the air and Sam thought he was going to try to dive into the ocean, a drop that he wasn't entirely sure that the man would survive, but Sam hadn't seen the rope that passed near the end of the spar. It was a rope that went straight down to the deck, part of the standing rigging holding the mast in place. Somehow the man caught onto the line and slid down it so quickly that Sam thought that he could see smoke coming from his hands. However, the man showed no sign of any discomfort as he landed almost gently on the deck and nonchalantly took off his black handkerchief and hung it with the rest, beating his rival by a good ten seconds.

Caesar's crew swarmed the man, cheering wildly and receiving the well-deserved congratulations of the other teams.

Sam couldn't believe what he had just seen; it was the stuff of comic books and action films, but the men around him were applauding the sailor as if for a job well done that was all in a day's work, not a feat of extraordinary skill and bravery.

Nonetheless, Sam felt that the man warranted further praise and he called out to his bosun. 'Mr Brown!'

'Yes, sir?'

'It looks like the first round goes to Captain Caesar's crew!'

'Aye, sir! That it does!'

'Here!' Sam took a small gold coin from his jacket pocket and tossed it to the bosun. 'Give this to that man with my compliments on an excellent run.'

'Aye aye, sir!'

There were cheers as Brown gave the coin to the man who had won the competition for Caesar's crew. He received the coin happily and touched his forehead in salute to the quarterdeck. Sam replied by doffing his hat, drawing further cheers, and some surprise, from the men at a captain's graciousness in deigning to acknowledge an ordinary sailor, who wasn't even one of his own crew.

When the men calmed down again Sam called out. 'Next round, Mr Brown! What do you have for us?'

'Well, sir, if you could spare a few cannonballs and a pinch of powder we would like to test our aim.'

'I think we can spare some shot for a good cause.'

'Thankee kindly, sir!'

Twenty minutes later three large barrels were bobbing in the ocean about a hundred metres apart and a couple of hundred metres from the side of the ship facing away from the town. It was fairly easy shooting for the three cannon crews who had been chosen to represent their ships; they didn't want to be hours trying to hit their targets, or waste too much shot and powder. The crews were all invited to pick a cannon to use, receiving advice from the crews who normally fired them as to which were the most accurate or reliable. The advice was genuine; Sam's crew wanted to win, but they wanted to win fairly and on their own merits. The only gun that wasn't available to the crews of the Vengeance and the African Queen was the one on the quarterdeck that Sam had fired against the French; that one was the exclusive province of Bosun Brown, who had been chosen to represent the Mermaid and refused to fire anything else but his trusty gun "Betsy".

Sam wandered over to Brown, who was standing by the gun supervising the preparations. The crew were weighing bags of powder to Brown's precise specifications while Brown himself was choosing cannonballs from a large pile, turning the heavy shot over and over in his hands to find the smoothest and roundest. He looked up and smiled as his captain approached. 'D'ya mind if I lay the gun this time, sir?'

'I wouldn't have it any other way, Mr Brown. Show them how it's done.'

'Aye aye, Cap'n.'

Since Brown was taking part in the competition Smithy had temporarily taken over his announcement duties. He stood by the rail of the quarterdeck and surveyed the contestants. 'The rules are simple! Shoot fast, shoot accurately and the first crew to destroy their target wins! Are you ready?'

Smithy received shouts from the three gun crews to indicate their readiness and this time it was Caesar who started the competition off with a pistol shot.

Immediately, the three cannon fired and Sam looked out to see the result.

None of the barrels were hit in this first round, but the shots were all fairly close - a testament to the quality of the crews' shooting.

'Over and a touch to the right...' Brown had been watching the fall of the shot closely and, while his men reloaded as fast as they could, he started making adjustments to the lay of the cannon.

Caesar's crew were the first to shoot again, but Brown ignored them, focusing on refining his own aim. He shot again at the same time as Bonny's crew.

Nobody hit the barrel on the second try either, but the splashes as the balls hit the water were creeping closer and closer to the barrels.

Brown tutted and shook his head, disappointment in himself, 'short and still off to the right!'

The crew from the Mermaid were still reloading when Caesar's men fired for the third time - they were shooting very fast, but they didn't seem to be coming any closer; their thinking appeared to be that it was better to shoot more times and hope for the best than to take the additional seconds required to aim the gun more carefully. That kind of thinking was fine in a ship to ship action at close quarters, when you were almost guaranteed to hit, but in this contest it was a mistake.

Brown was almost ready. He used a large wooden mallet to minutely adjust the cannon, tilting it up by scant millimetres at a time. Sam couldn't see that he had actually made any noticeable adjustment, but Brown was satisfied. He stood back and smiled at Sam. 'This time, Captain.'

He touched the slow match to the touch hole and the cannon flew backwards on its small wheels.

Brown didn't even have to look. He knew that he had hit the target and the sounds of cheering from the Mermaid's crew confirmed it. Seconds later Bonny's crew shot again and there was more cheering as they in turn destroyed their target, but it was too late; Brown had won and was already being borne on the shoulders of the crew of the Mermaid for a lap of honour around the ship.

Brown was finally deposited, grinning from ear to ear, in front of Sam and his fellow captains.

'Well done, Mr Brown, but I hope that you didn't deliberately choose that event because you knew you were going to win it.'

'Perish the thought, sir!'

'Well, that's one round to the Mermaid and one to the African Queen. What do you have in store for us next?'

"Next" was a hornpipe competition. Groups of men and women danced in perfect coordination; hopping and skipping, doing nautically themed steps, all to music provided by fiddles, flutes and an accordion that one of Bonny's men had brought along and happily agreed to play for all of the crews. The competition was judged by a group of older sailors, chosen from all of the ships. They were apparently looking for such things as authenticity, style, and something called mugging, which in this case didn't mean beating someone up for money, but rather playing up to the crowd and supposedly added an extra dimension to the entertainment.

Even though Sam understood very little of the technique involved, he could appreciate the skill and athleticism of the men and women, and the practice and dedication that it took to be able to dance in unison, especially seeing as none of them were professional dancers; they all had jobs to do aboard their respective ships. He himself would not have been able to say who had won, he thought that everybody was very good, but the judges had no doubts and gave the win to Bonny's crew.

This meant that each of the ships had won one event and Sam called for a tie-breaker.

There had been nothing planned, but a quick discussion among the crews resulted in a simple and elegant finale to the competition - one sailor was selected from each crew and they were presented with a collection of pieces of wood: bits of flotsam, the blade of a broken oar, a couple of spars from a barrel, part of an old chair. All bits and pieces that Sam knew would have gone straight into the bin in the modern world, but had been kept here just in case there was ever a use for it.

The three sailors, two men and a woman from Bonny's crew, gathered around the junk, inspecting it, touching it, knocking it with their knuckles, even stroking it somewhat lovingly. Sam had no idea what they were looking for, but eventually they seemed satisfied and each chose one of the pieces and carried it away to a patch of deck below the quarterdeck, where a sail had been laid down for them to catch the scrapings. A hushed silence fell over the ship as everyone waited for this final, deciding round to begin.

Brown approached Smithy. 'Would you be timekeeper for us please, sir?'

'Of course, Mr Brown.'

Brown turned and spoke to the three sailors who were waiting patiently for the signal to start. 'You only have thirty minutes, I'm afraid, but do the best you can. Off you go!'

Brown nodded to Smithy, who took note of the time, and then all eyes were on the three competitors.

Chips flew as they carved confidently into the pieces of wood, each of them using their knives with a precision and an elegance that spoke of decades of practice. Shapes started to take form, gradually turning lumps of rubbish into art in a way that no contemporary artist could ever dream of doing, and it was all done so swiftly and confidently that it was as if they were only revealing the secrets that were already hidden within them.

The work was done in complete silence; each crew watching intently, showing the utmost respect for a skill that only came from true talent.

Sam found himself leaning forwards in his seat on the quarterdeck. He was so mesmerised by what they were doing that he had no idea how much time had passed until he was startled by Smithy shouting out, 'time!'

The sailors stopped carving and they placed their works on a crate set in the centre of the main deck to be seen and judged.

Sam led his fellow captains down to inspect the scrimshaw sculptures. The true judges of the competition were mostly the same old sailors that had judged the hornpipes, but he wanted to have a closer look at the statuettes nonetheless.

The transformation of the scrap wood was incredible, even given the limited time of the competition; a rampant unicorn and a mermaid were the contributions of the competitors from the Mermaid and Vengeance, but what truly took Sam's breath away was what Caesar's man had done to a thick chair leg - he had no idea how the man had had the time to do what he had done; five men, sculptured in miniature, hauled together on a rope.

Sam looked closer. Despite not having had time to get even close to fully completing his work, the man had still been able to put an incredible amount of detail into it. 'Why, Captain Caesar, I believe that's you; I would recognise that grin anywhere!' Indeed the man at the front of the rope was the image of Caesar, down to the last bulging muscle.

This sculpture was unanimously declared the best, to universal acclaim, although Sam gave all three of the competitors a small gold coin and asked them to complete their works at their leisure before delivering them to him as keepsakes, something that they were very glad to do.

As the winners, Caesar's crew lost no time and hurried off to prepare their entertainments. They laughed and joked with the other crews as they put together costumes, ingenuously using whatever was at hand, organised songs and singers, and found musicians and instruments, some of which had to be brought from the African Queen. Very soon, however, they were ready and the entertainments began; skit followed song, and the audience found themselves alternately laughing and crying as their emotions were taken on a roller coaster ride.

Sam looked back on that afternoon as one of the most companionable times he'd ever had and he remembered it fondly for many years after. He didn't have very many good friends; other boys tended to stay away from him because they didn't want to be bullied as well, so he was a bit of a loner and he didn't have chances to socialise like this.

Also, the contest and subsequent entertainment had helped him to completely forget his momentary homesickness; those family get-togethers were good, but very often they were with people who were there almost as an obligation and not friends like these, who genuinely wanted to be there.

All too soon, though, the sun started to go down, the day was no longer quite as hot and the shadows were lengthening inch by inch. It was time to face reality; all good things have to come to an end eventually.

Smithy leaned in to talk discreetly to Sam, not wanting to spoil the mood. 'Captain, it's time to go.'

Sam nodded his thanks. He waited for the end of the current entertainment, a sketch involving a huge bearded man in a skirt and a mop head wig being wooed by a tiny man who was trying to physically carry his "bride" away from her parents, then stood and addressed his fellow captains. 'Thank you all for coming and helping to take my mind off things for a while, I have had a wonderful afternoon, truly, but I'm afraid that it's time for me to get back to Blackbeard's game.'

There was disappointment from the captains and their crews, but they all understood and while the men squared away the ship, Sam thanked the captains for coming. The captains were profuse in their gratitude in return and he received another bone-crushing hug from Caesar and an overly-friendly embrace from Bonny that made him turn bright red.

The sailors also bade each other farewell and Sam was pleased to see that the three crews were closer than ever - there were gifts and handshakes exchanged among the men and women, as well as a few furtive kisses, before they scrambled down the sides of the ship. The entire crew of the Mermaid lined the sides to wave them goodbye as they rowed away, but before long, Sam sighed and wandered away to go to his cabin, leaving them to it; he suddenly felt the need to be alone for a while.

Twenty minutes later he was sitting at the tiller of his boat, steering automatically as he was rowed to the docks.

His thoughts had gone racing back to Blackbeard's contest after Caesar and Bonny had left; his own common sense had already told him that he was in danger, but the multiple warnings and concern from the captains during lunch had gotten to him, and the joy he had felt during the afternoon's get-together had evaporated far too quickly. Having Swallow as an opponent was going to be vastly different from Bonny; he knew that if Swallow had to bend or break the rules in any way in order to win, then he wouldn't hesitate to do so. Sam also knew that he would be lucky to get out of this with his crew and himself alive and in one piece.

All thoughts of this being a dream had now gone, he had banished them from his mind because in the end it really didn't matter how he had gotten here, what mattered was that he could no longer afford to have the doubts and questions, that had plagued him since he had arrived, distracting him; the stakes were far too high now to face Swallow with anything less than certainty and dedication.

Despite his resolution to concentrate on the task in hand he was so lost in his thoughts that he didn't notice when they approached the shore and only the quietly urgent 'Captain!' from Smithy stopped him from guiding the boat headfirst into the jetty. He quickly adjusted and the boat swung round and settled against the dock so smartly that it appeared that that was what he had wanted to do all along.

Sam smiled wryly, his mood considerably lightened as the absurd image of a ship's captain crashing his boat into the docks and sinking flashed through his mind. 'Thank you, Smithy. What would...?'

'Don't mention it, Captain.'

They shared a grin and Sam leapt up the stairs to the town square and sauntered light-heartedly towards the coming danger.

CHAPTER 11
THE BIG FINAL

The crowd had grown considerably in size since the morning and they found it difficult to make their way across the square to where the other captains and Blackbeard were already waiting for them. Obviously the word had got around of what was happening and people had travelled from far and wide to witness the event.

Sam was accosted every few steps by well-wishers. Flowers were given to him, his back was slapped over and over and his hand was shaken so many times it began to hurt. He lost count of the number of girls he was kissed by and, if he hadn't been so focused on the final round of the contest, he might have died of embarrassment. He was also kissed by a good few women old enough to be his grandmother, a couple of whom were so persistent that Smithy had to pull them away gently but persuasively.

Eventually, after what seemed like an eternity, Sam and his party made it to the stands and stood in front of Blackbeard's throne.

It appeared that Swallow still wasn't back in Blackbeard's good graces, instead, he was standing to one side speaking with a huge, bald sailor with scars across both cheeks.

The two men looked up at Sam in unison as he approached, then quickly looked away again when they realised that he was watching them, which just served to increase Sam's worry; it seemed that Swallow was no longer going to rely on Blackbeard's help in making mischief, but create some on his own.

Blackbeard was swivelled around in his throne, arm draped across its back, laughing and joking with some town elders sitting in the stands just behind him. One of them pointed out that Sam had arrived and Blackbeard turned his head and smiled at him.

'Be right with you, Captain Vives.'

It seemed that Blackbeard was still trying to assert his dominance in whatever way he could, no matter how trivial, and Sam was forced to wait patiently as the pirate lord leisurely finished his conversation.

He passed the time by watching a nearby jester - the man was juggling three flaming clubs somewhat unsuccessfully and it was a hell of a lot more fun to watch than if he'd been doing it neatly. Sam reflected that his clumsiness might in fact have been deliberate - a ploy to keep the audience off guard and entertained. The juggler always seemed to be just an inch from disaster, but never completely lost control and Sam couldn't take his eyes off him. It really did seem to hold the interest much more if you were always waiting for disaster to strike, and the man was doing it so well that the crowd around him thought it was accidental. It reminded him of what Uncle Andrew had said about magic tricks a few years back when he was entertaining him and Violeta at Christmas in England - that the most important part in any trick was misdirection; you have to give the audience something to watch so they don't see what's *really* going on.

A few minutes later Blackbeard turned in his seat and waved the captains over to him.

'Sorry about that, gentlemen and lady, town business, something that will have to be taken care of by whoever wins and takes over from me. It's not all plunder and pillage in my seat, you've got to take care of the people as well.' He looked pointedly at Sam. 'Do you think you can do that, Captain Vives?'

Sam considered carefully before answering. He nodded. 'Yes. Yes, I believe I can.'

'What about you, Mr Swallow, do you think you can?' Blackbeard called out, interrupting Swallow's conversation with the thug. Swallow looked up and blinked, lost, not really knowing what had been said.

'Sorry? Er, yes, I'm ready, let's do this!'

'Right... Good answer, Mr Swallow.' Blackbeard gave the listening audience a knowing look and a shake of the head.

The crowd laughed and Swallow reddened in a combination of anger and embarrassment, but mostly anger. He didn't understand why they were laughing at him, but that didn't matter to him; the *fact* they were laughing at him was enough to make him furious. He turned and snarled a quiet word to the bald thug, who disappeared into the crowd.

Sam wondered how much worse the mocking of the crowd was going to make things for him in the coming event.

Blackbeard just grinned, though, enjoying Swallow's discomfort.

'Anyway...' Blackbeard climbed up onto his throne and held up his arms for the attention of the crowd. 'Ladies and gentlemen, or as close as we get to them in this part of the world, it's time for the final round of my little contest!'

A big cheer rose up from most of the people watching, although some of them just groaned, disturbed from the state of unconsciousness that had been brought about by having drunk too much.

'My own first mate, Jack Swallow, will face off against brave Captain Vives and the winner will take all!'

Another cheer, this time much larger, was enough to wake up those people who had not already done so, which was probably for the best because Sam knew that they would not want to miss the excitement just for the sake of an hour's sleep.

Blackbeard stepped down from his throne and sauntered over to the captains. He looked at Swallow and Sam in turn and then pulled a coin out of his pocket. 'So then, laddies, who's going to call it?'

Sam opened his mouth to answer, but Swallow beat him to it. 'Heads!'

Blackbeard raised an eyebrow and gave Sam a half smile, but tossed the coin anyway. 'Heads it is! Seems that luck is with you today, Mr Swallow. What's your pleasure?'

Swallow smiled confidently. Obviously he had something planned, something he hadn't revealed in the previous round. 'I'll defend.'

Blackbeard chuckled and shook his head wryly before turning away to announce the result of the coin toss to the crowd. 'Captain Vives will attempt to board, while Mr Swallow defends!'

While Blackbeard's back was turned, addressing the crowd, Swallow leaned forward and whispered in Sam's ear. 'Win and you're dead, Vives.' He straightened up again and smiled evilly at Sam.

Sam was a little taken aback at the sudden vehemence and open threat in the man's words, but he didn't have time to reply as Blackbeard turned back to the contestants. 'Good luck, gentlemen. Mr Swallow, get to your boats if you please, your ten minutes have already started!'

'But, I....' Swallow stammered, at a loss. The confident smile disappeared instantly from his face. It seemed that he still hadn't fully realised that he was no longer being given the same kind of preferential treatment from Blackbeard as he had before.

'Well? Go on then!' Blackbeard made shooing movements to Swallow, who eventually got the hint and ran off to the renewed mirth of the crowd.

Blackbeard grinned and watched him scurry away. 'I really do not like that man...'

Sam saw the opportunity to resolve some of his doubts and he seized upon it, 'then why, may I ask, Captain, have you been favouring him so far?'

Blackbeard turned to Sam. He stood there silently for a second, sizing him up, staring him fiercely in the eye.

Sam met the stare without blinking, staying firm despite the fact that his brain was telling him to run away from this dangerous brute of a man. He wondered if he had gone too far at last.

The pirate lord's expression softened slightly, though, and he spoke quietly so that only Sam could hear. 'I saw in Swallow the kind of man that I used to be; ruthless, determined, strong, but just a bit rough around the edges and needing polishing. I thought that if he was given the opportunity to lead then he would learn to control his cruel side and start thinking of the good of others, not just himself, maybe become more sympathetic. I thought that a fun competition like this would make him lighten up and play to the crowd a bit, work at getting them to like him, but sadly the opposite seems to be happening - he's getting worse, more vindictive. And blowing up Wong...

Blackbeard shook his head sorrowfully. 'Lord knows I've done some bad stuff in my time, and I love mischief and mayhem as much as the next man, but I like to think that I've never done anything truly malicious like that... Well, except to the French, but that's another matter entirely.'

He looked up at where Swallow was being rowed out towards the brig and scowled. 'Right now I'm not seeing the qualities that I wanted to find in him, instead they are staring me in the face whenever I look at you. I haven't given up on him yet; he would still make a good, albeit callous, leader, but now I know that there is another option available that might well prove to be the wiser choice. At least now I know that, whatever happens today, I can be sure that I will be leaving the people in good hands. And that's all I wanted.'

Blackbeard smiled, a simple gesture that took away all menace from his face. He still had the coin from the toss in his hand and he threw it to Sam.

Sam caught it and raised an eyebrow at Blackbeard.

'For luck, Captain.' Blackbeard turned and walked away without waiting for a reply. He made his way back to the throne and sat down, immediately resuming his conversation with the town elders.

Sam looked at the coin and turned it over in his hand. He chuckled.

Smithy wandered over when saw his captain laughing. 'Sir? What's going on?'

In reply Sam handed him the coin.

Smithy looked at it. 'It's...'

'Yes. Two heads. Blackbeard and Swallow were making their own luck all along, it seems. It makes no difference now, though.'

Sam looked out over the bay at the boats swarming towards the ship. 'Are the men ready?'

'Yes, sir.'

'Good, thank you. Have them standby at the water's edge then, please. Blackbeard might make another mistake in telling the time and I want to be ready to take advantage of it.'

'Aye aye, Captain.'

Sam paused a second to think. 'And I want you to pick out your best swimmer, someone who can climb well. Also, I need you to find me something about three feet long and hollow, like a reed or a pipe.'

Smithy smiled, understanding immediately. He nodded and went to join the rest of the crew.

Sam glanced back at Blackbeard who was now having what looked like a serious discussion with the town elders. After what he had just said, Blackbeard might actually be happy to see him win, but if he did, would he really step aside and let Sam take over? And would Swallow just accept it and let him? He supposed that he would find out soon enough.

Sam wandered over and joined his men at the boats. 'Right, here's the plan. Have any of you ever seen a magic trick...?'

A few minutes later Sam and his men were in the boats and rowing hard out towards the ship. Blackbeard had sent them to attack after almost exactly ten minutes, something that Sam took as another sign of his growing neutrality.

As usual Sam was sitting in the stern steering the boat, but this time he had the tail of his jacket draped over the rail, dangling almost to the water. He looked down and adjusted it to better cover the two hands that were clinging there, checking quickly to see if the man Smithy had chosen was still with them and managing to breathe comfortably through the reed in his mouth.

The ten boats quickly took up positions surrounding the ship, as if they were going to attack in the same way that everyone else had, with Sam's boat on the far side of the brig away from the docks. Sam waited until everyone was in position and then patted the hand of the man holding onto the boat. He waited for the hands to slip off the rail before he stood up. He raised his hand in the air and pointed forwards, signalling the attack. He didn't make the same mistake as Swallow had, though, and stayed on balance as the boat surged forward.

Out of the corner of his eye he could just about make out the end of the reed poking out of the water as the submerged man stayed in place. Everything was going according to plan so far, but if something happened to the man they'd left treading water it was going to be a very short and very humiliating fight.

They approached the ship at full speed, but at the last minute all the boats on Sam's side veered away. Instead of going directly to the attack and assaulting the ship from all sides, they rowed back around to the side of the ship facing the docks and joined the others, moving into position as quickly as possible as if trying to catch the defenders off guard.

The men from the Mermaid swarmed up the side, trying to overwhelm Swallow's crew. However, there wasn't room for all of the boats to nudge up to the small brig at the same time so Sam found himself holding off and watching the fight from a short distance away as he waited for his own chance to attack.

As he had expected, his men didn't do very well - most of them were beaten down before they got to the rail and he saw that a good few of them weren't getting back up again. He was angered, but not very surprised to see that most of Swallow's men, led by the bald and scarred thug he'd seen with Swallow earlier, had completely removed the padding from their weapons and were hitting out with the plain wooden poles, which were more than enough to do serious damage.

What his sailors were succeeding in doing, though, was to draw all of Swallow's men over to this side of the ship. Consequently, there was nobody there to see a single out of breath and very wet man come slithering over the gunwale on the far side of the ship and start to climb silently up the rigging towards the flag. Just like the juggler in the square, the crew of the Mermaid was holding the attention of their rivals by deliberately doing so badly that they couldn't look away. They were making a desperate sacrifice of blood and pain for a chance to win.

This was the critical moment, when the already tired man was only just beginning his climb. It would still be possible for someone to catch him if he was seen, so something had to be done to make sure that none of the enemy had time to look around and notice what was happening.

Sam made a quick decision and spoke urgently to Smithy and the rest of the boat crew. 'Come on, follow me.' He stood up and made the highly dangerous leap from his boat across a short gap to one of the empty boats that was against the ship. He slipped and almost fell, scraping his shin badly on one of the rowing benches, but caught himself before he tumbled into the water. Ignoring his injury he made the shorter hop to the ship and began the short climb up the low side of the brig.

'Come on, men, let's go!'

His shout was answered with a roar from his crew and they redoubled their efforts, following the example of their captain, exactly what Sam had wanted - additional noise and chaos to keep the attention of Swallow's crew firmly fixed on them.

Misdirection. So that they didn't see how the trick was done.

Smithy climbed at Sam's side and they got to the rail at the same time. They were lucky; the defenders at the side were momentary occupied, ganging up on one of Sam's crewmen to heave him into the water, and the two friends used the distraction to leap aboard.

As soon as their feet hit the planks of the deck they struck out fiercely at the enemies around them and managed to create enough space for more sailors to leap over the rail behind them and in short order Sam found himself joined by the familiar figure of Bosun Brown.

Brown protected Sam's left side while Smithy took care of his right and together the three of them forced Swallow's men back a couple of paces.

Five more sailors from the Mermaid's crew joined them, and together they gained some space on the deck along with some time to breathe.

Sam took the opportunity to look down over the rail. Below them the remainder of his men were lying exhausted and bloody in the bottom of the boats or were clinging to them, floating in the water like drowned rats. He was relieved to see that none of them were in immediate danger of drowning, but none of them were in any shape to continue the fight. They were on their own.

There was silence as the two sides faced off; Sam's eight men, already tired, completely outnumbered by Swallow's thirty relatively fresh thugs.

Sam glanced quickly around his faithful crew. He could tell that they knew they had no hope of winning the coming fight, but, even so, none of them wavered or showed any sign of doubt - they just stood there with him, weapons raised, defiantly staring down an implacable enemy, firm in the belief that their captain knew what he was doing.

The bald thug that Swallow had been talking to before the contest was standing directly opposite Sam. He met Sam's gaze with wide eyes and a slyly confident grin while he struck his bare stick into his palm with a slap and smoothly shifted his weight from one side to another, balancing easily on the balls of his feet. He was obviously someone who enjoyed fighting and was good at it. Sam wasn't looking forward to going up against him, but he wasn't about to send one of his men into a danger that he wasn't willing to face himself, so he steeled himself, preparing to face the coming pain.

The silence drew out as the two crews glared at each other, unmoving, as if none of them wanted to do anything that would spark off the attack. It was like something out of a spaghetti western, and again, Sam was almost surprised not to hear music or enigmatic whistling.

Suddenly, laughter broke the silence, and Swallow made his way through his men. He shoved the scarred thug aside and planted himself opposite Sam. Unlike his men, who all sported some marks from the fight, he was completely untouched - there wasn't a single scratch or bruise on him. Obviously he had stayed as far away from trouble as possible and even now he didn't come within reach of the weapons of the crew of the Mermaid, but kept his distance, staying among his men for safety.

He taunted Sam, his face screwed up in a mocking expression. 'Are you going to surrender now, Vives? Or do my men have to whip you and send you packing like the scruffy little puppy you are?'

Sam was trying very hard not to look up at the main mast and give the game away, but out of the corner of his eye he could just about make out the man almost at the top - a dark blob against the sky approaching another dark blob that was the flag. He only needed to hold Swallow and his men's attention a little bit longer.

He smiled and raised an eyebrow. 'Are you feeling brave now, "Jack Swallow"? Are you feeling unbeatable, now that you have more men than I do?'

Swallow looked around arrogantly. He grinned, supremely confident. 'Well, actually... Yes!'

The two dark splotches in the corner of Sam's eye became one and he straightened up, coming out of his ready stance. He had stalled for long enough and he had no desire to prolong the fight any further; he had crew members in the water below that needed taking care of. He shrugged and relaxed the tension from his shoulders. 'You're right, we can't beat you in a straight up fight.'

Swallow smirked and Sam watched, fascinated, as the man's eyes defocused slightly and his tongue flicked over his thin lips, wetting them. His hands spasmed briefly; he was probably already imagining them caressing the huge diamond that would be his prize.

Sam gave him all of three seconds to savour the taste of his victory before bringing him crashing back to reality.

'But...'

Swallow started and came out of his daydream, his eyes snapping back into sharp focus. 'But what?!?'

'But, I think you should look up.' Sam lifted a finger and nonchalantly pointed towards the top of the mast behind Swallow.

'I'm not falling for some cheap trick like that.' Swallow scoffed and crossed his arms over his chest, but he couldn't ignore the man tugging insistently on his sleeve and his head involuntarily turned, his eyes going towards the mast. He craned his neck to look up and finally saw what everyone else had already seen.

The heroic sailor had made it to the top of the mainmast, unclipped the flag, and was waving it furiously over his head.

A cheer went up from Sam's men on the deck and was echoed tenfold by the crowd on the docks.

Swallow was not about to accept defeat so easily, though.

'YOU CHEAT!' he bellowed. He pulled a wicked looking knife out of his belt and lunged at Sam, closing the gap incredibly quickly.

Sam was taken completely by surprise by the man's treachery and all he could do was watch as the gleaming knife came closer and closer.

Suddenly, there was someone in front of him, protecting him. It was Smithy, face to face with his captain and holding him in a protective embrace.

The knife slipped silently up to the hilt into Smithy's back. He stiffened, quite literally transfixed.

Sam and Smithy held each other's gaze, both with wide open eyes, but one in shock and surprise, the other in pain.

'What... would you do... without me... Captain?' Smithy managed to force the words out before his eyes fluttered and closed and he went limp, unconscious.

Sam caught him and lowered him gently to the floor.

A shadow fell on him and he looked up.

Swallow was standing over him, the bloody knife still in his hand, looking down at Smithy in anger. 'How is it you people always inspire such loyalty wherever you go?!? Won't you ever learn? I thought I'd taught you meddlers a lesson already, but it looks like I'm going to have to do so again!'

The Mermaid's crew finally came out of their stupor and sprang into action to defend their captain as Swallow started to lunge forward again, but it was his own men who grabbed the man and pulled him back. He struggled against them, but they were just too strong and he had the knife ripped out of his grasp.

'MR SWALLOW!' Blackbeard's angry bellow froze the dramatic scene in place and everyone looked up at him as he loomed over them, standing on the rail of the brig. The pirate lord had seen the pause in the action and then the flag being waved and had come to congratulate the winner, thinking that the game was over, but he had arrived just in time to witness Swallow's latest act of treachery.

He jumped down from the rail, thudding heavily on the deck, and stalked towards Swallow. He glanced down at Sam and the unconscious Smithy as he passed and a look of compassion and grief briefly came over his face, but it was quickly replaced by one of sheer fury as he stood in front of Swallow.

'Let him go.' Blackbeard's voice was low and full of menace.

The men around Swallow released him and he stood up and brushed his clothes down. 'Thank you, I was just...'

'SILENCE!'

Swallow rocked back on his heels, as did the men around him, such was the fury projected by this giant of a man.

'Jack Swallow, you are expelled from my crew and banished from Port Royal for the rest of your days.'

'But I...!'

'BE QUIET!!!' Blackbeard neither needed nor wanted to hear excuses. 'If you are seen in this town again after sunrise tomorrow you will end your days in my cage being roasted by the sun and fed on by the carrion birds, is that clear?'

Swallow nodded silently, utterly defeated.

'Good. You have ten seconds to leave the ship before I have my men throw you off.'

Swallow opened and closed his mouth as if he was going to speak, but saw that every single man on the brig was glaring at him with murderous intent in their eyes, even his own shipmates. He clearly realised that if he was thrown off the ship he might not be guaranteed a soft landing in the water, or even be conscious, and he scrambled to get away, pushing roughly through the crowd and disappearing over the rail. Moments later they heard the splashes as he frantically and ineptly rowed away.

Blackbeard turned to Sam. 'Is he still alive?'

'Barely.'

'Come on, let's get him to shore and to a doctor; I want him to live long enough to be rewarded for his bravery. Meanwhile a celebration is in order - we'll have a few rounds, then I'll announce your win. And I really think you owe your men a drink.'

There were some cheers from the Mermaid's sailors at that, but they were subdued and the men quickly fell into silence as they left the ship, carrying the limp body of Smithy with them. They gently placed the first mate in the bottom of a boat and Sam used his own jacket to prop his head up. Only then did he spare a thought for the rest of his men. He was relieved to see that they had already been rescued from the water and there were smiles all around through the bruises, blood and broken bones; they had survived worse and in their minds it had been worth it to see their captain triumphant.

Smithy had briefly woken up on the journey back, but had fallen back into unconsciousness when he was being lifted out of the boat, overcome by the pain. At the dock they were met by some of Blackbeard's men who put the first mate on a stretcher and carried him up the steps to where a grey-haired man in a rough suit was waiting. The man looked at the wound and tutted, shaking his head, but nonetheless assured Sam that his first mate would most likely survive, although he would have a long recovery period.

After Smithy had been carried away, Sam finally had some time to catch his breath and only then did he notice that his hands were covered with blood and that there were red stains on his breeches. He wandered back down to the docks and washed the blood off as best he could in the water before slowly going to join his crew in the square, all the time wondering if winning the competition had been worth the pain and suffering that had been caused.

The crowd didn't care anything for Smithy's injury or for Sam's doubts and were in a jubilant mood. They plied him and his crew with drinks and food and again Sam was the target for the affections of the women. However, now they were sizing him up in a way that was making him all too uncomfortable, like a gambler sizing up racehorses before a meet, or a farmer choosing which cow to slaughter for lunch. Apparently, Sam had already been something of a crowd favourite and they had been rooting for him to beat Swallow, but now that he had won and was Blackbeard's heir apparent, he was even more popular than ever and there were a good many mothers in the town who were looking at him as a good catch for their daughters.

Sam hadn't really been in the mood for a celebration after all that had happened, but the doctor's favourable prognosis of Smithy's condition had comforted him somewhat, and the congratulations of the people around him almost completed the job of restoring him to his old self and brought a half-smile to his face.

It was looking like it was going to be a great party. He just wished that his friend could have been there to enjoy it with him.

CHAPTER 12
CHOSEN

The sun was going down and the sky looked as if it was on fire as the three captains gathered in front of the throne.

An expectant silence fell as Blackbeard climbed up onto the seat of his throne, faced the crowd and held up his hands.

'I hope you've all enjoyed the contest as much as I have and what a show it's been! But, as you know, today has been about more than just a bit of fun. I've been thinking of retiring for a while now...'

Many of the people in the audience hadn't heard his announcement before, having either not been present, or been so drunk as to not remember, so it again drew disappointed noises from the crowd and he paused accordingly, putting his hands up and nodding in sympathy with them.

'Come on! You all knew this was going to happen sooner or later; either the British would get me or Davy Jones would. At least this way we can all be sure that Port Royal will be in good hands and protected once I'm gone! So let's all stop moping around, shall we? And give a cheer for the winner of our little competition and my worthy successor - Captain Samuel Vives!'

Blackbeard held out his hand and beckoned for Sam to come up next to him on the throne. Sam was doubtful about how dignified it would be for both of them to stand on it together, but once there he found there was plenty of room for both of them, despite Blackbeard's impressive size.

The pirate lord wrapped an arm round Sam's shoulder and whispered out of the side of his mouth, 'Take a bow, laddie; you've earned it!'

Sam didn't bow as such because he was tired after the day's events and couldn't trust himself not to fall off the big chair, instead he just waved and bobbed his head.

Blackbeard followed his lead and waved as well, roughly pulling Sam into his side as if they were the best of friends.

The reason why the pirate lord had invited him up to stand next to him now became clear - he was giving the town an image of the two of them together, making sure that his successor was forever associated with him, allowing some of his own popularity to rub off on the newcomer.

With that revelation came another and a better understanding of the motives behind Blackbeard's contest itself. On the face of things, the contest had been far too arbitrary to really choose the best candidate for the job. It didn't particularly seem to matter much who the candidate ultimately ended up being, beyond the fact that he or she would have had to demonstrate a modicum of skill or luck to win, and Sam had wondered why Blackbeard hadn't just given the job to someone. However, finding the best replacement had never been the real purpose of the contest; it had been more about entertaining the town, introducing them to the heir to the throne and gaining their acceptance of the chosen man or woman.

Sam turned his head to glance at the elders sitting behind the throne, they were the ones who had most needed convincing of his suitability as a leader and they were beaming up at him, evidently already confident in Blackbeard's choice.

It looked like the plan had worked in full, Sam just hoped that he could live up to everyone's expectations; after all, he knew even less about running a town than he did about sailing a ship.

'By the way...' as Blackbeard leaned in and whispered in Sam's ear, he felt a hand slip into his jacket pocket and something heavy settle there, '...this is yours. I don't think we want to display it in public again and risk starting a riot, do we?'

For a second Sam didn't know what Blackbeard was referring to, but then he remembered the diamond that had been the winning captain's prize. He had no idea what on Earth he was going to do with such a big and presumably valuable stone, even if he could take it home. He wasn't sure how he was going to explain it to his mother for a start. He didn't think that 'oh, by the way, I found this while I was walking home from school' or 'would it be OK if I kept this priceless diamond on my bedside table, please?' were going to cut it somehow. Not to mention that the police would be quite interested to know where it had come from and he hadn't got a clue what he was going to tell them; he was pretty sure there weren't any diamonds to be found naturally in Catalonia and certainly not just lying around in a city waiting to be picked up by passersby.

He shrugged and decided to worry about it later. For now he was just going to keep it in his pocket while he enjoyed the party, then when he got back to the ship he'd put it in front of a lamp and watch the rainbows.

'Now, give them a big smile and let's go have a drink!' Blackbeard jumped down from the throne leaving Sam alone in the limelight.

Sam gazed around as he smiled and waved at the crowd again. There was thunderous applause and cheers from townspeople and ship's crews alike and he grinned down at his loyal men, who were crowding close around him. He was glad to see that his fellow captains were applauding also; there were definitely no hard feelings there, and he felt warm inside when he saw Caesar's arm go around Bonny's shoulders - it seemed that something good had come from Blackbeard's contest, not just tragedy and loss of life.

The townspeople and pirates didn't need much excuse for a celebration, but they had one and made the most of it.

Sam had given his crew permission to drink and they had taken his words to heart, doing about as much of it as they could. They were a decent lot, though, and not many fights broke out, unless you count the odd kind of nautical "dance off" that some of them got into with the crew of Caesar's ship, to the general amusement of the locals.

Right from the moment he jumped off of the throne, Sam was the centre of attention and throughout the night, men and women alike were asking him questions and trying to get close to him. They also plied him with drinks, but he politely refused them, sticking to pineapple juice all night.

Many of the women asked him to dance, still obviously trying to attract him, but he was very reluctant to encourage them. The dances themselves were energetic, involving a lot of jumping and hopping around, as well as some thigh slapping and the occasional "hey!" Admittedly, it looked like fun, but he felt he would just make a fool of himself if he tried it and, despite the assurances of his men that he wouldn't look at all silly, he contented himself with watching.

Eventually, though, a girl about his own age shyly asked him to dance with her and she looked so different from the others, seemingly without their ulterior motives or the assessing look in their eyes, that he reluctantly agreed. To the cheers of his men and many dirty looks from the other young women he had refused, she grabbed his hand and led him out onto the area of the square that had been set aside as a dance floor. Too late, Sam noticed Bosun Brown talking to the men playing the music, grinning mischievously as he handed over a small coin, and as the band started playing a slow song, he realised he'd been set up.

The girl pulled him in and held him tightly in a way that wasn't very shy or particularly innocent and they stumbled around the floor for a while, until Sam started to get the hang of the simple movements and was able to take the lead a bit more. The rest of the dance was actually quite enjoyable, at least when he was able to avoid thinking about how she was rubbing up against him whilst they were going around in circles.

The song ended, Sam bowed and she curtsied back. He held out his hand in order to lead her off the floor, but she all but leapt into his arms and planted a kiss firmly on his lips.

Sam was completely taken by surprise and his arms went around her automatically. This was Sam's first ever real kiss; it wasn't that he wasn't interested in girls, it was just that they didn't seem particularly interested in a victim of bullying, just like the boys stayed away in fear as if he was a leper. Here, though, he wasn't a victim, he was a winner, and that was a whole other matter.

The blood rushed to his head and he lost himself in this new sensation, wondering what the hell that was she was doing with her tongue.

They stayed locked in the kiss for what felt like an eternity, but was in reality only a few seconds, until the sound of the men cheering and clapping got through to Sam. He gently pushed her away, the blood rushing to his face and ears in embarrassment. He blinked at her in shock, not entirely unpleased, and was about to ask her if she wanted to dance again when he saw her sharing triumphant looks with a woman standing at the edge of the dance floor who he assumed was her mother. The girl was nodding slyly as the woman gave her "keep going" gestures and Sam realised that she was just another woman with her eyes on the prize after all. He was disappointed, but not too surprised, and when she turned back to him he smiled and thanked her profusely, bowing again, all the while backing away.

He turned to leave the dance floor, but found his way blocked. Several young, and not so young women had witnessed the kiss and evidently now believed that they had a chance at the dashing captain with loose morals. They grinned at him wolfishly, flashing teeth in varying stages of disrepair.

'Uh...'

Sam again started backing away, but came up sharply as he bumped into the girl he had been dancing with. She tried to wrap her arms around him, but he managed to dodge her and hurried off in the other direction, heading across the dance floor. He glanced over his shoulder as he dipped and ducked around the dancers and found that the girls were in hot pursuit. He sped up, but still didn't quite break out into a run; he didn't want to call too much attention to himself because he didn't think that the sight of him being chased by a gaggle of girls would do his reputation very much good - he would most likely find it hard to command his men with dignity if they knew that their captain had run in panic from a few kisses.

He pushed his way through the onlookers surrounding the dancing area and continued past the viewing stands, searching for a place to lose his stalkers. He spotted some kind of tent in the shadows underneath the wooden construction and leapt at it gratefully, pulling the heavy fabric closed behind him hurriedly and peering out through the gap as the hunting girls went past one by one outside.

'There is power in you.'

Sam jumped, startled at the voice that came from behind him, but somehow rang out in his head at the same time.

He turned and squinted against the light of a tiny lantern hanging overhead, taking in the rags and the herbs hanging everywhere, searching for the source of the voice.

He finally found it: a woman with skin as dark as Caesar's was sitting on a stool behind a small table on the other side of the tent. She was gazing up at him with shockingly blue eyes that didn't at all fit with her skin colour and seemed to blaze from her dark skin.

'Excuse me?'

'I said "there is power in you". Such power.'

Sam blinked, puzzled. 'Of course; I'm the captain of the Mermaid.'

The woman laughed and Sam found himself mesmerised by the beautiful sound and drawn into the humour of her startling eyes. 'If you say so, child! Now, come closer and sit yerself down.'

'No need, I was just looking...'

'For a place to avoid unwanted advances for a while and you have found it.'

Sam blinked. 'What? How...?'

'No-one will disturb us; they know better. In the meantime, why don't you sit? Cross my palm with silver and I will tell you what you want to know.'

Sam finally understood and shook his head, smiling wryly. The woman was a fortune teller, one of those charlatans who made vague predictions based on the clues and reactions they got from the gullible people who went to them, or worse, did tarot readings on the television. She had undoubtedly recognised him, seen his behaviour and come to easy conclusions about why he was in her tent - there was nothing mystical about her pronunciations, anyone with even an ounce of intuition could have done the same. Sam passionately disliked people who preyed on the desperation of others and, even though he had the money to spare, he'd rather take his chances with the girls outside than waste his time listening to any nonsense she might have to say. 'No, thank you, I don't....'

'Even if you don't believe in what I do, don't you think that the next pirate lord can afford to indulge an old woman?' She chuckled. 'It's not as if it's your gold anyway, is it, *Samuel James Vives Hudson*?' She pronounced his full name carefully, rolling it on her tongue and savouring it, even down to his mother's surname that nobody had used before in Port Royal or seemed to even know.

She saw his consternation and laughed again. Her head tilted backwards gracefully and her eyes closed as the sound filled the tiny space and reverberated in Sam's mind. Suddenly, though, she fell silent and Sam staggered, as if the ground had moved beneath him. Her head dropped and her eyes snapped into focus on him, the intense blue flaring with a cold fire. 'Sit!'

The woman's voice was gentle, with a Jamaican lilt, but there was an incredible strength to it and Sam found himself obeying her command against his will. He all but fell onto the stool at the table opposite her.

Now that he was closer he could see that some of what he thought were herbs hanging behind the woman actually had crude human forms - they were voodoo dolls, things he'd thought only existed in movies, and he briefly toyed with the idea of getting one of Rafa to see if it could do anything to make his life easier.

The woman saw the direction of his gaze and chuckled, shaking him out of thoughts of pins and private parts. 'You do not need one of those to take care of your childish problems, Sam. You just need to trust in yourself more.'

Sam frowned as he leaned forward on the stool to stare at her; she knew far more about him than he had given away. 'Who are you?'

He studied her face, taking in the smooth skin and the clear eyes that spoke of a young person, in stark contrast with the long white hair that curled about her shoulders that told of someone much older. There was a vitality to her that spoke of someone in the prime of their life. However, at the same time, he got the sense of someone very wise and very *very* old. It was the same feeling he got from his grandfather, in fact, on those few occasions when he turned serious.

She met his frank gaze with a slight smile, not taking any offence at his scrutiny. 'I am nobody, just a soul, adrift on the seas, searching for answers and providing them when I can.'

He wasn't quite sure what she meant, but at least she wasn't spouting the normal, self-assured, "I will make your life better" stuff that fortune tellers always seemed to come out with. He realised he had nothing to lose indulging the woman and it actually might be fun, so he started to fumble in his pocket for a coin.

However, she stopped him with a wave and a smirk. 'I think that, in your *very special* case, I will waive my normal fee. Maybe that will help prove to you that I am not some *charlatan fortune teller*, I practice voodoo and I give my advice when I feel like it, to those who need it the most. And you, boy, are in dire need.'

'Um... Thank you?'

'Don't thank me yet; not all who come to me are glad when they hear what I have to tell them.'

'As long as you don't tell me that I'm going to meet a tall dark stranger.'

'Of course not!' She laughed then smiled at him mischievously. 'She'll be blonde, actually. But she will be a touch taller than you, yes.'

Sam wasn't sure how to respond. His instinct was to laugh and leave because he didn't believe in people predicting the future. However, if there was any way she could tell him what he really wanted to know, then he couldn't go just yet.

He wet his lips, hoping against hope, and asked the one thing that had been on his mind since the moment he had appeared on the deck of the Mermaid, what seemed like a lifetime ago. 'Can you tell me how to get home?'

The woman shook her head and looked at him sadly. 'Oh, my dear child, I'm sorry, I can't, I am not a party to those kind of secrets, but don't worry; you will find out soon enough that your home is where you make it.'

Sam sighed; once again her words were unhelpful and unclear, and he was still no closer to getting back to his family.

'Do not be disappointed; that is not what you have really been brought here to learn.'

She reached out and took his hands, her eyes boring into him, as if piercing his soul.

They sat there for long seconds and Sam quickly began to feel uncomfortable under her unblinking gaze. She kept eye contact with him, never once looking down at his hands, and he wondered why she needed to hold them if she wasn't going to read his palms.

He was about to pull them away when she finally spoke.

'Well, I can say one thing; you're going to be popular with the ladies, so maybe you should get used to attention like what's waiting for you outside.'

She laughed as she saw the horrified look on Sam's face, showing teeth that were as bright as the white in her eyes. 'Oh, dearie, you may fear it now, but it's not such a bad thing and you'll be glad for it when the right woman comes along, you mark my words.'

The woman shuddered suddenly and her eyes defocused as if she were looking through him instead of at him. Her hands tightened on his, gripping them painfully with sudden strength.

Her voice was vastly different than before, infinitely powerful and *ancient* somehow, and it resounded throughout the tent, vibrating his bones and making his teeth hum. He didn't so much hear her words as they were burned directly into his brain.

'The time of need is upon us and you have been chosen.

'You must be strong. You will be the rock around which others gather and who they look to in order to deliver them from the coming storm.

'Do not be afraid to lead, even when the path ahead is fraught with danger, for the way will be made clear to you, even if those around doubt you.

'Never give in to your fears and never shy from sacrifice; that way lies destruction as clear as if you had extinguished all hope yourself.

'Beware of those who walk in the light, because they will drag us all into perpetual night if they can, but trust in the snake; it will be your friend and provide you with allies on whom you can rely.

'Above all else, you must find your love and keep her close, for there you will find our salvation and only together will you see us all through this darkest of times and pave the way for the peaceful present that was promised.'

The voice came to a sudden halt as the woman's mouth snapped closed, her teeth clicking together. Sam reeled as the world tilted around him and, suddenly dizzy as if he'd been in the sun for too long, he would have slipped off of the stool if not for her death-like grip on his hands.

She convulsed and her hands jerked away from his as she used them to support herself with the table. Her head dropped forwards onto her chest and her body heaved up and down as she struggled to breathe, wheezing as if she were trying to pull air through a constricted windpipe.

He reached out and tentatively put his hands on hers, squeezing them gently. 'Miss? Are you alright? Miss?'

After several long, tension-filled seconds she shuddered then slowly lifted her head. She seemed to come back to herself and her eyes refocused on him as the tension seemed to flow from her and her back straightened with an audible creak.

Sam's mouth flopped open. He stared at her, not sure if he was supposed to run away screaming or applaud; it had been an impressive piece of theatre and if it weren't for the fact that they wouldn't be invented for centuries he'd be looking around, trying to spot the hidden speakers that had made her voice so powerful.

'Thank you for your concern, Sam. It always hurts my throat a bit when that happens, but don't worry; I'll be fine after a few mugs of rum.' She smiled at him, but it didn't last long before she turned serious, her eyes once more capturing his. 'Now, I'm not going to pretend to know what any of that meant; I am just the conduit for powers greater than me to talk to you and it is for you to decipher their words as best you can.'

He forced a grin, trying to make it seem as if he wasn't scared half to death by everything that she'd just said. 'Can't you ask the higher powers to speak a bit clearer, then, please? Because I have no idea what they're talking about.'

'I'm afraid you'll find out soon enough that that's not how these things work.' The woman smiled knowingly. 'I will tell you this, though: be strong, Sam, I see sorrow, hardship and pain in your future and you will need all of your power and resources to survive the months and decades to come. And never let your guard down because you will be surrounded by treachery and the attacks will come from where you least expect them, when you least expect them.'

She reached out to touch his cheek, cupping it gently, reassuringly.

Sam found himself falling into blue eyes that were as timeless as the ocean, spiralling down into unimaginable depths, being pulled out of himself and into an infinity that would swallow him without noticing.

She blinked slowly, deliberately, and with that the spell was broken, the moment lost forever. He frowned, wanting to ask so many questions, but she just shook her head and went on.

'However, as I said before, there is great power in you. Trust in yourself and trust in the friends you make on your way; together you can defeat any foe and maybe, just maybe, things will turn out how they should have all along.'

She sighed and gazed at him sadly, but it was only for a couple of seconds and then she chuckled and pinched his cheek, just like his Catalan grandmother always did. 'Oh and by the way, don't worry about those girls outside; they are not for you - you belong to another and the love you find will shine through the ages. Farewell, Sam Vives.'

She patted him one last time then gestured and Sam found himself leaping to his feet, his body obeying her as if he were merely a puppet. Unable to look back and accompanied by her musical laughter, he staggered out of the tent and back into the noise and chaos of the revelry. His legs carried him all the way to the edge of the stands and dumping him unceremoniously on his arse on a bench before the invisible hand finally released him.

He was almost immediately surrounded by the gaggle of young women who had apparently been lying in wait for him. This time, though, he was more firm in declining their invitations and they quickly lost all hope that he was going to get drunkenly trapped into marriage with any of them. They soon gave up pestering him and flounced away in a huff, going in search of easier prey and leaving him alone with his thoughts.

He remained where he had been put and distractedly watched the fun while he tried to make some sense of the voodoo woman's words.

On the face of things what she had said just seemed to be a jumble of random statements without very much connection between them, although they all did all have one common factor that he didn't like and that was that he was going to be in a lot of danger. Quite possibly for decades to come, if the woman was to be believed.

The more he thought about it, the more he was convinced that it had all been nonsense spouted by someone who was half mad, for example, it was ridiculous that he had to watch out for "those who walk in the light", while befriending snakes - it would be far more logical if it had been the other way around. Her insistence that he had some kind of power was equally bizarre - yes, he was the captain of a ship and heir to Blackbeard's empire, but he got the feeling that it wasn't that kind of power that she had been talking about, as if she'd been hinting that he had abilities like her own or something. And as for finding his love - that was supposed to be almost impossible at the best of times and besides, he didn't even have a girlfriend.

After about an hour of slowly driving himself crazy, mulling things over and over without coming to any conclusions, he couldn't take it anymore and went to look for answers. However, when he got to where the tent had been it was no longer there. In its place was a makeshift bar, already surrounded by drunken pirates singing bawdy songs.

More than a little frustrated and not at all in the mood for a party anymore, he slowly made his way to a quiet corner of the square near the sea front and sat down against a wall.

It was there that one of the doctor's assistants found him shortly after and told him that Smithy was awake and asking for him.

The woman and her words were instantly banished from his mind and completely forgotten as he hurried to see his friend.

CHAPTER 13
WINNERS AND SORE LOSERS

Smithy was looking pale and weak, but was in good spirits. He was lying on his stomach, wrapped in bandages and tried to get up as Sam came in, but Sam immediately waved him back.

'Captain, thank you for coming.'

'Don't be silly, Smithy. What kind of captain, indeed what kind of man would I be if I didn't come and see the person who saved my life. Thank you for that, by the way.'

Smithy waved away his thanks with a weak smile. 'Actually, I'm pretty sure I ran into his knife. He probably would have missed you completely if I'd just let him try.'

'Yes, probably, but it was best not to tempt fate.'

'Maybe. Speaking of which, I wanted you to have this back.'

Smithy held out his hand. In it was the two headed coin that Blackbeard had given him earlier.

'It brought me luck; I'm still alive. Now it's time for it to protect you.'

Sam took the coin. A tear almost came to his eye, but he hid it with a smile. 'Thank you. I'll make sure to keep it close.'

Smithy stiffened in pain and groaned. He looked away, not wanting his captain and friend to see him in pain.

Sam felt himself wince in sympathy and waited until the man turned back to him before continuing. 'You're missing a good party out there. I even danced.'

'You'd better get the doctor back, Captain; I must be delirious because I think I just heard you say that you'd danced…'

'Don't be cheeky, Mr Smith, or you'll find yourself demoted to powder monkey.'

'I'm terribly sorry, Captain, I'm sure you were the belle of the ball.'

'You'd better believe it!'

They laughed together, but Smithy's face screwed up in fresh agony and he gasped as the movement jolted his back. He put a brave face on, but Sam could see the sweat beading on his forehead, the strain in his expression and the trouble his eyes were having focusing, and he knew that Smithy was close to passing out again.

However, before he could say anything Smithy grinned feebly, preempting him. 'Thank you again for coming, Captain, but if you don't mind, it's a bit past my bed time.'

'Of course. Get some rest, Mr Smith, that's an order. I want you back on board as soon as possible.'

'Aye aye, Captain.'

Smithy's eyes fluttered closed and he drifted off into unconsciousness.

Sam stood by the bed for some time looking down at him, until the doctor came in and told him that he had to leave.

He didn't feel like going back to the celebration, but he also knew he wouldn't be able to sleep, so he wandered down to the shore and along the beach, trying to find some peace.

He sat on the sand and stared out to sea, listening to the party going on in the distance, calming his nerves and recalling the day's events. It had been an adventure he would never forget, but good things too often came with a heavy cost.

The sky was just beginning to glow in the east when he finally decided to call it a day and go back to the Mermaid.

He got to his feet and wandered slowly back towards the town. The celebrations were winding down now and the silence of the early morning was broken only by a single group of sailors singing some song about Spanish ladies and laughing, obviously reluctant for the day to come to an end. Sam was glad to see that they were a mix of sailors from his crew and those of Bonny and Caesar; the good relations between the crews continued to spread.

He made his way across the square, stepping carefully over people who had just dropped and fallen asleep where they were, and was almost at the jetty when he came across Bonny and Caesar. They were sitting on the edge of the dock with their feet dangling over the water, passing a bottle of something back and forth. They were sitting very close, not quite touching, but still a lot closer than would have been comfortable under normal circumstances. It looked like they were having an intimate moment and Sam didn't want to disturb them, but the only way for him to get to his boat was right past them.

Caesar looked up as Sam approached and beamed his huge smile at him. 'There you are, Captain Vives! We didn't see you at the party, we were a bit… busy.' As they struggled a bit unsteadily to their feet, the two captains shared a sheepish and self-conscious grin which Sam found very cute, but a little strange on the faces of two hardened pirate captains. He supposed they were just human beings after all, with the same feelings that everybody else had.

Caesar offered the bottle to Sam, but he refused with a smile. The big African just shrugged and took a swig himself before giving it to Bonny and wiping his lips on the back of his hand. 'We were afraid we wouldn't have a chance to say goodbye to you; we've decided to merge our fleets and we sail on the tide, so I'm afraid I will have to owe you that meal.'

Sam beamed at them, looking back and forth from one to the other. 'That's great! I'm sure you'll do wonderful things together. And don't worry, we can get together and swap stories next time we're all in port together.'

Bonny smiled shyly and reached out to take Caesar's hand. 'We'd like that! We figure that in a couple of years we should have enough plunder to retire back here and start our own crew.'

'Your own crew?' Sam was puzzled for a second, but quickly realised what they meant and coloured slightly. 'Oh, uh, yes, well… Good luck with that, and if you ever need a godfather you know where to find me!'

Caesar flashed his brilliant white smile. 'We will, you can count on it, my friend!'

Sam reached out and took the bottle from Bonny; he figured it was a special occasion and he needed something to toast his friends with. He raised the bottle. 'Here's to a successful cruise, a happy retirement and a peaceful future!'

He took a swig and swallowed it down then handed the bottle back.

Two seconds later he felt like his throat had exploded. He coughed and gasped, unable to breathe, and doubled over, clutching his chest and staggering, his legs suddenly shaking.

The two captains laughed and Caesar started pounding him on his back, almost knocking him into the harbour.

'It's good!' Sam managed to wheeze out finally. He straightened up, taking in huge gulps of air, his eyes streaming.

Bonny took a step forward and kissed him. It was just a small kiss, between friends, nothing like the one the girl had given him earlier, but it meant much more. She put her hand on his cheek and looked him in the eyes. 'Thank you for everything.'

Sam stood there speechless as they turned and walked away hand in hand, disappearing back the way he had come, heading for the beach.

He watched them until they were out of sight, smiling to himself; even in rough times like these it seemed there was still a chance for romance.

With a last look around the square at the aftermath of the celebration he turned and went down the wooden steps to the jetty, where he found the men from his crew who had volunteered to remain sober to guard the boats. He asked one of them to row him out to the Mermaid, leaving the rest of them to sleep for a little bit longer.

Sam wearily climbed up the side of the Mermaid and stepped onto the main deck. The ship was silent except for the usual soft creaking as it swayed gently at anchor - with most of the men at the party on shore, he was alone apart from the skeleton crew that had been left on board in case of emergencies and there were none of the usual sounds that a large number of men in close quarters made.

He returned the salute of the officer of the watch on the quarterdeck as he made his way towards the stern and entered his cabin. He closed the door and leaned against it, yawning - he was beyond tired and more than ready for bed, but there was something he wanted to do first.

A lantern had been left on the table for him and he sat down in a chair next to it, then took the diamond from his pocket and held it up to the light.

He could almost understand the fascination that some people had with these stones. It was so beautiful, but at the same time so cold and, after all was said and done, it was just a thing, an object, certainly not worth killing or dying for. He turned it over in his hand, watching the rainbows it sent around the room shifting and merging... glinting off the blade of the dagger as it stabbed towards his ribs.

Sam threw himself to one side and fell heavily on the floor, his tiredness evaporating as adrenaline surged through his body. His chair tipped over on top of him and blocked the thrust of the knife, giving him time to look up at his aggressor, now revealed in the pool of light cast by the lantern.

Swallow's face was twisted with fury as he wielded the blade, pulling it from the upholstery of the chair where it had caught and drawing it back to try again. He had evidently been hiding in the shadows of Sam's cabin on the deserted ship for who knew how long, waiting patiently for his chance to assassinate his rival.

Sam thrust his legs out with all the strength he'd developed in hours of fencing practice and kicked the chair off of him. It hit Swallow in his shin and knocked him off balance, giving Sam time to scramble away and gain his feet. He rushed to get the table between him and his attacker.

Swallow recovered and faced Sam across the table. He brandished the knife and hissed in fury. 'Give me that diamond!'

Sam looked down and realised that he still had the huge gemstone his hand.

'Give it to me! I'm not going home empty handed!'

Sam grimaced at Swallow defiantly. 'Not a chance, murderer!'

Swallow began to edge around the table, but Sam matched him, making sure that it stayed squarely between them.

'How long are you going to keep up this charade, boy? Aren't you getting tired of playing at being a pirate? Or is this really just some kind of game to you?' Swallow was smirking sarcastically as he edged sideways around the table, his gaze fixed on the diamond, the glow of greed in his eyes. He licked his lips, his desire clear on his face, but then his eyes flicked to Sam and hardened. 'Well, I intend to show you how serious this really is - I've spent the last year getting to where I am now, a whole bloody year without a decent toilet or any toilet paper, and I'm not about to let one of *you* just waltz in and take what's rightfully MINE!'

Swallow shouted out the last word, using it as impetus to lunge over the table. He pulled himself forward on his stomach, wildly slashing out with the knife, but Sam was too quick for him and leapt back, only just staying out of range. He scurried around the table and put it between them again.

As Swallow regained his feet awkwardly, Sam had a moment to catch his breath and he frowned as he realised what the man had said. 'What do you mean "one of you"?'

Swallow snarled and began advancing round the table once more, but suddenly halted as what Sam had said got through to him. His face briefly registered his surprise, but it was almost instantly replaced by a look of insane hatred and absolute rage and he screamed at Sam. '*You mean you don't know?!? I've been fighting with a BOY who doesn't even know WHAT HE IS?!?*

Swallow had completely lost control of himself and he lunged forward, scrambling ferociously to get to Sam, who realised that if there was any time to be afraid it was now; when confronted for the first time in his life by someone whose every intention and thought was towards one thing and one thing only: killing him.

The chase around the table had brought Sam back around to the door. He yanked it open and tumbled through with Swallow only a few steps behind, closing the gap fast.

The sun was just peeking above the horizon, covering everything with an appropriately blood-red glow, as Sam ran out onto the main deck. He stumbled over ropes and chains and raced to the nearby capstan. He took refuge behind the large cylindrical object, putting it between him and the hysterical Swallow, who came rushing after him, panting and foaming at the mouth, swinging the dagger wildly.

Swallow stabbed repeatedly around and over the capstan and Sam barely managed to dodge each time, sometimes only by inches. He knew that it was only a matter of time before the man got in a solid hit, but Swallow's patience was apparently at an end and he gave into his frustration, going for a huge lunging dive. The knife ripped through Sam's jacket and tore his shirt, narrowly missing his ribs - it was the closest Swallow had come to his target yet, but it put him off balance and he was slow to recover.

Sam saw his chance. He twisted, knocking the knife to one side, then lashed out with his hand, the hand that still held the diamond, hoping for the best.

It slammed into the side of the man's head, knocking him to the floor.

Swallow was taken completely by surprise and he sat on the deck where he had fallen, staring up at Sam, his mouth open and bleeding from a deep gash in his forehead.

Sam hadn't been able to put much strength behind the blow, though, and it wasn't long before Swallow struggled back to his feet. Suddenly he was calm again, focussed, as if the blow from Sam had woken him from a momentary lapse in concentration. The madness was gone from his eyes and in its place was a cold light that scared Sam far more.

He wiped the blood from the side of his head and inspected it before looking back up at Sam and grinning evilly.

'Not bad, boy, but it's obvious that this is your first time; you don't have the instincts. You are way out of your depth and terrified, the stink of it is on you.' Something occurred to him and he laughed. 'I'm betting you don't even know how you got here, do you? And you probably have no idea how to get back! Am I right, or am I right? Right?'

He chuckled, shaking his head. 'So, what happened? Did you have a wet dream about Kiera Knightley? Or Johnny Depp maybe? Actually, never mind, I don't think I want to know!'

The man laughed and began to weave his knife slowly from side to side. The blade shone in the red light of the rising sun, making it look as if it were already covered in blood and Sam found his eyes drawn to it irresistibly.

Swallow resumed his advance, but slower and more carefully this time. 'Oh, and one last thing - despite your fancy swordwork earlier today, it seems you have no idea about how a real fight works...'

It was only when his back bumped up against the rail of the ship that Sam realised that he had made a disastrous mistake. He'd been as surprised as Swallow by the success of his punch and in his shock he had forgotten to make sure that the capstan was between them again. Now he had nowhere else to run.

Swallow stopped a couple of steps away and the grin left his face to be replaced by a look of such murderous coldness that Sam felt his legs would have given way beneath him if it weren't for the solid wood of the side of the ship propping him up.

'The way I see it you've got three choices, boy. One, I'll stick you with this knife, just like I did your friend, and you have no idea how much that's going to hurt or how much pleasure it's going to give me. Two, you jump over the rail there and swim for shore. That way you get to keep the diamond, but you stay here for the rest of your life to rot. Or three, you give me the diamond and I'll tell you all you need to know in order to run home crying to your mummy.' The man bared his teeth in a snarl. 'I'm not sure which of those I prefer, but the longer you make me wait the more I'm leaning towards option one.'

Sam realised that the man was right, he *was* frightened, much more than he'd ever been facing Rafa, or even when he'd gone into Blackbeard's garden. It was an awful feeling, as if he was no longer in control of himself, as if his instincts had taken over and were screaming at him to flee, to give in to his cowardice and find a safe place somewhere to hide where he could cry and wish that he did indeed have his mother there to comfort him. At the same time, though, there was another voice at the back of his head that was crying out in protest, that was begging for him to stand up for himself and face down this man, this *bully*. It was a strong voice, stronger every day, but tonight it was being completely swamped by the fear and by the fact that Sam knew that he didn't have the strength or the ability to win, or even survive a fight with Swallow.

He had done everything he could, but it would be stupid to press his luck against a man who had so readily murdered hundreds already, so Sam took a deep breath and prepared to go against all his principles and give in to a bully for the first time in his life.

The hateful words were left unsaid, though, as his attention was caught by motion in the corners of his eyes. Shadows moved, coming closer and becoming more distinct in the growing light.

The way out of the situation had presented itself.

Sam straightened up and pushed himself away from the rail, once again in full command of himself. He smiled. 'I think you left out an option - four, my crew overpower you and force you to tell me everything.'

Swallow retreated a step in the face of Sam's renewed confidence and looked around. He had been so intent on his target that he had forgotten about the rest of the men on board.

Even though there was only a skeleton crew aboard they still outnumbered him ten to one and they were slowly advancing on him from all sides, armed with belaying pins and knives.

Swallow snarled angrily, his gaze going from Sam to his men and back again. He shifted, obviously weighing his chances of snatching the diamond before they caught him and coming to the conclusion that it was going to be impossible.

'Enjoy the rest of your life here, then, runt.' He sprinted past Sam towards the rail and leapt headfirst over it, dropping the short distance to splash into the water of the bay.

Sam rushed to the rail and looked down into the water.

His crew rushed to join him.

'Shall we go after him, Captain?'

Sam didn't hear the question, he was too busy staring into the placid, completely undisturbed water. He waited, watching for more than a minute for some sign of the man, but it never came, and he slapped the wooden rail, furious with himself at not having prevented the loss of another life.

One of the crew, the officer of the deck, leaned over the rail to peer down into the water before looking at Sam with some concern. 'Er... what's the matter, Captain? Is everything alright?'

He gestured at the water. 'Didn't you see that?'

'What, Captain?'

Sam finally turned away from the ocean and look around at his men. They were all gazing at him strangely, quizzically, and he blinked, not quite believing that he had to explain himself. 'He just disappeared! Didn't you see?'

'Who, Captain? Who disappeared?'

'Jack Swallow! The man we just chased off the ship!'

'Jack Swallow? That's a funny name for a pirate! I've never heard of him, is he one of Blackbeard's men?' The man looked puzzled.

'Yes! He lead Blackbeard's team in the competition, surely you remember him!' He looked around the men, but they just gave him blank stares.

The officer shook his head. 'I think you're mistaken, sir; it was Bill Jones leading the Queen Anne's men. Big bald man with scars on his face. Can't mistake him for anyone else.'

Sam was about to try again, but he saw the expressions on the men's faces and he realised that they probably thought he was crazy. While that was most likely a good thing for a pirate to be, it wasn't really what he wanted them to think about him, so instead he laughed and made light of the situation.

'Never mind, I guess I just drank too much last night!'

His men laughed as well; that was something they could all relate to, and wandered back to their posts, leaving their captain alone at the rail.

Sam turned back to the sea and stared down into the water that had, for want of a better way of putting it, swallowed Swallow and tried to make some sense of the bizarre events of the past few minutes.

The way the man had vanished without a trace was inexplicable, but somehow in keeping with the whole mystery of how Sam had become a pirate in the first place. It wasn't just that his men, good, steady, sober men had never heard of the man, it was as if the very act of him disappearing had erased him from their memories - Swallow hadn't just stayed under the water and drowned, he had gone as if he'd never existed. Sam realised that he wasn't too unhappy about not having to deal with the man anymore, but he *was* worried that the answers he needed to get home might have gone with him.

He yawned and slumped against the rail, using it to keep him on his feet. He groaned and propped his head up in his hands as his exhaustion hit him full force, along with a bit of a headache from whatever it had been that he'd toasted Caesar and Bonny with.

There was undoubtedly some clue as to how he could get home in the way Swallow had disappeared, but he was far too tired to work it out - thinking would have to wait until after he'd slept.

The sun was free of the horizon now and sweat was already prickling in his armpits, making the thought of the huge, comfortable bed in the cool, dark room even more appealing than it already was. With a supreme effort he summoned the energy to push himself away from the rail and staggered back to his cabin.

He closed the door and leaned against it, looking around at the mess. Even though in his men's minds it was like Swallow had never been there, it looked like Sam was still going to have to clean up after him.

He fully intended to leave everything as it was, but only made it half way to the bed before his mother's voice sounded in his head and began nagging him to tidy up his room, like she'd done so many times at home. He cursed, using one of the particularly funny ones he'd learnt from his men, knowing full well that he wouldn't be able to sleep if he didn't at least make an effort to clear up.

He wandered around, picking up the chairs from the floor, straightening the table and rounding up the fruit that Swallow had sent flying in his lunge across the table. Finally, with his conscience salved, he took the diamond out of his pocket where he'd stuffed it after Swallow had jumped overboard. He used the French captain's handkerchief to wipe away a small smear of blood then placed it on the table in the lamplight.

He glared at the stone, hating it suddenly, irrationally. It and the greed it represented were the root of all his troubles and the cause of the destruction of the last few days. Given the chance he would swap it, and all the treasure in the chest next to the bed, for the knowledge of how to get home, and he knew that if he could do everything all over again, he would just give the damn thing to Swallow if it meant being able to see his family again.

He sighed, knowing that it was useless to wish for the impossible, and turned his back on the stone.

Without bothering to get undressed he flopped onto the bed and was asleep within moments.

'Captain! Captain!'

The words brought Sam out of one of the deepest sleeps he'd ever had.

'Wake up, Captain!'

He desperately tried to ignore the voice, to brush it away, but it was insistent and he reluctantly rose from the depths. His eyes slid gummily open and he found himself looking up into the smiling face of Smithy.

Suddenly wide awake, he propped himself up on his elbows and looked at his first mate in wonder. 'Why aren't you still at the doctor's?'

Smithy gave him a puzzled look. 'Why would I be, Captain? Has somebody been hurt?'

Sam looked his first mate up and down. The man seemed fine, as fit and healthy as he had been before the fight with Swallow. He certainly didn't look like a man who had been stabbed. 'No, I guess not!' Sam grinned, more than happy that Smithy was fit and healthy again. 'So, what's happening?'

'Blackbeard is on his way, he sent a signal asking his "heir" to join him on a tour of Port Royal's fortifications.'

Sam groaned. 'Oh, goody! A day out with Blackbeard and his mood swings, just what I needed...' He swung out of bed and stood up painfully on feet that had been confined in boots for far too long.

'I have your oilskin coat ready, it's blowing up a storm out there and looks like rain.'

'Rain? But it was sunny this morning!'

Smithy grinned. 'That was yesterday, Captain. You've slept for a whole day again... I've never known anyone to sleep like you! But you certainly earned it and none of the crew wanted to disturb you - they've been padding around the ship on tiptoes and have banned anyone from going on the quarterdeck above your cabin so as not to disturb you.'

Sam shook his head in wonder at this new evidence of how much his crew cared for him. 'Thank them for me, would you, please, and if they haven't had enough to drink these days then give them an extra tot of rum from me.'

'I'm fairly sure they won't say no, Captain!'

Sam walked towards the door, but stopped as something caught his eye - the diamond, sitting on the table right where he'd left it. He picked it up and looked at it in the dim light coming through the window. He shook his head. Yes, it was truly beautiful, but he still couldn't fathom how a simple rock could possibly provide enough motivation for a person to kill someone - its value was purely artificial and faded to nothing when compared to the love of his family and the esteem of his crew.

He knew that he should probably lock it in his treasure chest to keep it safe, but he really didn't think that one of his loyal crew would steal it, so, with a grin, he just placed it in among the oranges in the fruit bowl then walked over to where Smithy was waiting impatiently for him by the door.

After Smithy had helped Sam on with the coat, they stepped out on deck where Sam met the smiles and nods of his men with smiles and nods of his own. He found he could greet most of his crew by name now; they had gone through a lot in the few days since he had arrived and, if not yet his friends, they were certainly much more than simple acquaintances.

He made his way to the rail and looked out across the bay towards the docks and the approaching boat. Blackbeard was standing in the prow, one foot up on the gunwale, balancing easily even as the increasing waves tossed it around wildly.

With some time to spare, Sam wandered over to the other side of the ship and gazed out to sea. That way the clouds were black, completely blocking the sun, and there was a haze and a disturbance on the water as a squall rolled in towards the land. It would reach them very shortly, probably before Blackbeard arrived and would make stepping down into the plunging boat a bit more of a dangerous proposition.

The first drops of rain were just starting to fall as Blackbeard's boat was pulling up alongside.

Sam tucked his jacket closer around him, suddenly chilled, and as he did so he noticed a splotch of white on his lapel. He lifted his hand to brush it off, but thought better of it as it occurred to him that it was probably from a seagull passing overhead. Rather than getting his hands dirty he decided to just let the rain wash it off instead.

However, far from washing away, there seemed to be more and more marks appearing on his chest and shoulders. On top of that, the sleeves were somehow becoming transparent and he could see his arms through them. He wondered if this was the acid rain he had heard about and, with a smile, it occurred to him that, even so, his mother would probably know how to get the stain out.

All of a suddenly the squall hit them and the rain began falling in earnest. In less than a second Sam's clothes and hair were soaked and he could barely see through the water streaming down his face.

Smithy called out from the opposite side of the ship, his voice barely audible over the noise of the downpour. 'Sir! Captain Teach is here!'

Sam began to walk back across the deck, but the rain was now so bad that he couldn't see and he had to stop. He pulled the handkerchief out of his pocket, bringing with it Blackbeard's coin, and started to mop his eyes.

'Ahoy! Captain Vives! Get your arse down here!' Unlike Smithy's, Blackbeard's voice had no trouble reaching him and he cringed at the burgeoning anger in it - it didn't matter that Sam was his heir, he obviously wasn't going to accept being made to wait by anyone. The big pirate lord was much like Sam's mother that way; she was British to the core, which meant tea and, above all else, punctuality.

'Samuel Vives! Come here this minute!'

Sam's eyes were closed against the rain, but he could tell that it wasn't Blackbeard calling him now, it was someone female and strangely familiar. Whoever it was, though, was equally annoyed and equally capable of making Sam wince at the promise of repercussions for any transgressions.

The rain lessened enough for Sam to take in his surroundings and he gaped in shock at what he saw.

Gone were the elegant masts and rigging and the smoothly polished wooden deck of his beautiful ship and in their place were the towering monstrosities and ugly rough concrete of the world he had grown up in - he was back on the street outside his home, exactly where he'd been when the rain had first started.

'Come on, Sam! You're going to catch your death!' His mother called out again from where she was standing with his sister in the doorway of the block of flats where he lived, waving insistently with her hand.

'Coming!' He didn't quite understanding what was going on, but he started running automatically anyway; he'd always done what his parents told him to, most of the time, anyway, but especially when it made sense, like it did now.

While his mother and sister made their way up the stairs towards their flat, Sam lingered behind. He stood in the hallway just inside the door and peered out through the glass panels at the same familiar street in Barcelona, with the same cars stuck in the same traffic jam that had been blocking the road when he'd left. Somehow it looked far more dull, grey and lifeless than usual, after the colours and dangers of Port Royal, and if it weren't for his family he was fairly sure he would rather be back on the Mermaid, with a life of adventure ahead of him, than here, with just the prospect of school and being bullied to look forward to.

The world outside, while familiar, seemed less real than the one he'd just left, like in the *Wizard of Oz* when the movie was in colour when Dorothy was in Oz, but black and white when she was at home, which just added to the sense that what he had gone through had been just a dream.

However...

He glanced down at the handkerchief and the coin in his hand.

He'd never heard of anyone bringing anything back with them from a dream.

CHAPTER 14
HOME

The evening passed very slowly. Sam was absolutely exhausted, but didn't want to sleep; Uncle Andrew was coming over for dinner and he wanted to talk to him about his experience when he arrived. He flitted from one distraction to another, trying to stay awake, but was unable to concentrate on anything for any length of time. It wasn't just that he was tired, though, it was more that he couldn't rustle up any interest in anything - his books and video games seemed boring all of a sudden and even the television seemed to have lost its usual stranglehold on him. Finally, as a last ditch attempt to stay awake, he shut himself in his room and sat down at his desk to do his homework. He had to write an essay on pirates for history and he thought that would be easy enough, given what he'd just been through, but, bizarrely, he was having trouble with it, unsure even where to start. He was about to give up and switch to his maths in desperation when there was a knock at the door.

'Come in!'

Andrew poked his head around the door. 'Evening, Sam! Your mum said you wanted to talk to me?'

'Yes, if you don't mind, Uncle Andrew.'

'Of course not!'

He came in, closing the door behind him and spoke in a quiet voice. 'Is it Rafa again?'

Sam thought back to his fencing match with the big boy. Despite the fact that the bout had been over a week ago he found that it was still fresh in his mind, unlike the bruise on his leg, which was long gone. However, his problems with the bully, which before had worried him so much, now seemed so trivial when compared to what he had gone through in Port Royal.

He shook his head. 'No. Well, yes... but no.'

Andrew laughed. 'And? Which is it?'

'I guess it's no.'

Andrew looked at him shrewdly. 'But there's something else bothering you, isn't there?'

Sam stayed silent; he wasn't quite sure what to say, or how to say it without sounding absolutely insane.

'These are interesting.' Andrew had noticed the other things on Sam's desk - next to his books were sitting the French Captain's handkerchief and Blackbeard's coin. Andrew ran his fingers over the fine embroidery on the handkerchief, the French flag and the initials, then picked up the coin, turning it over in his hand. 'Hmmm... Looks new... Two heads...' Puzzled, Andrew looked from the coin to Sam and back again, but then his face lit up with a huge smile. 'You did it, you've been into the past, haven't you?'

Sam just nodded mutely.

'Ha! I thought I felt something this afternoon, but I wasn't sure. So? Where did you go?' Andrew looked down at Sam's laptop on the desk and the open Wikipedia page displaying information on Blackbeard. His eyes went wide. 'I thought I recognised this coin! It's Blackbeard's lucky coin, isn't it? How the hell did you get it?'

'He gave it to me for luck... Wait, you've met Blackbeard too?'

Andrew sighed. 'Let's just say that I've had the pleasure.' He chuckled, shaking his head as he flipped the coin into the air and caught it with a flourish. 'Well, well, well, you met Blackbeard on your first time and you survived. Well done, Sam, well done indeed!'

'So, it was real and not just a dream?'

'Of course it was real and, before you ask me, no, you're not going mad!' He sighed. 'You should have been told all about this before anything happened to you. I wanted to, believe me, but I wasn't allowed to; rules are rules, you know, even if they are bloody stupid. Um, do you mind if I sit down? I'm knackered.'

Without waiting for an answer, Andrew slid down the wall near the door to land heavily on his backside with a groan of satisfaction. He still had the coin and he started turning it over in his hand, making it jump from knuckle to knuckle like a magician. He stared into nothing while he did it with a faint scowl on his face.

'Uncle Andrew?'

Andrew started. 'What? Oh, yes. Sorry, I was miles away - just remembering my own run-in with Edward Teach. I barely survived. Almost ended up in that cage of his...' He shuddered. 'You said you thought it was a dream?'

'Yes. When I found myself on that ship in the middle of the ocean I was convinced that it was just a dream, so I played at being a pirate - swinging on ropes, shooting cannons, swashbuckling...' Sam stopped as he had a sudden, chilling thought. 'Hang on. *What* did you just say? You barely survived? Does that mean I could have died?'

Andrew sighed and nodded. 'Of course. All too easily I'm afraid.' He gathered his thoughts. 'We call it "Displacing" and ourselves "Displacers". It's not dreaming, it's time travel.'

Sam sat up straight, his exhaustion completely forgotten in his eagerness to get answers. 'How does it work? Will I be able to do it again? Last week, I mean, today, I… I guess I don't know when it was exactly, but I went out in the rain and found myself commanding a pirate ship, and then when it rained again I came back home. Is this kind of thing going to happen every time I get wet from now on? Do I have to stop showering?'

Andrew laughed. 'Slow down, slow down! One question at a time! And don't look too happy, of course you don't have to stop showering.'

'Aw...' Sam faked disappointment and they grinned at each other.

'OK. Where to start.' Andrew considered briefly. 'Displacing is insanely complicated and none of us really fully understands it. It's impossible to control completely, but some people can do so better than others. There are a few of us who need to get wet in order to Displace properly; the immersion helps the process, but being in the rain or bath won't automatically make you jump into the past unless you want it to. So no, you'll only Displace when you decide to. It was your first time today and it was probably triggered by you thinking about something - getting soaking wet just gave you a shove and got you on your way.'

'I had a lesson on pirates at school today, I'm pretty sure I was thinking about that on the way home.'

'There you go then, that would do it. Now, why don't you tell me everything, that way I can connect my explanations to your own experiences and they'll be easier for you to understand. Try not to leave out any details; you never know what might be important.'

For the next half an hour, Sam told Andrew everything that he remembered.

Andrew scowled when Swallow came up and he interrupted to ask for a better description of the man. His face darkened even further when Sam elaborated and he got the sense that his uncle knew the man. Then, when Sam told him about beating Swallow in the final challenge, Andrew smiled and nodded, adding a quiet 'well done' for the distraction tactics he had used.

Eventually, Sam finished and fell silent. He watched Andrew, shifting in his seat, impatiently waiting for him to sort his thoughts out and begin.

'Chuck me a pencil, would you?'

Sam threw him a wooden pencil from his desk and Andrew twirled it between his fingers as he spoke, making it dance like he had the coin before. 'Displacing is pretty hard to describe, but we like to imagine it as being like driving a wedge into a time and a place.' He demonstrated, holding up one hand with the fingers firmly together like a blade, 'let's say that this is the past. At first glance it seems set in stone,' he held up the pencil in the other hand, 'but then a Displacer comes along. He turns up in a time-line and pushes aside whoever is already there.' He pushed the pencil through his fingers, creating a gap between two of them, 'From what you told me, this Mr Smith must have been the captain of the Mermaid and when you arrived you pushed him aside, *displaced* him, so to speak. You took over the captaincy and made him your first mate, which was why he knew so much and could do so much to help you. The Displacer does what they are there to do and then, when they leave, everything goes back to how it was before - the time-line bounces back.' He pulled the pencil out again and the gap between his fingers closed, leaving it as it was before. 'That's why nobody could remember Swallow being there after he'd left and why Smith was no longer hurt. Just like your leaving will mean that Smith will once more be the captain of the Mermaid and it is he who will be Blackbeard's successor. And, I'm sorry, but he won't remember you.'

Andrew threw the pencil back to Sam, who frowned at it, thoughtfully. 'So, everything will go back to how it was before I went there. Does this mean that a, er, *Displacer* can't change the past?'

Andrew laughed. 'Of course we can! There would be no point in us existing otherwise, would there? We don't *just* go into the past to have fun, we actually have a job to do while we're there - we are the protectors of time, of *history* itself. The past isn't nearly as set in stone as you might think; it can change and it can *be* changed, it's just hard to do, and we have to be very careful how we do it.'

'I knew it wouldn't be as easy as I made it look.'

Andrew laughed. 'Always so modest! Well, hold on to your hat, Sam, because this is where it starts to get *really* complicated. You see, whether you affect a change or not depends on direct or indirect influence. For example, Swallow's attack on Smith was a *direct* action by him, so when he left it became as if it had never happened. Also, the two ships he destroyed and all the men he killed on them would come back to life, as if by magic. However, your winning the competition was *indirect* because throughout it all you were aided by Smith, who would have been taking part in it if you weren't there anyway. That means, when you left, he would not only have gone back to being captain of the Mermaid, but he would also be Blackbeard's heir.'

Sam tried to work out what his uncle was saying and groaned as he failed dismally. 'I think I'm getting a headache...'

Andrew slapped his thighs and stood up. 'Then, I think that's enough for now.'

'But I have so many questions!' Sam protested; he wanted to understand what had happened to him, but also, and more importantly, he wanted to know how to do it again so that he could have another adventure, or better still, continue the one he'd had. Among other things he really wanted to see how Bonny and Caesar got on.

'I know, I know! But they can wait. You won't be able to Displace again for at least a month anyway; your body needs time to recover and build up its energy again. For now, let's go and find out if dinner is ready, shall we?'

'Please! Just one more thing!'

Sam's pleading tone made Andrew pause, and he stood with one hand on the door knob, looking at him quizzically.

'Um, well, since I got back I don't feel comfortable... It's like this isn't my world any more, like, I don't know, it's not my life.'

Sam searched for the words, not quite knowing how to put it, but Andrew seemed to know exactly what he was talking about and he nodded sadly. 'I'm afraid that's a downside of being what we are. It will fade this time, don't worry, but the more you Displace the more you will get the feeling that you're only really alive when you're in the past.' He gave Sam a sympathetic smile. 'For now, be with your family, watch telly, play games and try to be a teenager while you still can. It won't last much longer. Sorry.'

He turned to go, but one last thing occurred to him. 'Oh, and by the way, you did a very important thing stopping Swallow. I'll tell you all about him soon, but for now, just make sure you don't daydream in the shower until I've had a chance to train you properly.'

Andrew winked and gave Sam a huge grin before walking out.

Sam sat staring at the closed door, trying to reconcile himself with the sudden prospect of a life that would be so different from the one he had imagined for himself. He was itching to burst out of the room and demand answers from his uncle; there was so much he wanted to know, so much he *needed* to know, but he restrained himself, barely, certain that Andrew would explain everything in good time. He knew he just needed to be patient, so he took his uncle's advice and went to see what was for dinner, determined to enjoy being with his family.

Andrew made his excuses as soon as dinner was finished, much earlier than he usually did when he was their guest, saying that he had a headache after a particularly tough day at work. With what had happened to Sam and the grief he would get from the other Displacers when he reported it, it was technically the truth, even if what the Vives family thought he did for work was in reality very different from what he actually did.

'Goodnight!' He waved to them, smiling widely as he went down the stairs towards the street entrance.

The smile vanished from his face as soon as the door to the flat was out of sight and he pulled out his phone. Opening WhatsApp, he frowned as he couldn't immediately see what he was looking for. He searched briefly and then found a group named *The Seven Samurai*, tutted and typed in a message.

Skype. 30 minutes. Urgent.

He was about to put the phone away, but sighed and continued typing.

And John, I've told you before - stop changing the group name!

Half an hour later, Andrew was in his study sitting in front of the computer monitors mounted on his wall. They were all on and each showed the face of at least one person connected to the conference call. A few of the monitors were divided in the middle to show two members, and one even displayed the three Elders who had been at headquarters when the call had come in and had squeezed together in front of a single camera.

Despite the fact that the WhatsApp group was only for active Displacers, the word had obviously spread, because every single Displacer and Elder had connected. Andrew wasn't surprised; they had all been waiting a long time for something to happen and an urgent message from him could mean only one thing. Nobody had wanted to miss the resolution of the long-standing mystery that was Sam Vives, no matter which way things turned out.

It was just as well the Society was paying for fibre optic broadband for everyone, otherwise it would have been a nightmare of grainy video, stuttering audio and lost connections.

Andrew nodded as the last person connected and spoke into the expectant silence. 'Thank you for joining me at such short notice. I have news - Sam Vives Displaced this afternoon.'

There were excited voices at that and general celebration; however, the dark-haired young woman in her late twenties occupying the bottom right corner screen broke in, puzzled. 'I thought you weren't going to teach him yet?'

'I didn't, Julia, he Displaced spontaneously in the rain.'

There were some gasps, although it was obvious that this in itself wasn't completely unprecedented.

'Where did he go?' The middle-aged dark-haired Indian woman in one of the middle screens in the top row spoke for the first time. Her accent was English, despite her appearance; her family lived in Slough, near Heathrow airport.

'Port Royal, 1718.'

'Blackbeard?'

'Yes.'

'And he survived? Completely intact?'

'By all accounts he acquitted himself quite well, Lisa.'

'My word!'

'Indeed! He is *very* mature for his age.'

There was silence as the group took in Andrew's information, but it was quickly broken by the brown haired man in his late thirties who occupied the screen in the top left corner. 'I knew it! He is... *the one.*'

A chorus of groans came from Andrew's speakers at this.

Andrew sighed. 'John, please. This isn't the *Matrix*, however much you want it to be. And stop changing the group name on WhatsApp! We're not *The Wild Bunch*, or *The Avengers*, or *The Seven Samurai* or even the bloody *Seven Dwarfs*! Just leave it, would you? This is serious!'

John was a movie enthusiast; several posters and a shelf full of miniatures could be seen in the background of his chat. He made movie references as much as he could and insisted on seeing their little group as super heroes. He also claimed that he was the inspiration behind

Quantum Leap, a TV series from the early 90's that had had some success, having met its creator once on a Displacement.

'He could easily pass for Dopey, though.' This came from the screen in the middle of the bottom row where a blond and blue eyed young girl was following the conversation and trying not to laugh. She was Andrew's niece by blood, Rachel Evans, about a year older than Sam.

Andrew sighed, 'thank you, Rachel, that's a huge help.'

Andrew tried to restore order and bring the conversation back to the matter at hand, but he had to wait for the laughter and calls of "Dopey! Dopey!" from the younger members and a couple of Elders who should have known better to stop before he could go on and give them the bad news that he had saved until last. 'There's more.'

'What can you possibly add that would surprise us any further, Andrew? Or better yet, distract us from your failure to properly prepare the young man in question?'

This came from the man on the screen in the middle on the right, Ralph Price. He was a sour-looking older man in his early fifties, his dark hair streaked with grey. He had small, round, wire framed glasses on his nose and was dressed in a dark suit with a white shirt and tie. He didn't like Andrew and Andrew didn't like him, but they were forced to work together so Andrew tried to put up with him as best as he could. He was right though, Andrew had failed Sam, but only because he'd been forbidden from telling him about what he could be by the rules of the Society.

He replied to Ralph coldly, making a plain statement into an accusation. 'Quentin was in Port Royal, Ralph. Your son is back in play.'

That really put the cat among the pigeons and everyone started talking at once, except for Andrew and Ralph, who just glared at each other in silence.

Eventually the hubbub died down and Ralph lost no time in leaping to his own defence. 'I have told you before, Andrew, I no longer consider him to be my son. I have disassociated myself from him completely.'

'I remember. My apologies.' Andrew gave him a cold smile and a nod.

Ralph didn't reply so Andrew just went on. 'Anyway, Sam forced Quentin to come back before he could obtain what he was apparently there for - a large diamond in Blackbeard's possession. There will be a full report available once I get around to typing it up and I will, of course, keep you all informed as I proceed. Any questions? Comments?'

'Well... You keep insisting that he's not "The One"...'

'Yes! Because there's no such thing, John!'

'But after his stunning success you have to admit that he's at least a little bit special.'

Andrew sighed, but nodded, yes he had to admit that at least; not many people had ever managed to do what Sam had done - survive such a dangerous first Displacement without any prior training, and none of them were in this chat.

'How exactly are you proposing to proceed?' asked James, ever the voice of reason and always concerned for his grandson.

'I'm going to train him normally. I refuse to start filling his head with expectations and prophecies until we know for sure he is who we've been looking for all these years; we made that mistake once before and look how that turned out.'

Andrew didn't have to tell them that it was Quentin he was talking about and Ralph's face went even redder than before at the reference to how he had so badly fouled up his son's training.

'At least test him! We want to know!' John insisted.

'All in good time. For now I think it would be a good idea to take things slowly and carefully. Rachel, maybe you could come over to Barcelona for the summer holidays and help me train him; I think Sam might respond better to someone his own age who has just gone through the same process.'

Rachel smiled. 'It won't be a problem; my mother will be happy to get me out of her hair for a while and pack me off to my *wonderful* uncle's place.'

Andrew laughed. 'Good, thank you. Well, that's everything for now, I will keep you updated. Thank you all and goodnight.'

There were variations of farewells from the group and they signed off, their faces replaced one by one by the crest of "The Honourable Society of Displacers", leaving Andrew alone, staring off to one side at nothing.

'Penny for your thoughts?'

Andrew was startled by the voice of an American woman and he looked up - one of the screens in the middle was still connected.

'Anne! I'm sorry I didn't notice you were still here.'

'Obviously not, otherwise you wouldn't have been so rude!'

She smiled warmly and Andrew smiled back. It was easy to forget that Anne was there sometimes; she didn't say much, preferring to watch, listen, then formulate her own ideas, which were usually spectacularly insightful. She was a beautiful woman in her early thirties, a native of Manhattan, with brown hair and hazel eyes and unfashionably pale skin that, in Andrew's opinion, suited her very well.

'Did you have any thoughts?' asked Andrew.

'Not especially, I just wanted to make sure you know that this wasn't your fault - there is nothing you should be blaming yourself for.'

'I'm the one who was supposed to be keeping an eye on the boy, I should have sensed him before now. I should have been certain. I dropped the ball.'

'And now you are picking it back up. The game is not yet lost.'

They shared another smile, the attraction obvious, but the distance preventative.

'Will you come and visit sometime? You've never been to Barcelona, have you?'

'Soon, darling, soon. I'm not sure about Barcelona, but I am going back to London for work in a couple of months, I'll see you then if you're around, but for now, "chin up" as you Brits say and take care of yourself; these are dangerous times.'

'Don't I just know it...'

There was a short, comfortable silence as they just looked at each other, sharing a moment. All too soon though Anne sighed. 'I have to go, I have a meeting.'

'Speak to you soon?'

'Of course!'

'Goodnight, then.'

'Good afternoon, actually!'

'Of course, I keep forgetting the time difference...'

'I know you do, and it's rather ironic in our line of work, don't you think?'

Andrew chuckled. 'Yes. Indeed.'

They shared a smile, but there was nothing more to be said, so with a look, they signed off.

Andrew was now truly alone with his worries.

Sam's spontaneous Displacement was one thing, but coinciding with Jack Swallow, better known as Quentin Price, was an entirely different matter, completely unheard of, and infinitely more mystifying.

Deep in thought, Andrew stood up and slowly went from screen to screen, turning them off. Something caught his eye, though, and he hesitated with his finger hovering over the button of the last one - the snake, twined around the hourglass and scroll on the crest of the

Society, which usually looked so sympathetic, now seemed to be staring at him accusingly.

'It wasn't my fault! He survived, didn't he?' He snarled at it and stabbed the button angrily.

'You failed.' As always the voice of the Master was unrecognisable, artificially distorted.

Shortly after Andrew had finished making his report, Quentin Price, the man that Sam knew as Jack Swallow, was angrily making his own.

He was perched on a sofa in front of a laptop in the living room of his flat. The room was cluttered with all kinds of electronic goods and items that were nominally "toys" but seemed to attract adults just as much as children. Fast food boxes were stacked by the door and empty cans of coke and energy drinks were everywhere.

The room screamed "bachelor" just as loudly as it did "nerd" and "slob".

As always the screen of the laptop was blank; the Master never let anyone see his face.

'I was there for a year, the prize was in my grasp and then that *child* turned up and suddenly everything was *fubar*! You should have told me about him!'

At the thought of Sam, his hand wandered to the plaster covering the bloody gash on his forehead, where the boy had hit him with the diamond. It was probably going to leave a scar.

'You should always anticipate a Displacer turning up and be prepared.'

Quentin snarled, 'you're supposed to warn me about this kind of thing, what use are you otherwise?'

'Mind your tongue! Remember who you are speaking to! Or do you want to be removed from existence?'

Quentin was furious, but he didn't dare answer back again; his boss was perfectly capable of carrying out any threat he made. Besides, it wouldn't pay to annoy him too much; he knew he would need help if he was going to get his revenge on the boy. He forced his anger away and moderated his voice. 'Can you at least tell me if Vives was sent or if it was just a coincidence…? Please?'

'Apparently it was just a coincidence - he really is the untrained boy that you thought he was.'

'What can you tell me about him? Where is he from?'

'Barcelona, but he's half English. He's related to Andrew, or at least he was…'

'The wife.'

'Indeed.'

Quentin laughed. 'It's going to be a pleasure taking even more of his family away from Andrew. When do we get started?'

'Oh, don't worry; we already have.'

EPILOGUE

The old man carved the woman's face into the white stone. Even after all these years her likeness was still firmly etched in his mind, how could it not be; in a few short years they had spent lifetimes together.

This was to be his last work, the culmination of almost thirty years of study with his friend, the Maestro. All his other efforts had just been practice runs for this.

He smoothed away the last rough edges and put down his tools. A tear ran down his cheek as he picked up the heavy sculpture and held it in his liver-spotted hands - normally steady, they were trembling now with emotion, as he saw the woman that he had loved so much looking back at him, freed from the marble block at last. It was still nothing when compared to the Maestro's work, but he didn't care; it would suffice.

The Maestro was there as always, surveying the work going on in his studio, keeping an eye on his apprentices, and he came over now, putting his hand on the old man's shoulder. 'It is wonderful, Andrew, your finest work. She is alive at last. Now perhaps you will tell me who she is? Over dinner tonight, maybe?'

'Thank you, Maestro. Of course, I will tell you all about her.'

Maestro Bernini walked away, inevitably drawn back to his own work, and for the last time Andrew watched him pick up his tools and consider his latest masterpiece. He had learnt much here in Rome, in the studio of Gian Lorenzo Bernini, but now it was time for him to go home.

The old man closed his eyes…

…and opened them, young again and sitting in the armchair in the living room of his flat in Barcelona.

Andrew stood, never taking his eyes from the bust in his hands, and walked slowly out of the room and down the hallway. He opened a door to reveal a small room. The room was bare, apart from three paintings on the wall and an empty plinth, ready for the new addition to the collection. He put the bust in its place and stood back.

All four pieces were of the same subject, the same beautiful woman. His only subject. There was one for every year since she had been taken from him and each of them had cost him a lifetime of learning to create.

She had loved art, but he hadn't, and so they had never gone to any of the places that she had wanted to; there was always something else that had to be done first, something more important.

This was the penance he had set for himself.

He had failed to protect her.

He wouldn't fail Sam.

AUTHOR'S NOTE

While most of the characters in this book are fictional the major piratical characters existed in some form or other. Blackbeard obviously was real and did in fact retire, for a little while anyway, but Caesar and Bonny are also based on known pirates from the time and I would invite you to find out about them for yourselves; it's much more fun than me telling you about them.

For a map of Port Royal's harbour showing the hazards that Sam has to navigate go to www.simonbrading.co.uk and look on the "Displacers" book series page!

ABOUT THE AUTHOR

Simon Brading tried his hand at many things before it occurred to him that he might have a few stories to tell. As well as the odd novel he writes screenplays and also does some acting every so often.

www.simonbrading.co.uk

For news of special offers, upcoming releases, exclusive content, competitions and events, please follow me on social media.

Instagram - @sibrading
Facebook - Simon Brading Author
Tiktok - @SimonBradingAuthor

ALSO BY SIMON BRADING

The "Displacers" series - a young adult time travel adventure series for all ages.
The Time Traveller's Nephew
The Secret of the Ancients
The Whitechapel Plot
The Price of Greed
The Time for Vengeance

The "Misfit Squadron" Series - a Steampunk series set in an alternate World War 2.
The Battle Over Britain
The Russian Resistance
A Misfit Midwinter
The Lion and the Baron
The Maltese Defence
Tales from the Second Great War
The Siege of Gibraltar
The King's Mission
The Home Front
Taking to the Skies
The Invasion of Britain

The "Twin Ambitions" series - ballet books for children ages 7 and up.
Fight to Dance
Back to Basics

The "Ni Hon - The Two Books" Series - a young adult series set in a dystopian future Japan.
The Black Book

Others
Public Enemy
Empath
The Lifeboat at the End of the Universe

www.ingramcontent.com/pod-product-compliance
Lightning Source LLC
Chambersburg PA
CBHW031241210726

48287CB00003B/854